9

M

Jl

THE
WRONG
GUN

THE WRONG GUN

J.P. Hailey

Library of Congress Cataloging-in-Publication Data
Hailey, J.P.
    The wrong gun / J.P. Hailey.
        p.   cm.
    ISBN 1-55611-333-1
    I. Title.
PS3558.A3275W76   1992
813'.54—dc20   92-53077
                                                                CIP

Manufactured in the United States of America

10 9 8 7 6 5 4 3 2 1

Designed by Irving Perkins Associates

For Lynn, Justin and Toby

1

STEVE WINSLOW LEANED BACK IN HIS CHAIR, cocked his head, and looked across his desk at the man holding the gun.

Russ Timberlaine looked like he'd stepped out of the road company of *Indians*. He could have played Ned Buntline, Buffalo Bill or Wild Bill Hickok, no problem. His blond hair hung to his shoulders. He was dressed in boots, jeans, denim shirt, buckskin vest and cowboy hat. He was a tall man, say six-six, broad-shouldered and solid. Looking at him, the term cowpuncher came to mind. He looked like he could stop a stampede just by standing there and letting the cattle run into him.

Completing the picture was a handtooled gun belt and holster. The holster was now empty, since Russ Timberlaine had drawn the gun.

"Know anything about guns?" Timberlaine said.

Steve Winslow shook his head. "Not a thing."

Timberlaine glanced over at Tracy Garvin. "What about you, young lady?"

Tracy shook the long blonde hair out of her face, pushed her glasses up on her nose. She smiled. "Only what I read in books."

"What kind of books?"

"Murder mysteries."

Timberlaine grinned and shook his head. "Then you know about as much as the boss. Ninety percent inaccurate, those things are."

Timberlaine chuckled, looked at the gun a moment, then turned it around and extended it to Steve. "Here, take a look."

"Is it loaded?"

"Yes."

"Then I'd better not mess with it."

Timberlaine nodded approvingly. "Good man. I wish more people had that attitude." He extended the gun. "Go ahead. Take it. It's not loaded. I just *say* it is, 'cause you should always handle a gun as if it *were* loaded. If your reaction is not to touch it, you've got the right idea. Here. Go on. Take it."

Steve took the gun, turned it over in his hand. Knowing nothing about guns, there wasn't much for him to observe. It was a revolver, that he could tell. And it seemed to go with the Wild West image Russ Timberlaine was attempting to cultivate. It had what appeared to be wooden handles, though again Steve couldn't tell if that's what they really were.

Steve noticed a flaw on one of them. Looking closer, he saw that it was a scratch. He tilted the handle, made it more visible. Sure enough, the letter *R* had been scratched onto the handle of the gun.

Steve looked up to find Russ Timberlaine watching him closely.

"Well?" Timberlaine said.

Steve pointed. "This R on the handle. Is that for Russ?"

Timberlaine winced. "Hell, no. You think I'd deface one of my guns."

Steve smiled. "Obviously not. So what's the R?"

"The R is for Robbins. As in Pete Robbins. As in Pistol Pete Robbins."

"You're kidding."

Timberlaine grinned. "Not at all. They really existed. The Kids and the Pistols. Hell, even the Deadeyes and the Two-guns and the Slims and the Reds. Anybody ever killed anybody got some kind of nickname laid on 'em."

"Like Pistol Pete Robbins?"

"Exactly. Now that son of a bitch, Pistol Pete, killed five guys that they know of, and lived to the ripe old age of twenty-six, when he was gunned down by, get this, Sheriff Montana Pride."

"Oh, no."

"Oh, yes." Timberlaine's eyes were gleaming. "The pride of Montana. He must have taken some kidding over that, which might explain why he was such a mean son of a bitch. At any rate, guess who this Montana Pride turned out to be?"

"Pistol Pete's boyhood friend?"

"Bingo."

"Jesus Christ."

"Hey, these things are documented."

"By whom? Mexican maidens who play guitars and sing?"

Timberlaine grinned. "It's not as bad as all that. There were newspapers back then. Some of the accounts written exist to this day. There's a lot of stuff on microfilm, and if you dig you can find it."

"Fine. So?"

"So the legend of Pistol Pete is an authenticated part of the history of the Old West."

Steve nodded. "I see. And this gun is therefore valuable."

"No, it isn't."

Steve frowned. "Why not?"

Russ Timberlaine shrugged and shook his head. "It's the wrong gun."

2

STEVE WINSLOW FROWNED. "I beg your pardon?"

"It's not my gun. I don't know how else to say it. It's not mine."

"You mean someone switched guns on you?"

"Exactly."

"How could that happen?"

"I don't know how it could happen. That's what I'm trying to figure out. The point is it did."

"So this gun is not Pistol-Pete-whoever's despite the R on the handle?"

"Of course not. Someone scratched the R on the handle to make it look like mine. It could have been done yesterday."

"Is that when the gun was stolen?"

"I don't know."

"Oh?"

"I noticed it last week. That's why I'm here now. Obviously that's the first time I noticed. But when was the last time I looked at the gun? I mean carefully enough to see the difference. I try to think back and I don't know."

"Where was the gun kept?"

"That's just it. In a display case. In my study. Along with a bunch of other guns. Glass enclosed. The gun sits in a rack. If I glanced at it lying there in the case I might not notice. I'm trying to think. When was the last time I took it out, picked it up? The last time I know for sure. And damn it all, I can't remember."

Steve held up his hand. "O.K.," he said. "Pardon me for a moment, but as I said, I know nothing about guns. How do you identify your gun, and how do you know this isn't it? Are you going by the serial number?"

Timberlaine shook his head. He pointed. "Turn the gun over. Look there, on the other side of the barrel in front of the cylinder. See those scratches?"

Steve turned the gun over and looked. The area Timberlaine had indicated was a crosshatch of metal scratches. "That's where the serial number was," Timberlaine said. "Only it's been filed off. On my gun and on this one."

"Why? On the real gun, I mean."

"Theory is Pistol Pete did it himself. Apparently a lot of cowboys did. Superstitious. Didn't want a number on their gun. The gun was their lifeline. Always workin' on it. Cleaning and oiling it. Carving things in the handle. So a lot of them took the numbers off."

"If there's no number, how can you tell this isn't yours?"

"How do you know one painting's an original and another's a copy? I know my gun, and that isn't it."

"Fine, but could you give me a concrete reason?"

"Sure. Just look at it. See the cylinder? You'll notice the metal on the cylinder's slightly lighter than the metal on the barrel. See that? Why, because this gun's been rebuilt and the cylinder's been replaced. See what I'm sayin'? The cylinder's newer than the rest of the gun, so it's lighter in color.

"That's one thing. For another thing, the whole gun is lighter in color. Than the real gun, I mean. That means the whole gun is probably more recent. My gun dates back to 1862. What this is I couldn't tell you."

"I see."

"Then there's the handles. To begin with, the wood's lighter. And if that weren't enough, look at the R. Whoever did this rubbed something in the scratches to try to age 'em, but you can tell the difference. No way that R is a hundred and some odd years old. That carving is fresh."

Timberlaine looked up. "You want more?"

"No, that's pretty convincing. All right, someone stole your gun and substituted a duplicate. I'll buy that. Tell me. The original—was it valuable?"

Timberlaine nodded. "Relatively. I paid twenty thousand dollars for it. And that was ten years ago. The price has doubtless gone up."

"Doubtless," Steve said. "Mr. Timberlaine, why are you here?"

Timberlaine frowned. "I beg your pardon?"

"A valuable gun of yours has been stolen. Why are you consulting a lawyer? Why don't you go to the police?"

"Well, that's a problem."

"What's a problem?"

"Well, for one thing, as I said, the serial number had been scratched off."

"Yeah. So?"

"Technically that makes the gun an illegal firearm."

"You paid twenty thousand dollars for an illegal gun?"

Timberlaine nodded. "With proper authentication. That's not unusual. With collectors it happens all the time. Yes, the guns are illegal, but it's not like we were buying them to hold up banks. A collector's not going to pass up a chance to own a rare gun just because it's technically illegal."

"That explains why you don't want to consult the police. It doesn't explain why you want to consult a lawyer."

Timberlaine nodded. "Good point. The fact is, I'm scared."

"Of what?"

Timberlaine took a breath, held up his hand. "Look, this is hard to explain, because it's mostly just a feeling. But it's basically this. If the gun were just missing, that would be one thing. I could say, O.K., it's valuable so someone stole it. All right, no big deal, a simple theft, let's try to find out who."

"But the gun wasn't just stolen. It was substituted. A duplicate was made and put in its place. And I have to keep wondering why."

"So you wouldn't notice the theft."

"Yes, but that's only a temporary measure. Because eventually I'm going to notice."

"Maybe that's all the thief needed. If you noticed the theft right away, you'd know when the gun was stolen and you'd know who must have taken it. The time of the theft was obscured so it wouldn't point to any one person."

Timberlaine held up his hand. "Fine, fine," he said impatiently. "I can see that, that's obvious, if that's all it is I hope you're right. I'll kiss the gun off, absorb the loss, and good riddance to it. That's not what worries me."

"What is?"

"Suppose that gun is used to commit a crime."

"What makes you think it would be?"

Timberlaine frowned. "Don't be stupid. Someone went to all the trouble of switching guns. I start tying to figure out why, and the obvious answer is what if someone's trying to frame me."

"Why would anyone want to do that?"

Timberlaine frowned impatiently. "That's not the question. Say someone is. I'm looking to protect myself. So what's the worst case scenario? A dead body turns up with my gun lying next to it."

"I can see that," Steve said. "That's obvious." He smiled. "Melodramatic as all hell, but obvious. All right, say that happens. First off, how would the cops know it was your gun?"

"What?"

"Well, you say the serial number's been filed off. How could they prove it was yours?"

"No problem," Timberlaine said. "True, not as easy as if it were registered and had a serial number. But the gun is known to be mine. In gun-collecting circles, I mean. There's collectors who could testify to the fact that I did own the gun and that they had seen it in my possession. And there are enough experts who would be able to testify to the fact that the gun in question was indeed the one that had been authenticated as Pistol Pete's.

"That's one way." Timberlaine reached in his pocket and pulled out a glass cylinder the size and shape of a cigar. "Here's another." Timberlaine looked at it, passed it over to Steve Winslow.

Steve took it, saw that it was indeed a cigar tube. Inside was a piece of rounded metal, obviously a spent bullet.

"Don't tell me," Steve said.

"Absolutely," Timberlaine said. "This is a bullet fired from my gun. The real gun, I mean, the one that was stolen. It happens I did some target shooting with it last month. That's a bullet removed from the target."

"When?"

"What?"

"When did you remove the bullet from the target?"

"This morning. Before I came here.

"Then how do you know it's from your gun? Was that the *only* gun ever fired at that target?"

"No, there were other bullets in it. But it's the only forty-five. That I'm sure of."

"Fine. So what's the point?"

"If that was the idea, to frame me by killing someone with my gun, then the fatal bullet will match this one."

"Naturally. All this is obvious, Mr. Timberlaine. The point is, what do you expect me to do about it?"

"I want you to take the bullet and the gun. I want you to give the gun to a ballistics expert and have him fire test bullets from it and then compare them with the bullet in that tube. I want him to be prepared to swear that the bullets *do not* match, and that therefore this gun, the gun that I have in my possession now, is *not* the gun that fired the bullet in this glass tube, and consequentially is not responsible for any crime that might be committed with the original gun."

Steve frowned. "I see. Would you want me to hang on to this gun?"

"No. That's the problem. The gun has to be returned to its position in the display case. Otherwise, whoever took it will realize I've caught on to the theft."

"So what? If it warns them off, that's what you want in the first place."

"Yeah, if it warns them off. But for all we know, whoever took the gun is just waiting for me to discover the substitution and remove the other gun from the case before they act."

"Yes, but who?" Steve said. "Who could have done such a thing, and why would they want to?"

Timberlaine scowled and looked at his watch. "I don't have time to get into that now," he said irritably. "I have a business appointment to get to. I'm noted for my punctuality. If I'm late, people will be surprised and want to know why. I happen to be a rather poor liar. I don't want to have to answer any questions.

"Now, I need the bullet compared and I need the gun back by tonight. The question is, can you do it?"

Steve glanced over at Tracy Garvin, who had been sitting there hanging on every word. If he said no, he'd have a mutiny on his hands.

"Of course I can do it," Steve said. "The question is, how sincere are you about wanting it done?"

Timberlaine frowned. "What the hell does that mean?"

Steve smiled. "Make me out a check for ten thousand dollars."

3

MARK TAYLOR FLOPPED his two-hundred-twenty pounds in the overstuffed clients' chair, ran his hand through his curly red hair and said, "Shoot."

Steve Winslow picked up the gun from his desk. "Interesting choice of words, Mark."

"Good lord," Taylor said. "What's that?"

Steve handed the gun to Tracy to give to him. "Here. Take a look."

Taylor took the gun, turned it over in his hands. "This goes back a few years," he said. "Colt .45, right?"

"Yes. How did you know?"

Taylor grinned. "Actually, I'm guessing. Colt's a pretty common gun. A revolver this vintage's apt to be a Colt. Forty-five's a common caliber, the barrel opening looks right for it."

Steve nodded. "Very good, Mark. What else can you tell me about it?"

Taylor looked at the gun again. "Not that much. What's this R carved in the handle?"

"That's to indicate the gun was once owned by the notorious gunslinger, Pistol Pete Robbins."

Taylor's eyes narrowed. "What?"

"That's right, Mark."

Taylor looked sideways at Tracy Garvin. "Is he shitting me?"

"Not at all, Mark. Tell him how he died, Steve."

"How who died?" Taylor said.

"Pistol Pete," Steve said. "The notorious gunslinger who shot down five men in his lifetime, and don't you want to know how he died?"

Mark Taylor looked back and forth from Tracy to Steve. "I'm afraid to ask."

Steve grinned. "You tell him, Tracy."

"O.K.," Tracy said. "Well, Mark, it seems the gentleman in question was gunned down by his boyhood companion, Sheriff Montana Pride."

"What?"

"That's right."

"Sheriff Montana Pride?"

"You got it."

"I don't think I wanna *know* what he was named for."

Steve grinned. "Pride is the family name, Mark. It's the Montana that's suspect."

"This whole story's suspect. Tracy said you had a case. You just havin' fun with me, or is there a point to all this?"

"A little of both, Mark." Steve took out the cigar tube with the bullet, had Tracy pass it over. "What do you make of that?"

Taylor took it, looked at it. Nodded. "Ah," he said. "Now we're getting somewhere. This is obviously a forty-five-caliber bullet. I assume you'd like me to prove it came from this gun."

"No, I'd like you to prove that it didn't."

"What?"

Steve gave Mark Taylor a rundown of his meeting with Russ Timberlaine.

"Well, what do you think?" Steve said.

Taylor shrugged. "It's a tough call. The guy's either paranoid or he's right. Just who does he think stole this gun, by the way?"

"He didn't say."

"No?"

"No. When I asked, he looked at his watch and remembered an important business engagement."

"Uh-oh," Taylor said. "That's a bad sign."

"Yes, it is."

"On the other hand, if he gave you a retainer, who gives a shit? You want me to check out the gun?"

"Yes, I do. And I want it done by five o'clock this afternoon."

"Oh?"

"That's when he'll be back in my office to pick it up. The gun has to be returned to its proper place so no one will notice he's discovered the substitution."

"Why does he care?"

"I don't know, Mark. As I say, the gentleman had to run. So we have an interesting situation here. A client's asked me to do something, he hasn't told me the whole story, so basically we're working in the dark."

"Yeah. So?"

"So I want to protect myself. You say a Colt .45's a pretty common gun, right?"

"Yeah. Why?"

"I want you to find a dealer who has one that matches the one you have there. I want you to buy it, fire test bullets through it, file the serial number off it, carve an R in the handle and have it in my office by five o'clock this afternoon."

Mark Taylor's jaw dropped open. "Are you kidding me?"

"Not at all, Mark. I said I wanted to protect myself."

"Great, but what about me? Filing a serial number off a gun happens to be a criminal offense."

"I'm sure there's a matter of intent involved."

"Right. Your intent is not to commit a felony. Your intent is only to deceive and defraud your own client." Taylor held up his hands. "*You* explain it to the cops. *I* am not filing any serial number off any gun."

"Fine," Steve said. "Forget the serial number. Just get the gun and fire the test bullets through it. You have no problem with that, do you?"

"Not at all. I have every right to own a gun." Taylor held up the forty-five. "Does that mean you don't want this one tested?"

"Not at all. Test them both. And you and the ballistics expert are very careful with the bullets. You get 'em labeled and you keep 'em straight."

"How do you want 'em labeled?"

"Same as this one. Put 'em in a glass tube and label the tube."

"This tube's not labeled."

"I know. Label it RT-ORIG for Russ Timberlaine original." Steve pointed to the gun Taylor was holding. "Label the bullets from that RT-SUB for substitute. I want two bullets from the gun in separate tubes—RT-SUB and RT-SUB–2. Same thing with the gun you buy. A bullet in a separate tube, labeled SW."

"For Steve Winslow?"

"Of course. Can you do that?"

"No problem," Taylor said. "As long as there's no serial number filing."

"Don't sweat it, Mark. If it's illegal, I wouldn't ask you to do it."

"And you need all this by five o'clock?"

"Well, that's the thing, Mark."

"What's that?"

"Now I need it by *four* o'clock."

4

Tracy Garvin watched while Steve Winslow filed the serial number off the gun. Steve blew the metal scrapings away, held the gun up for her approval.

"What do you think?" he said.

She frowned, looked from one gun to the other. "Damned if I can tell the difference."

"What about the R?"

She shrugged. "Your R looks like his R. Whether it looks like the original, I couldn't tell."

"Yeah, but it doesn't have to. This gun doesn't have to pass as the original, just as the substitute."

"Think Timberlaine will notice?"

"There's no reason why he should."

"He's an expert."

"Yeah. He could tell a copy from the original. But to tell a copy from a copy? Unless there's some particular flaw in the first copy that he's noted—which I have no way of knowing—well, there's no reason why he should."

"You sure *you* can tell 'em apart?" Tracy said.

Steve grinned. "Good point, Tracy. This is where I mustn't fumble." He picked up the gun he'd been working on. "This is the substitute gun. I mean, this is the *substitute* substitute gun. The one Mark bought. This gun I set aside."

14

Steve set the gun down on his desk. He picked up the other one. "This is the *original* substitute gun. The one Russ Timberlaine brought." Steve gestured to the antique safe in the corner of his office. "This gun gets locked in the safe."

Tracy frowned. "Are you sure? Last time you locked something in that safe it got stolen."

"That was entirely different," Steve said. "In this case, no one even knows we *have* the gun, and no one will know that it's there. No, that wouldn't be enough to stop me."

"What would?"

"Not finding the combination."

"No problem," Tracy said. "After turning the office upside down to find it last time, you will pardon me, but I didn't leave it with you. You want it, I got it."

"Fine," Steve said. "Get it, and let's lock this sucker up before Timberlaine gets here."

Tracy went to the outer office, copied down the combination and brought it back. Steve took it, spun the dials, opened the antique safe.

"O.K.," he said. "The gun goes in here. So do our share of the bullets."

He went back to his desk, got the gun and the glass tubes marked RT-SUB–2 and SW, put them all in the safe and locked it.

"There," he said. "That leaves us with the substitute gun Mark bought, the original bullet Russ Timberlaine brought, and the bullet fired from the gun he brought us, RT-SUB."

"Why isn't it marked RT-SUB dash one?" Tracy asked. "Aren't you telling him there's a dash two?"

"He's a busy man," Steve said. "No need to bother him with too many details."

"Like the fact you switched guns?"

"Exactly."

"Why?"

"What?"

"Why did you switch guns, and why aren't you telling him?"

"Isn't that obvious?"

"Not really."

"The man is not telling me the whole story, so why should I tell him the whole story?"

"That's no answer."

"Maybe not, but it's the reason. If I don't know what's going on, I have to protect myself."

"Bullshit," Tracy said.

Steve raised his eyebrows. "I beg your pardon?"

Tracy smiled. "Give me a break. Protect yourself? Protect yourself from what? No, I'll tell you what happened. Timberlaine came in here and told you his problem. And he didn't just ask you to solve it, he told you *how* to solve it—take the gun and fire test bullets through it." Tracy smiled again. "Well, it's a real good solution, but it's not yours. You're not being anything but a messenger boy. Which you're not willing to do. So you take charge of the situation by substituting a gun and not telling him you're doing it."

Steve grinned and shook his head. "That's very interesting, Tracy. Were you a psych minor, by any chance?"

"Hey, this doesn't really require study." Tracy pointed to the Colt .45 lying on the desk. "Little boys playing with guns. And you substituting yours for Timberlaine's." She shook her head. "Freud would have had a field day."

5

STEVE WINSLOW HANDED THE GLASS TUBE to Russ Timberlaine. "Here's your original bullet back. You'll notice what's marked on the tube."

Timberlaine took it, looked at it. "RT dash ORIG?"

"Russ Timberlaine Original. That designates the bullet you gave me, the bullet you *claim* came from the original gun."

"It *did*."

"I'm sure it did. But the ballistics expert is not taking your word for it. In terms of evidentiary value, the ballistics expert is prepared to testify that this is the bullet supplied by me. Or rather, by my private detective."

"And this seal across the top?"

"On that you will find the signature of the ballistics expert. With that seal in place, the tube itself has evidentiary value. In other words, that seal validates the label RT-ORIG, and guarantees that the bullet in the tube is the one you gave me."

"But if that seal is broken, we can't prove it?"

"Not at all. The ballistics expert has also marked the base of the bullet and would be prepared to identify it from that." Steve smiled. "But as long as it's in the tube, it's a lot easier for *us* to identify."

"I see."

Steve passed over the second glass tube. "This is the bullet fired from the gun you gave me. The gun you claim was substituted for your own."

Timberlaine looked at it. "RT-SUB?"

"For Russ Timberlaine Substitute," Steve said. "Now, if you'd like me to keep these bullets for you, I will. I would probably even advise it. What was your intention?"

"No," Timberlaine said. "I'll hang on to them."

"Fine," Steve said. He picked up a gun from the desk and extended the handle toward Timberlaine. "Here," he said, and when Timberlaine reached for it, added, "Be careful, it's loaded."

Timberlaine drew his hand back. "What?"

"It isn't really," Steve said, "but you should always treat a gun as if it were."

Timberlaine frowned. "Damn it," he said. "*I* know how to handle guns."

He took the gun, opened his briefcase and stuck it in, along with the two glass tubes. He snapped the briefcase shut.

Steve Winslow stood up.

Tracy Garvin, who had been sitting taking notes, looked up in surprise. She had expected Steve to draw Timberlaine out on the subject of who could have substituted the gun. Instead he had stood up to indicate that the interview was over.

However, the reverse psychology worked.

Timberlaine frowned. "Just a minute."

Steve looked at him. "Oh? Was there something else?"

"Well, damn it, yes there was."

"I beg your pardon. I thought we'd finished." Steve sat back down. "What is it?"

"Well, I've been thinking about who could have taken the gun."

"Any ideas?"

Timberlaine frowned. "No, that's the problem. I have no idea who took it. But I have a pretty good idea when it was taken."

"Oh? When was that?"

"A week and a half ago. At the auction."

"What auction?"

"The rare gun auction. That's when it must have been."

"And where was this?"

"At my house, of course. That's how the gun could have been taken."

"And where's your house?"

"I didn't tell you? Oh, no, I guess I didn't. Well, I got a house on Long Island. Mansion, really. One of the old estates. Bought it twenty years ago. Got it for a song. Crumbling, broken down. Had it rebuilt. Anyway, I hold auctions there."

"Why?"

Timberlaine frowned. "Why? Because I like to, that's why. And I got the space to do it, so why not? They're famous, my auctions are. In gun circles anyway. The top dealers show up, auction their wares. The top collectors come. From all over the country."

"Just for one day?"

"No, the whole weekend. I put 'em up."

Steve frowned. "You're saying they stay with you?"

"Absolutely. I told you, it's a mansion. I got forty-eight rooms. Sure I put 'em up. Anyway, that's when it must have happened. Over the weekend when everyone was there and everyone had access."

"I see," Steve said. "And who do you suspect?"

Timberlaine hesitated a moment. "I don't suspect anyone in particular. It's just that's when it must have happened."

"You hesitated," Steve said.

"I beg your pardon?"

"You hesitated before you answered."

"I was thinking."

"You may have hesitated because you were thinking, but the fact is you hesitated. I'm wondering who you were thinking of."

Timberlaine took a breath and blew it out again. "All right," he said. "You can't hide anything from a lawyer. All right. Melvin Burdett."

"Who?"

"Melvin Burdett. That's the name that flashed to mind. But it isn't him."

"What do you mean, it isn't him?"

"I mean I don't seriously think he took the gun."

"Then why does his name flash to mind?"

Timberlaine took a breath. "All right. Melvin Burdett is a thorn in my side. You know how that is? He's a collector. A rival collector. Accent on the word rival."

Timberlaine held up his hands. "Understand, I've never done

anything to him. But the man has taken it upon himself to make my life a living hell."

"Why?"

Timberlaine shook his head. "No reason. There are just people like that, you know. Burdett's one of them. He's aggressive and competitive. I'm fairly well established as a collector. I have a reputation. So he's made me his target and he's out to get me."

"In what way?"

"In any way. He's always trying to annoy me, compete with me. If there's a gun I want, he'll make it a point to outbid me for it."

"He has the money to do that?"

"He has money. To outbid me, no. But to bid me up, sure. If there's a gun I particularly want, he's quite prepared to keep bidding to the point where I either let him have it, or wind up paying more than the gun is worth."

"I see. And you think he might be involved in the theft of the gun?"

"No, I don't," Timberlaine said irritably. "That's why I didn't want to bring it up. The man is a royal pain in the ass, but that doesn't make him a thief."

"Then who is?"

"I don't know."

"You must have some ideas."

"No, I don't. That's the point. I absolutely don't. I look back to the weekend, there must have been twenty, twenty-five people staying there. It could have been any one of them, but there's no one I suspect."

"Why are you telling me this?"

Timberlaine frowned. "What?"

"What's the point? I did what you wanted, you were ready to go, you made a point of staying to tell me when the gun might have been taken—which isn't any help at all if you have no idea who took it. So what's the point? What are you getting to?"

"That's just it," Timberlaine said. "I have another auction planned for this weekend. Most of the same people will be there."

"So?"

"So, if it's the worst case scenario, if someone took the gun to frame me or at least put me in an embarrassing position, well, that's when it would logically happen. One, because whoever took the gun would be there. And, two, because enough people will be there that they could work undetected."

"That's obvious," Steve said. "The question is, why are you telling me?"

"Because I want you there."

6

"IT'S THE PERFECT SETUP," Tracy Garvin said as Steve Winslow piloted the rental car along the Long Island Expressway.

"What is?"

"This whole weekend. I mean, you couldn't have written it better. You got a stolen gun. You got a substituted gun. You got a bunch of previously identified bullets. And you got all the suspects gathered together in one spot for the weekend. Plus you got the client's crack lawyer/sleuth on hand to solve the crime."

"Not to mention his attractive, mystery-loving secretary," Steve said.

Tracy smiled. "It was kind of him to extend the invitation."

"Kind, hell," Steve said. "The poor man never had a chance."

"Oh?"

"As I recall, you coughed loudly twice and began squirming as if you were about to jump out of your chair."

"I was not squirming."

"Let's not quibble. The fact is, you made your wishes known."

"Well, I wasn't about to miss it. A setup like this. By rights, by tomorrow morning there should be a corpse on the library floor."

"Assuming he *has* a library."

"Are you kidding me? Forty-eight rooms, the man's going to have a library."

"Maybe so. Did we pass our exit?"

Tracy consulted the directions in her lap. "This is it coming up."

Steve got off the highway, followed Tracy's directions over a series of back roads, turned in at a marble gate.

"Good lord, is this it?" Tracy said.

"Damned if I know. I'm just following your directions."

"Then this is it."

It certainly was impressive. Timberlaine had three hundred acres, and his mansion was set a quarter of a mile back from the road. The driveway wound through spacious front lawns and an apple orchard, and ended in a circle in front of a sprawling, three-story marble mansion.

About a dozen cars were already parked in the circle. Steve got a space as close to the front door as possible, and he and Tracy got out and retrieved their suitcases from the trunk.

There was no one outside, but the front door was open. Steve and Tracy walked in and found themselves in an immense front hall, with marble floors, wood-paneled walls, and a wide circular staircase leading up to the second floor.

A young man in a white suit with a clipboard came bustling up. "May I help you?" he said.

"Steve Winslow and Tracy Garvin," Steve said.

The man consulted his clipboard, made a check. "Yes, yes, of course," he said. "You're on the third floor. Just one moment, I'll have you shown to your rooms."

He stepped to the side wall, pushed a button. "The boy will be here in a minute. I'm Martin Kessington. If there's anything you need, just ask. You'll find a house phone in your room. Just pick it up and ask for Martin."

As if on cue, a voice said, "Martin!" A strident, preemptory voice, obviously not pleased.

Steve and Tracy looked up to find a plump, bald man waddling down the staircase from the second floor. A teenage boy in slacks and a short-sleeved white shirt trailed behind him, carrying a suitcase.

"Martin," the plump man said again. "What is the meaning of this?"

"Excuse me, sir?" Martin said.

"Excuse me, hell," the man said. He wheeled on the boy with the suitcase. "This boy refuses to take me to my room. He's trying to take me to the third floor front."

Martin coughed discreetly. "Yes, sir. I'm very sorry, sir. That is where I have you down."

"Nonsense," the man said. "I have the second floor corner room overlooking the bay. I *always* have that room, now switch me there at once."

Martin coughed again. "I'm very sorry, sir," he said. "But there's a problem. Miss Timberlaine's fiancé has been staying in that room."

"He had no right to do that. You shouldn't have given it to him. Get him out of there."

Martin, who seemed to have infinite patience, smiled and shook his head. "In the first place, I didn't put him there, sir. I wasn't consulted. And in the second place, I don't have the authority to make him move. Unfortunately, that room is not available. If you are not happy with the one you have been assigned, perhaps you would care to choose another."

"I want the second floor corner."

"I understand, sir." Martin flipped over a page on his clipboard. "Let me show you what's available. Here's a nice second floor room with a view over the back lawn to the bay."

"It's not what I want."

"I understand, sir."

Steve Winslow, who had been watching the scene with some amusement, smiled and nudged Tracy Garvin. "It appears we have been forgotten."

"Shh," Tracy said. "Pay attention. Don't you see what's happening here?"

"What?"

"Pay attention. This could be important."

Steve frowned. "Tracy," he said. "What are you talking about? How could this possibly be important?"

At that moment Martin snapped his finger and said, "Timothy. Please show Mr. Burdett to his new room."

7

TRACY GARVIN COULD HARDLY CONTAIN HERSELF. "Don't you see?" she insisted. "It all fits."

"What all fits?"

They were in Steve's room on the third floor front, a room theoretically less desirable in that it overlooked the driveway and the front lawn instead of the backyard and the bay. Unlike Burdett, Steve had not complained. As far as he was concerned, the view he had was magnificent. Not that he gave a damn about the view anyway.

Nor had Tracy complained about her room, which was next door to his and commanded the same view. Instead, the minute she'd been installed in it she'd come banging on Steve's door to advance her theories.

"Are you kidding?" Tracy said. "It's the last piece of the mystery. Here's Burdett, Timberlaine's hated rival. He's here for the weekend and he's just switched his room."

"So?"

"So?" Tracy said. "Don't be a dunce. What's the next thing that happens? Either he gets murdered, or the person he switched rooms with gets murdered."

Steve looked at her. "Why?"

"Why? Why do you think? Because it screws everything up."

Steve frowned. "You'll pardon me, but that's hardly an answer."

"Oh, come on. You know what I mean. Timberlaine hates Burdett. If Burdett gets killed, Timberlaine's the main suspect. Timberlaine's gun's been stolen, and he thinks someone's trying to frame him. If someone's going to frame him, what better way than to kill Burdett? Can't you see that?"

"Of course."

"And now Burdett's switched rooms. Which, in the vernacular, fucks everything up. If the murderer kills Burdett, Timberlaine would have an alibi if he didn't know Burdett had switched rooms. On the other hand, if the killer kills the guy Burdett switched rooms with, then Timberlaine is dorked *unless* he can prove he knew Burdett switched rooms. See what I mean?"

"Yeah, but—"

"Plus, you got a third joker in the deck. This fiancé. Did you know Timberlaine's daughter had a fiancé?"

"I didn't know Timberlaine had a daughter."

Tracy rolled her eyes. "You're hopeless. Timberlaine's a widower, he has one daughter. Apparently she has a fiancé. So what about him?"

"What *about* him?"

"Suppose he's murdered?"

"Oh, come on."

"No, it fits just fine. He's staying in Burdett's room. Suppose he's killed. Then the cops can figure Timberlaine did it, thinking he was Burdett."

"Give me a break."

"What's wrong with that?"

"Come on. The fiancé's been there for some time. Timberlaine would know where he's staying."

"Why should he? What's he got to do with room arrangements? This guy Martin seems to be in charge of it. So there's no reason he'd have to know, and the cops can figure he did it."

Steve sighed. "Oh, dear."

"Plus, there's the other way around."

"What other way around?"

"The fiancé gets killed and the cops figure it's because he was sleeping in Burdett's room. But actually he gets killed for himself."

"What?"

"I mean, he's the guy the killer meant to kill."

"What killer?"

"Timberlaine. Who killed him to keep him from marrying his daughter."

"Oh, good lord."

"What's wrong with that motive?"

"Isn't that a little extreme?"

"Murder *is* extreme."

Steve took a breath. "Tracy."

"What?"

"If Timberlaine did it, who substituted guns?"

"Timberlaine did it himself."

"Why?"

"As a smoke screen. To divert suspicion from himself."

"Good lord."

"No," Tracy said, excitedly. "It's perfect. He goes to you. He gives you the substituted gun. He gets you to compare the bullets. Puts you in a position to establish he doesn't *have* the original gun. So when the murder's committed with the original gun—as he intended all along—you can show that he didn't have it in his possession." Tracy nodded in agreement with herself. "That would explain it."

"Explain what?"

"The retainer. He's got ten thousand dollars invested in you. What do you think it's for? A retainer? Hell no. It's an alibi."

Steve frowned.

"Well," Tracy said. "What do you think of that?"

Steve took a breath. "Tracy," he said. "I think you've got a vivid imagination."

She opened her mouth to protest. Steve held up his hand. "I'm not putting it down. I'm not saying you're wrong. I'm just saying what you're giving me is a scenario straight out of a detective book. There's nothing wrong with detective books, but they're usually a lot more interesting than real life. Otherwise they wouldn't have gotten published. That doesn't mean you're wrong and it doesn't mean nothing's going to happen this weekend. All I'm saying is, the odds are the disappearance of the gun is nothing more than that—a disappearance—and has nothing to do with the people staying here. And even if it did, absolutely nothing is going to happen to them on this particular weekend."

Steve smiled. "See what I mean?"

There came the sound of a gunshot.

8

TRACY GARVIN CAME PELTING DOWN the circular staircase and found Martin standing in the front hallway calmly consulting his clipboard. In her agitation, Tracy couldn't remember his name. So she clattered down the stairs crying out simply, "Gunshot!"

Martin looked up, saw her, smiled. "Yes, ma'am," he said. "That would be Mr. Timberlaine and I believe Mr. Nigouri at the pistol range. I know he had a gun Mr. Timberlaine wanted to check out."

Tracy blinked. "Pistol range?"

"Yes, ma'am." Martin pointed. "From the patio take the path off to the left."

Steve Winslow came walking calmly down the circular stair in time to hear the last exchange. Tracy looked up, caught his eye and he smiled.

Tracy flushed slightly, then turning back to Martin and mustering what dignity she could, said, "And how do we get to the patio?"

Martin pointed again. "Right through there."

"I suppose you knew it all along," Tracy said, as she and Steve followed Martin's directions and stepped out onto a marble terrace running the length of the back of the building.

"Not at all," Steve said. "That gunshot could just as well have been the murderer firing Pistol Pete Robbins's Colt .45 into the

28

heart of Russ Timberlaine's archrival, Melvin Burdett. And I think the fact that it wasn't in no way diminishes any theories you've advanced so far."

"Fuck you," Tracy said. "How did you know it was nothing?"

"I didn't."

"You walked calmly down the stairs as if nothing had happened."

"I walked calmly down the stairs because running wouldn't have helped."

"Why not?"

"Because unfortunately killers don't stand over their victims holding the murder weapon, they flee the scene. Once they do, they leave a tableau that basically does not change. The matter of a few seconds in viewing it is not going to make any difference whatsoever."

"We might have seen something."

"What?"

"Someone fleeing the scene."

"If there had been, I'm sure you would have seen them and told me."

"Yes, of course, but—"

"And," Steve said. "If I'd gone racing down those front steps, I'd be feeling as foolish as you're feeling now."

"Exactly," Tracy said. "That's what pisses me off. You're developing into a conservative old fogy. You're so concerned about what people might think of you that you'd risk missing a murder scene so as not to appear foolish."

Steve frowned. "Not a very charitable interpretation of my actions."

There came the sound of a gunshot up ahead and to the left.

Steve looked at Tracy. "What do you think? Should we run, or stroll along like old fogies?"

"Hey, fuck you," Tracy said.

Steve nodded. "Right. Yet another hostile sexual reference. Tell me, are you upset because I'm so cool to your theories, or because they gave us separate rooms?"

Whatever crushing comeback Tracy may have had was forever lost, for at that moment they rounded a bend in the path and emerged at the pistol range.

The range was simply a small clearing in the wood. Two men stood in the clearing, Russ Timberlaine and a Japanese gentleman. They were looking down what appeared to be a path off to the left. As Steve and Tracy approached, Russ Timberlaine raised a gun, sighted and fired down the path. He lowered the gun, turned to the Japanese gentleman and said something.

Steve and Tracy came walking up.

Timberlaine saw them, turned, smiled, "Ah, Mr. Winslow. Miss Garvin. Glad you could make it." He turned to the Japanese gentleman. "Mr. Nigouri, Mr. Winslow."

As they shook hands, Mr. Nigouri said in perfect English, "Are you a collector, Mr. Winslow?"

"Afraid not," Steve said. "And you?"

Nigouri smiled. "I'm selling, not buying. I'm here to auction off several weapons. Including that one," he said, pointing to the one Timberlaine was holding. "So you won't be bidding on it?"

"Afraid not," Steve said.

"Then, perhaps you, Miss . . . ?"

"Garvin," Tracy said, taking his hand. "I'm afraid Steve and I are just looking."

"Do you know anything about guns?"

"I'm afraid not."

"Ah, then let me show you," Nigouri said.

He led Tracy off to one side of the clearing where there was a circular marble alcove and bench, obviously part of the original estate. On the bench was an open leather box. Nigouri began opening drawers, removing guns and showing them to Tracy.

Timberlaine smiled at Steve. "You watch out. He'll sell her two pistols before dinner."

"I don't think she's in the market," Steve said.

Timberlaine shrugged. "You'd be surprised who's buying guns these days."

"What's with you?" Steve said.

"What do you mean?"

Steve jerked his thumb. "Your outfit."

Timberlaine was dressed in shorts and a T-shirt, and his hair was parted and pulled back in a ponytail. He grinned. "You mean what happened to the Wild West getup? Well, I have to admit that's a complete affectation. I put it on when I'm carryin' Pistol Pete's gun. Or in this case, the substitute." Timberlaine hefted the gun in his hand. "Now this baby's a derringer. It's French. Dates back to 1820. I'd look stupid firin' it in cowboy boots. Plus, the other guns in the auction will be from all different countries, periods, what have you."

"You bidding on them?" Steve asked.

"Oh, definitely," Timberlaine said. "I always bid. I'll be bidding on several." He looked at the gun in his hand. "Though I think this baby's the one I really want."

"Why is that?"

"Well, there's a story with it. I'm a sucker for stories. This gun was once owned by Marie LaBlanc, who was the victim of a tragic love affair. Her lover, Pierre LaTour, left her for a cafe singer. In despair she blew his brains out, then turned the gun on herself."

"You're kidding."

Timberlaine frowned. "Why should I kid about a thing like that?"

"This gun here?"

"That's the one."

"You'll pardon me, but how do you know that?" Steve jerked his thumb at Nigouri, who was still pulling out guns and bending Tracy's ear. "I mean, how do you know your friend there isn't buying old guns wholesale, then coming out here telling fancy stories and auctioning them off for record prices?"

Timberlaine shook his head. "Couldn't happen. The guns' histories are authenticated. Everything's double-checked. And we have our own independent expert on hand, hired specifically for these auctions. And of course any of the guests are free to bring their own experts. Believe me, the guns are genuine."

"I see," Steve said.

"Dad," came a voice.

Steve looked up as a young blonde bounced into the clearing. Steve smiled as he realized that's how he'd describe it. The girl was young enough and lively enough that she gave the impression of bouncing. She had short, curly blonde hair, twinkling blue eyes, and a turned-up nose. She was wearing a halter top and shorts and was barefoot.

She ran up to Timberlaine and kissed him on the cheek. "There you are," she said. To Steve she added, "Always know where to find Dad. Just follow the gunshots." She turned back to her father. "Donald and I are going out. I need money."

"Money?" Timberlaine said. "So why don't you stop at a cash machine?"

"Oh, it always takes so long. Just give me some money, Dad."

"Where are you going?"

"Shea Stadium. The Mets game."

"Oh," Timberlaine said. He fished in his pocket for his wallet.

The girl, having accomplished her purpose, now turned her attention to Steve. "Who's this?"

"Oh," Timberlaine said. "Steve Winslow, this is my daughter, Carrie. Carrie, Steve Winslow."

Carrie Timberlaine extended her hand. "Are you a collector, Mr. Winslow?"

Steve smiled. "Everyone asks me that. No, I'm not."

"Mr. Winslow is the attorney I told you about," Timberlaine said.

Carrie's eyes widened. "You're kidding. Oh, I'm sorry, Mr. Winslow. You'll pardon me, but you don't look like a lawyer."

Steve smiled again. "Believe it or not, you're not the first person to tell me that."

Tracy, who had observed this, managed to excuse herself from Mr. Nigouri and materialize at Steve's side, prompting another round of introductions.

Steve watched with some amusement. Tracy and Carrie, who were about the same age, did not exactly hit if off. Observing them, the phrase "shake hands and come out fighting" came to mind. They certainly eyed each other like adversaries, and without actually moving, still gave the impression of circling each other.

At about that point an athletic-looking young man with wavy brown hair and a soap opera star's plastic good looks arrived and proved to be Donald Walcott, Carrie's boyfriend, and the whole round of introductions began again.

"Steve Winslow's the lawyer," Carrie put in.

"Oh," Donald said. "Then you're here about the gun."

Steve raised his eyes to Timberlaine. "This is public knowledge?"

"Well, *they* know, of course," Timberlaine said. He nodded at

Nigouri, who was packing up his guns on the other side of the clearing. "But, no, there is no reason to tell everyone."

"My apologies, Russ," Donald said. He put his hand to his mouth, made a twisting motion. "My lips are sealed. Still," he said to Steve, "I think it's a good idea you're here. To find out what the hell is going on. But we'll be discreet, we won't tell anyone. Come on, Carrie. I don't wanna miss the first inning."

"Oh, yeah? If you're late, it's your own damn fault," she said, and turned and ran up the path.

Donald smiled and ran off after her.

As soon as he did there came a thump and a curse, like an offstage sound effect in a sitcom. Moments later, Melvin Burdett came into view. He was rubbing his head, and looked slightly peeved when he came around the corner, but when he saw Timberlaine his face brightened.

"Ah, there you are," Burdett said. "I might have known. Getting a jump on the competition. And Mr. Nigouri."

Burdett's eyes went straight to the gun in Timberlaine's hand. "And which one have you got there?"

Timberlaine's instinct was to hide the gun, but it was way too late. He took a breath, glowered in helpless frustration.

"Ah, yes, of course, the derringer," Burdett said. "Is that what you plan to bid on? Excellent. Excellent choice." Burdett nodded with complete satisfaction. He rubbed his hands together. "All I can say is, may the best man win."

9

DINNER DID NOT, as Steve had feared, consist of all the guests seated around one huge, long, solid oak table. Instead, half a dozen small tables were scattered throughout the spacious dining room. As some of the guests were not due to arrive until Saturday, and as Timberlaine's daughter and her fiancé had gone off to the Mets game, only four of the six tables were filled.

Seating was not left to chance. Steve and Tracy were met at the dining room door by Martin, who guided them over to Timberlaine's table.

Timberlaine hesitated just a beat as they sat down. He had told them to dress for dinner. Tracy, in a floor-length gown with her hair up and earrings, looked quite stunning. Steve Winslow had exchanged a T-shirt for a white shirt with collar and had thrown on a tie. Otherwise, he was still wearing his corduroy jacket and jeans. It was what he wore in court, and as far as he was concerned, that was as formal as he was going to go. Timberlaine did not comment, but he did hesitate perceptibly before introducing him.

The tables were round and seated eight. With Mr. Timberlaine was Mr. Nigouri, a middle-aged couple introduced as Mr. and Mrs. Crumbly, a trim, high-powered woman executive, introduced as Ms. Ebersol, and a white-haired gentleman with bifocals, introduced as Mr. Potter.

The guests quickly sorted themselves out. The Crumblys and

34

Ms. Ebersol were collectors. There the resemblance stopped. The Crumblys were in bubbling spirits and seemed to treat the whole thing as a lark, as if coming up for the weekend and bidding on guns was a form of amusement for them, delightful, whatever the outcome. Ms. Ebersol seemed to regard the whole thing as a business venture and find the Crumblys' attitude irritating.

Mr. Potter turned out to be the expert brought in by Timberlaine to authenticate the various items up for bid. Having ascertained that, Steve was amused to find that his occupation carried over into his social life as well, and he had a tendency to render judgment on everything, from the guests to the weather to the veal.

Steve and Tracy's introduction to the table caused a slight ripple of surprise, especially since Timberlaine introduced Steve as "my attorney." Obviously Timberlaine had not discussed this before and no one knew they were coming. There were a few raised eyebrows and polite smiles of inquiry. The only actual comment was from Mr. Potter, who nodded judiciously and said, "Good idea."

Ms. Ebersol frowned and cocked her head. "Winslow?" she said. "The name is familiar, but I can't quite place you."

She squinted across the table at him. Of course, in shoulder-length hair and corduroy jacket, he was not the sort of thing she would expect to find in a boardroom. Or in Timberlaine's dining room for that matter.

"It's unlikely that we have met," Steve said. "I have a limited practice, and there's no reason why you *should* know me."

"What sort of lawyer are you?" She caught herself, smiled. "I'm sorry. That didn't sound right. I mean, what sort of practice do you have?"

"I have my own, small, private practice. For the most part, I handle only one client."

Mr. Crumbly, who had a booming laugh, said, "Whoa, that sounds like Robert Duvall in *The Godfather*, doesn't it? I'd watch out you don't find a horse's head in your bed."

"And who is your client, Mr. Winslow?" Mrs. Crumbly asked.

"Sheila Benton."

Ms. Ebersol frowned. "Sheila Benton?"

Mrs. Crumbly's eyes widened. "Sheila Benton?" she said. "Oh, of course. You're the attorney for the Baxter Trust." She turned and plucked her husband by the arm. "You know. Maxwell Baxter's estate. Sheila Benton was his niece. *Is* his niece. Or however you say that. *He's* dead, she's not, if you know what I mean."

Ms. Ebersol got it. "That's why I know the name," she said. "Then . . ." She looked at him. ". . . You're a *criminal* attorney."

"Guilty as charged," Steve said.

She turned to Timberlaine. "You have a *criminal* attorney here, Russ?"

Timberlaine smiled. "It would appear I do."

Potter nodded judiciously. "Good idea."

Burdett came bustling up, gave a perfunctory nod to the rest of the table and grabbed Potter around the shoulder. "Jack," he said, "I got two guns I want you to look at after dinner."

"Oh?" Potter said. "Which two?"

Burdett held up his finger and smiled. "Tut, tut. Tell you after dinner." He pointed at Timberlaine. "But you don't tell him."

Potter shrugged. "I'm his expert."

"Yes, but you know the rules." Burdett grinned. "What, have I got to bring my own expert to these things? I get independent examinations and you don't tell anyone, that's the deal. Right?"

Potter shrugged. "Right."

"Then why do you say, I'm his expert?"

Potter shrugged again and his eyes twinkled slightly, "Because I'm his expert."

Everyone laughed, Burdett included. Everyone but Timberlaine, who couldn't hide his annoyance.

Burdett waggled a finger at Potter. "Now, now. You talk, I talk. I put it around gun circles you're not to be trusted, how many of these cushy weekend assignments you gonna get?"

Crumbly's laugh boomed again. "Good move, Burdett. Threaten the man you're counting on for confidential advice."

Burdett smiled. "Threat? What threat? I'm merely reminding him of the rules. The game isn't fair if you don't play by the rules, right?"

"This is not a game," Ms. Ebersol said.

Burdett's teeth flashed. "Of course it's a game. That's the whole point. If it weren't, it wouldn't be any fun. Right, Russ?"

Timberlaine didn't answer, just glowered at him.

"See," Burdett said. "The strong, silent type. That's how *he* plays the game. Me, I don't fit the image, I gotta play it my own way. But I certainly intend to play it." He turned to Mr. Potter. "Jack? After dinner?"

Potter shrugged and smiled. "At your service."

Burdett nodded, scuttled back to his own table and sat down.

Ms. Ebersol watched him go. "Insufferable," she said.

"Now, now," Mrs. Crumbly said. "If you don't take him seriously, he's sort of amusing."

Timberlaine nodded grimly. "Sure," he said.

When the meal ended, Burdett materialized at the table like an evil specter and grabbed Potter. "Come on, Jack," he said. "You too, Nigouri. We want to look at a couple of your guns."

"Which ones?" Nigouri said.

Burdett raised his finger. "Oh, no. I know you're reporting back to Russ. We'll see the whole batch." Burdett shook his head. "Always trying. These guys. Always trying."

Burdett corralled Potter and Nigouri and herded them out of the room. When they were gone, Steve managed to draw Timberlaine aside. "Look, I have to tell you," Steve said, "I feel like a damn fool about this whole thing. But if you got a few moments, why don't you show me and Tracy where you keep the guns."

"Sure," Timberlaine said. "Let me show you the layout."

They went from the dining room into the main hall.

"My study's in the west wing," Timberlaine said. He grinned. "Bit of a jaunt, actually. One hell of a house, huh? Come on."

He led them off down the hall.

"Are we apt to bump into Burdett and the gang?" Steve said.

"No, the viewing rooms are in the east wing."

"Viewing rooms?"

"Two rooms set aside for dealers and collectors to display and examine wares."

"What's the big deal about secrecy?" Tracy asked.

Timberlaine frowned. "I beg your pardon?"

"At dinner. Burdett going on and on telling your expert not to tell you."

"Of course," Timberlaine said.

"But a gun's a gun," Tracy said. "I mean, your expert's going to tell you the same thing he tells Burdett."

"Of course."

"So what's the point?"

"It makes a big difference to know what someone's going to bid on in advance. We're all relatively rich, but it's not as if anyone had unlimited funds. We're auctioning off close to two hundred guns tomorrow. No one is going to buy them all. You save your money and bid on what you really want."

"So?" Tracy said.

"So," Timberlaine said irritably, "if you know what a person's going to bid on, and if you're a pain in the ass who wants to make it tough on them, you save your money to bid against them on that item."

"Well, here we are."

Timberlaine stood aside and ushered them through a wide double door to the left. Steve and Tracy stepped in and found themselves in a room nearly as large as the dining room. The walls were lined with bookshelves and display cases. The cases were glass-enclosed and held gun racks, filled with rifles and pistols. In addition to the cases on the walls, there were numerous glass-topped table display cases scattered throughout the room. It was hard to estimate at a single glance, but there were literally hundreds of guns in the room. The effect was overwhelming.

"Good lord," Steve said.

Timberlaine grinned. "Yes. Pretty impressive, isn't it?"

"I'll say," Tracy said. "Are these guns all valuable?"

"That depends what you mean by valuable. They're all worth money, some more than others." Timberlaine pointed to one of the cases on the wall. "Now this is what you might call valuable. Flintlock, supposedly once owned by Alexander Hamilton. I paid twenty thousand dollars for it. That was ten years ago. I couldn't tell you what it's worth now. But I've been offered fifty."

"Fifty thousand dollars?" Tracy said.

"That's right," Timberlaine said. "Naturally, I wouldn't touch it."

"Where's our gun?" Steve asked. "The Pistol Pete imitation."

"Oh," Timberlaine said. "That would be over here."

He led the way to one of the table-top display cases in the middle of the room. "There you are," he said, pointing to it.

Steve and Tracy looked. The gun was lying in a little rack in the display case. It was lying so the R in the handle was facing up. A small typed card in front of it identified it as Pistol Pete Robbins's gun, just as if it had been an exhibit in a museum.

"Is this where the gun was stolen from?" Steve said.

Timberlaine nodded. "Far as I know. I mean, the substitution could have been made some time when I had it out and was showing it around and I simply didn't notice and returned it to the case myself. That's possible. But the odds are it was taken from this case."

"These cases locked?"

"Absolutely."

"Who has the key?"

"I do, of course."

"Where are the keys kept?"

"In my office."

"Your office?"

"Yes, my office off the front hall."

"Who has access to your office?"

"That, of course, is the problem. Practically anyone. The office is unlocked, most of the day no one's there, anyone could go in and out as they pleased."

"What about at night?"

"At night the office is locked. But anyone could have taken the keys during the day. And they'd have to have taken the gun during the day too."

"Why is that?"

" 'Cause there's an electronic burglar alarm system activated at night."

"Oh?"

"Yeah. So the substitution must have been done during the day."

"Unless someone knew how to switch it off," Steve said.

"Yes, except the switch is in the office and the office is locked."

"Who would have a key?"

"I do. Martin does. But what's the big deal?" Timberlaine said. "Anyone who could have stolen the key to the cases, could have stolen the key to the office. So maybe the gun could have been stolen at night, but it would be a damn sight easier to have stolen it during the day. At any rate, the fact is it was. And I want to take every precaution to see somebody doesn't use that fact to get me into trouble."

Steve took a breath. "By shooting someone with your gun," he said dryly.

Timberlaine looked at him sharply. "I get the feeling you're not really taking this seriously."

"Of course we're taking it seriously," Tracy said quickly. "I assure you, Mr. Winslow will take every precaution to see that you are protected."

Timberlaine took a breath. "I'm sorry," he said. "It's just this whole thing is getting on my nerves. And then that goddamn Burdett!" Timberlaine's face reddened as he said the name. He took another breath, blew it out. "Well," he said, "feel free to look around. I've got to join the other guests."

Timberlaine nodded and went out.

Tracy turned on Steve. "See?" she said. "It's not just me. He can tell you're not taking this seriously too."

"Oh, for God's sake," Steve said. "Isn't it enough I'm here?"

"No, it's not enough you're here. This man is counting on you. You've accepted a big retainer. You're here, yes, but you think the whole thing's a big joke. So you're basically goofing off for the weekend and not acting on any of the things you should be acting on."

"What do you mean?"

"If there's one thing you know for sure, it's that this man is obsessed with Melvin Burdett. And having seen Burdett, it's easy to tell why. Burdett's going out of his way to be a pain in the ass and needle Timberlaine every chance he gets. Timberlaine hates him, and what's more, everybody knows it. If Melvin Burdett were to die, I bet you couldn't find a person here who wouldn't think Timberlaine had done it."

Steve looked at Tracy. "Yeah? So?"

"And," Tracy said "Melvin Burdett and Timberlaine's daughter's fiancé have switched rooms. Well, not exactly switched rooms. But the fiancé is sleeping in Burdett's room. Burdett isn't sleeping in the *fiancé's* room. We don't *know* where Burdett's sleeping. We know he's not sleeping where he usually sleeps, and we know he's not sleeping where he was originally assigned."

Steve looked at her. "So?"

"So, on the one hand, you haven't found out where Burdett *is* sleeping, and on the other, you haven't found out if Timberlaine knows."

"Good lord."

"Which you *would* do, if you were taking this thing seriously."

Steve thought that over. "All right, if those are your criteria, I'm guilty as charged."

"I rest my case," Tracy said.

Steve sighed. "All right. Come on."

They found Martin still in the dining room, supervising the dinner cleanup. He seemed somewhat surprised by the request, but stated that Mr. Timberlaine had instructed him to give them whatever help was needed, and proceeded to check his chart.

"That's right," Martin said. "Burdett was originally assigned Room Thirty-four, a third floor front. He was switched to Room Seventeen, a second floor rear. What he wanted, of course, was Room Twelve, the second floor corner, occupied by Donald Walcott, Miss Timberlaine's friend."

"And who was originally assigned the room where Burdett is now?"

Martin consulted the chart again. "That would be Mr. Potter."

"Jack Potter? The expert?"

"Yes, sir."

"Where is Potter now? In the room you originally assigned for Burdett?"

Martin nodded. "Yes, sir. Room Thirty-four, third floor front. I simply switched rooms." Martin cocked his head, looked at Steve somewhat quizzically. "Was there anything else?"

Steve shook his head grimly. "No, that will do it. Have you seen Mr. Timberlaine?"

"I believe he's on the patio."

"Great," Steve said. "Come on, Tracy."

He grabbed her by the shoulders and piloted her outside.

There were about a dozen people on the patio talking in small groups. Steve looked around, spotted Timberlaine in one corner talking to Potter.

Steve turned back to Tracy. "You really want me to do this?"

She gave him a look.

He sighed, walked up to the two men.

"Excuse me," Steve said. "Mr. Timberlaine. If I could just talk to you for a minute."

Timberlaine frowned, said, "Excuse me," to Mr. Potter, and moved off with Steve. "What is it?" he asked.

Steve took a breath. "I'm sorry to bother you," he said, "but did you know that your daughter's fiancé is sleeping in Melvin Burdett's room?"

Timberlaine's eyes widened, his jaw dropped open, and he looked at Steve Winslow incredulously. "What the hell are you talking about?" he demanded.

As expected, Steve felt like a total idiot.

10

IN THE BACK ROW of the seats in the grand ballroom, Tracy Garvin grabbed Steve Winslow's arm. "Look at that."

Steve looked up from his auction program just in time to see Russ Timberlaine come striding through the double doors. For the auction, Timberlaine had reverted to his full cowboy regalia, with hat, vest and boots.

"Good lord," Steve said. He looked back at Tracy. "I don't want to stare, but from where you're sitting, can you tell if he's wearing a gun?"

"He certainly is."

"You don't suppose it's the one I think it is?"

"Bet you a nickel."

It was two o'clock on Saturday afternoon and Steve and Tracy were in good spirits as they waited for the auction to begin. That was partly due to the fact that the weather was gorgeous and they had spent a very pleasant morning strolling around the grounds, and partly due to the fact that no one had died in the night. Donald Walcott, the boyfriend, didn't get shot in his bed by someone thinking he was Melvin Burdett. And Jack Potter didn't get shot in his bed by someone thinking *he* was Melvin Burdett. And Melvin Burdett didn't get shot in his bed by anyone thinking he was Melvin Burdett, Jack Potter or Donald Walcott for that matter. All of these were not only alive and well, but had been present and accounted for at brunch that morning. So aside from feeling slightly foolish, Steve and Tracy were feeling particularly well.

"If that's the gun," Tracy said, "he hasn't noticed the substitution yet."

"A credit to my craftsmanship," Steve said.

"Oh, bullshit," Tracy said. "It's no trick to copy a copy. Now if you could make a copy that could pass for the original, that would be something."

"Too late for that," Steve said.

"Tell me something."

"What's that?"

"You're convinced that being here's totally stupid, nothing's going to happen and we're wasting our time?"

"That's one way to put it."

"On the other hand, you went to the expense of the elaborate precaution of switching guns."

"True. So?"

"So, how do you justify those two positions?"

"Easy," Steve said. "While I have no expectations a crime is actually going to be committed with Pistol Pete's original gun, I have to figure there was *some* purpose for the substitution—if there *was* a substitution, since I only have Timberlaine's word for that. Since I don't know whether his story is true, or what he or anyone else is planning, I attempted to take some measure of control of the situation by introducing a factor into the equation that only I would know. See?"

Tracy shook her head. "Bullshit. You're just like me. You think something's going to happen."

"Shhh," Steve said. "It's starting."

Tracy looked where Steve was pointing and saw that a man in a red jacket now stood at a lectern that had been set up on the stage at the front of the ballroom. On either side of the lectern were tables. At one sat an accountant with a ledger and cash box. At the other sat two assistants with lists of the items to be auctioned.

Also on stage, but further back, were long tables at which the dealers stood with their wares. There were five dealers on stage, including Mr. Nigouri.

The auctioneer tapped the microphone, said, "Good afternoon, ladies and gentlemen. Please be seated, let's get right to it."

There was actually a couple of minutes of shuffling and finding chairs before the auctioneer said, "Very well. The first item up for bids. Number one in your program. From Mr. Nigouri. A Smith and Wesson thirty-two-caliber revolver."

As the auctioneer droned on, Steve Winslow slumped down in his seat looking bored, but Tracy Garvin, who had never been to an auction before, perked right up. Tracy found the whole process fascinating. Particularly an auction of this kind, where the auctioneer was not jabbering away a mile a minute in some sort of doubletalk the uninitiated couldn't understand. Instead, the whole thing was rather calm and sedate and easy to follow.

Plus, the bidders all turned out to have different styles. Some never said a word, but would bid just by raising a finger or inclining the head. Ms. Ebersol fell into that category. She seemed to bid with her finger and her chin. In fact, once, Tracy could have sworn she bid just by raising an eyebrow.

Others were verbal. Some would raise a hand and say, "Here," to indicate that they were making the bid requested by the auctioneer. Others shouted out the actual amounts. Mr. Crumbly was one of those. He seemed to take delight in booming out the figures. Tracy noticed he never said the number alone, but always punctuated it with the word dollars.

The bidders Tracy was really concerned with, of course, were Timberlaine and Burdett, but in the early going, neither of them bid. None of the guns seemed to generate much interest, and the bidding was low key at best.

Tracy had just begun to shift restlessly in her seat when Steve poked her in the arm. "Here we go," he said. He pointed to the program. "Item Fourteen. The derringer."

Tracy's eyes widened. "Is that it?"

"I think so."

It was. The auctioneer produced Item Fourteen with a bit of a flourish, and actually told the story of Marie LaBlanc in describing it.

Other guns had been starting in the thousand, two thousand dollar range, but in this case the auctioneer said, "Let's start the bidding at ten thousand dollars."

Russ Timberlaine bid and Tracy smiled. He was, as she'd expected, one of those bidders who both gestured and spoke. He raised his hand and said, "Ten thousand."

On the other side of the room, Melvin Burdett rose to his feet. His smile was a challenge. "Fifteen," he said.

There was an audible reaction in the room, a common intake of breath. A five-thousand-dollar jump was by far the largest raise of the afternoon.

Timberlaine scowled.

The auctioneer frowned. "I have a bid of fifteen thousand."

"Sixteen," Timberlaine said.

Burdett smiled at him from across the room, turned to the auctioneer and said, "Twenty."

"Twenty-two."

"Twenty-five."

A pause.

"I have twenty-five thousand."

"Twenty-six."

"Twenty-seven," Burdett said promptly.

Another pause.

Timberlaine took a breath. From way across the room, Tracy could see the fire in his eyes. She expected him to bid.

Then he slowly blew it out again. Clamped his lips together.

"I have a bid of twenty-seven thousand," the auctioneer said. "Do I hear twenty-eight? . . . Twenty-seven thousand going once . . . Going twice . . . Sold to Mr. Burdett for twenty-seven thousand, mark it down."

Tracy leaned over, grabbed Steve's arm. "Why'd he let Burdett outbid him?"

Steve shrugged. "You'll have to ask him."

"Don't you know?"

"I would assume Burdett bid higher than Timberlaine was willing to pay."

Tracy made a face. "That's obvious. I mean—"

"I know what you mean. The answer is, I don't know. You can ask him at the break."

"The break?"

"It's a long auction. There's an intermission."

"Oh."

Tracy settled back in her seat to see if anything else interesting would happen. Nothing did. Neither Timberlaine nor Burdett bid again, and the rest of the bidding was decidedly lackluster.

At the intermission, Steve and Tracy got up and went out in search of Timberlaine, who had actually slipped out before the end of the bidding. They found him on the patio talking with his daughter.

"I hope we're not interrupting," Steve said.

"Not at all," Timberlaine said. "We were talking about the Mets."

"Oh. How was the ballgame?" Steve asked.

Carrie made a face. "Terrible."

Timberlaine smiled. "She says terrible. The Mets won, one nothing. A great pitchers' duel."

"Oh, men," Carrie said. "That's what Donald said too. Pitchers' duel. You know what a pitchers' duel is? It's a game where nothing happens. Boring, boring, boring."

Steve and Tracy laughed, and Timberlaine smiled indulgently.

"So," Timberlaine said. "How do you like the auction?"

Steve pursed his lips judiciously. "It's a pitchers' duel."

Timberlaine laughed. "Glad to see you've got a sense of humor. You're right. It's been pretty dull."

"Except for the derringer," Tracy said. "Hope you don't mind my asking, but why did you let it get away?"

Timberlaine frowned. "Because it was a no-win situation. That's the way it is with Burdett. Yeah, I could outbid him, but I get too high, see? I have to pay much more than the gun is worth. See why it's no-win? I'm either a fool for paying way too much for the gun, or I'm a loser for letting Burdett outbid me."

"I see," Tracy said. She frowned. "That's terrible."

"Yes, it is," Timberlaine said. He smiled. "Now you see my problem."

"Yes, I do," Tracy said. She looked at him. Frowned again. "But I don't understand."

"Understand what?"

"Pardon me, Mr. Timberlaine, but considering Melvin Burdett just outbid you, and considering what you just told me, you don't seem that upset."

Timberlaine smiled. "Is that so." He looked around the patio to see who was in earshot, then leaned in conspiratorially, said, "Well, just between you and me, the auction ain't over yet."

11

TRACY GARVIN WAS ON THE EDGE of her seat for the second
half of the auction. Russ Timberlaine hadn't said what he meant
by the auction not being over yet, but Tracy knew damn well he
must have some surprise in store for Melvin Burdett, and the way
Timberlaine was acting, she figured it was going to be good.

What that could be in the course of an auction, she had no idea.
The only thing that came to mind was Cary Grant making ridiculous
bids in the auction in *North By Northwest*. Which, of course, would
make no sense here. Unless, the next time Burdett bid, Timberlaine intended to make nonsensical bids to mock him. Which
didn't seem practical on the one hand, or in character on the other.
So what the hell was he up to?

As the auction progressed, Tracy had no idea. Because a Tim-
berlaine-Burdett confrontation simply did not materialize. In fact,
Timberlaine bid on no guns at all. Neither did Burdett, until nearly
the end of the auction. That was when the auctioneer announced
what sounded like a particularly choice item, a pistol reputed to
have been carried by one of the cavalry at the battle of the Little
Big Horn. Burdett bid ten thousand and Tracy perked right up.
Surely this was the gun where Timberlaine was going to take him
on.

Only he didn't. Mr. Crumbly was the only other bidder. He bid
twelve thousand. Burdett came back with fifteen. Crumbly offered

48

sixteen. Burdett bid twenty thousand. Crumbly bid twenty-two, Burdett twenty-five.

Tracy was annoyed. It was the most spirited bidding of the afternoon, but without Timberlaine in the auction it seemed dull.

There was a pause while Crumbly conferred with his wife. Since that was obviously what he was doing, the auctioneer waited, did not prompt.

Crumbly turned back. "Thirty thousand," he said.

Once again there was a common intake of breath. A five-thousand-dollar jump at that level was somewhat unprecedented. It was to all intents and purposes a close-out bid.

Not to Burdett. "Thirty-one thousand," he said.

A murmur of voices greeted that bid. Burdett was bidding over and above Crumbly's close-out?

Crumbly frowned.

The auctioneer repeated the bid, asked if he heard higher, did not, went through the going once, going twice routine and said, "Sold to Mr. Burdett for thirty-one thousand, mark it down."

Tracy wasn't watching the auctioneer at the time. Nor was she watching Crumbly, nor Burdett. She was watching Timberlaine.

His face was murderous. Earlier, he'd been angry when Burdett had outbid him for a gun. But that was nothing compared to this. The man was furious.

As the gun was marked down, Timberlaine turned on his heel and stalked out of the grand ballroom.

"What was that all about?" Tracy said.

"Damned if I know," Steve said.

"I thought the auction was almost over."

Steve checked the program. "It is."

"Then where the hell is he going?"

"I have no idea."

Steve and Tracy sat there while the next few items were knocked down. Tracy expected that at any moment Timberlaine would return to deliver the fireworks he had promised at intermission.

As the auctioneer called the next bid, there suddenly came the sound of a gunshot.

Tracy jumped, started to get out of her chair, then thought better of it. She turned to Steve. "Pistol range?"

"Sounds like it."

"Is that Timberlaine?"

"Probably a good bet."

"What the hell's he doing?"

"Most likely letting off steam."

"Yeah, but—"

"Hey, you know as much as I do."

Tracy shook her head. "How many items left?"

Steve checked the program. "Three."

"Are they interesting?"

He looked again, shook his head. "Don't appear to be."

They weren't. Not one of them fetched more than five thousand dollars. Timberlaine did not return, and just like that the auction was over.

12

STEVE AND TRACY CAUGHT UP with Carrie Timberlaine and Donald Walcott right outside the grand ballroom door.

"What happened in there?" Tracy demanded.

Carrie looked around. The guests were streaming out of the ballroom all around them.

"Dad's very upset. We can't talk here. Come outside."

She and Donald led them out onto a corner of the patio.

"So what happened?" Tracy said.

"It was just like Dad told you. Burdett would never let him have a gun. Not for a reasonable price."

"Yeah, so?"

"He wanted that cavalry piece. From Little Big Horn. Burdett would outbid him if he knew he wanted it, so he got Crumbly to bid for him."

"So that's what he was talking about at intermission?"

"Yeah, that's it."

"Only it didn't work. Burdett outbid him."

"Right. Dad's furious."

"Why?"

"He figures someone tipped him off."

"Who?" Steve said.

Carrie smiled. "Hey. I haven't talked to him. I saw him storm out just like you did. I'm guessing this from knowing Dad."

"Who *could* have tipped him off? Who knew?"

"Besides me and Donald?" Carrie said. "The Crumblys, of course, but they wouldn't have, they were in on it. The only other one it could have been is Jack Potter."

"Why him?"

"He'd have known, because Dad would have had him check out the gun."

"How well does your father know Potter?"

"That's just it. Not that well. This is the third or fourth time he's used him. His regular expert, the guy he relied on, moved to L.A."

"Who recommended Potter?"

"I don't know. You'd have to ask Dad."

"Surely not Burdett."

"There again I don't know."

"O.K., thanks." Steve took Tracy by the arm. "Come on, Tracy. Let's check out the pistol range."

Steve led Tracy off the patio and down the path toward the range.

As they went, Tracy looked up at him and shook her head. "I don't understand you," she said.

"Oh, why's that?"

"I've been knocking myself out all weekend to get you to take an interest in this thing and it's like pulling teeth, you don't wanna hear about it. Suddenly you're all gung-ho to find your client like it was a matter of life and death."

"I wouldn't go that far, but I would like to find him."

"Why?"

"Because the guy is really pissed off and is probably out running around with a gun I had Mark Taylor buy and then filed the serial number off of. If so, he just fired it at the pistol range, which means he's running around with it loaded. Now, if that gun winds up back in the display case where it belongs, we have no problem. But until it does, I must admit I am somewhat less than happy."

Tracy smiled up at him. "You weren't prepared to see Timberlaine come walking in wearing that gun, were you?"

"No, I must admit that was a bit of a shock. But keep your voice down. We're almost there."

They came around a bend and reached the clearing, but to no avail. The pistol range was deserted.

"O.K., what now?" Tracy said.

"O.K., we missed him and there's no telling where he's gone."

"Assuming he was here at all."

"Right. But I think that's a pretty fair assumption. Anyway, if he was, he's long gone. He could be walking around the grounds just to let off steam, or he could have gone back to the house. There's a lot of different paths. We could easily have missed him."

"So?"

"Let's go back to the house, see if we missed him along the way."

They made their way back to the house.

By the time they got back, the patio was filled with guests who had filtered out from the grand ballroom after the auction. Steve and Tracy looked around, but couldn't see Timberlaine. His daughter and her boyfriend were no longer there either. They saw Burdett, who had a small cluster of guests around him, and who seemed to be pontificating on some subject or other, but there was no sign of their host.

"Damn," Steve said.

"What do we do now?"

"Well, no use getting worked up over nothing. Now we check the gun room, make sure the gun he's running around with is the one we think it is. I'll feel like a damn fool if all this time it's sitting there right in its case."

"Right," Tracy said. "But I don't think it is."

They went inside, walked down the long hallway toward the gun room.

The almost walked by it. The huge double doors were closed.

Tracy had to grab Steve's arm.

"Wait a minute. Isn't this it?"

"Isn't what it?"

"The gun room. Isn't this the gun room?"

"Oh. I thought it was the next door."

"No, that's the last room down. The gun room wasn't the last room down. This has to be it."

"Then why are the doors closed?"

"Maybe it's locked."

"Why would it be locked?"

"Maybe they keep it locked during the auction, and they forgot to open it when it was over."

"It's not locked," Steve said, twisting the doorknob.

Steve pushed the double doors open. He and Tracy stepped into the room and stopped dead.

The body of Jack Potter lay face up beside the display case in the middle of the gun room floor.

He'd been shot in the head.

Next to the body lay a Colt .45 with the letter *R* carved in the handle.

13

Russ Timberlaine wouldn't stop talking.

"It's the wrong gun," he insisted.

Lieutenant Sanders cocked his head. "Oh? What do you mean by that?"

Steve Winslow held up his hand. "As your attorney, I advise you not to answer any questions or volunteer any information until we have had a chance to talk."

Sanders frowned. "Mr., ah, Winslow is it? No one wants to step on anyone's toes here or deprive anyone of their rights, but I would like to point out Mr. Timberlaine has been given a full Miranda warning. He *knows* he doesn't have to talk to us. He *knows* anything he says could be used against him. And if he wishes to cooperate, we are delighted to have his cooperation.

"Now, at the moment, I believe Mr. Timberlaine wants to explain how this gentleman came to be shot with his gun."

"That's not my gun," Timberlaine said.

Timberlaine, Sanders, Steve Winslow and Tracy Garvin were standing in the hallway outside the gun room. A strip of yellow tape ran across the gun room door. On the other side, a Crime Scene Unit was processing the room for evidence. Photographs had already been taken, the medical examiner was just finishing up with the body, and detectives were dusting for prints.

55

A young officer ducked under the yellow tape and emerged from the crime scene carrying a gun in a plastic evidence bag.

"The murder weapon, sir," the officer said to Sanders.

"Thanks. That's what I wanted," Sanders said. He took the bag, held it out toward Timberlaine. "There. Mr. Timberlaine. The murder weapon. A Colt .45, fully loaded, one shot fired. You've already denied this is your gun, but you haven't seen it yet. So look and tell me. Is this your gun or isn't it?"

Timberlaine barely looked at the bag. "That's the whole point, officer. Yes, this is my gun, but it has not been in my possession for over a week. It was stolen from me over a week ago, and I have not seen it from then until now."

"So when witnesses state they have seen you wearing this gun in a gun belt this very afternoon . . . ?"

"Not *this* gun. Don't you understand? This gun was stolen from me. This gun is a valuable antique. It was stolen from me, and a substitute left in its place. The gun I was wearing today was the substitute."

Sanders held up the bag. "And this is the genuine gun?"

"Yes, sir."

"A valuable antique?"

"That's right."

Sanders pointed. "The serial number's been filed off this gun."

"That's right. That was done over a hundred years ago by the original owner, Pistol Pete Robbins."

Sanders didn't crack a smile. "Is that right?"

"Yes, sir."

"Then how can you prove it's the real gun?"

"The gun is well documented. Any expert could authenticate it."

"Do you have such an expert here?"

Timberlaine smiled slightly. "Yeah, but he's not going to help you any."

"Why is that?"

Timberlaine jerked his thumb at the body bag the medical examiner was zipping up. " 'Cause that's him."

Sanders grunted. "Aha. And the substitute gun you claim you were wearing—where is that?"

"Upstairs in my room."

"And why is that?"

"I was wearing my Western outfit for the auction. Hat. Vest. Gun belt. Boots. The works. After the auction I didn't feel like wearing it anymore, so I changed out of it."

"Oh?"

Timberlaine was wearing a short-sleeved shirt, sneakers and jeans. "Well, actually," he said, "these are the same jeans. I changed my shirt and changed the cowboy boots for sneakers."

"And the gun?" Sanders prompted.

"On the gun belt, up in my room."

"Mind getting it for me?"

"Now just a moment," Steve said. "That gun had absolutely nothing to do with the death of Jack Potter. I see no reason for confusing the issue here."

"No one's confusing the issue," Sanders said. "We're clarifying the issue. Would you like to have your client give me that gun, or would you like us all to stand here in the hallway until I can get a warrant issued?"

"No need for a warrant," Timberlaine said, irritably. "Mr. Winslow, I appreciate your trying to look out for my interests. But the point is, I have nothing to hide. And it is in my best interests to see that these guns are identified, marked and kept straight, before anything happens to mix them up."

Timberlaine turned back to Sanders. "So I'm delighted to give you the gun. I'd appreciate it if you'd put it in an evidence bag and label it, so there's no question but that that is the gun I wore all afternoon. Then, if necessary, I will be able to demonstrate, first of all, that it is not my gun, the original rare gun that I purchased and, second, that it is not the gun that killed Jack Potter. So by all means, lieutenant, let me give you that gun."

"Fine," Sanders said. He handed the plastic evidence bag back to the young officer. "And just to make your position stronger, I'll go with you when you get it. I'll be able to verify the fact that the gun was in the holster where you said it was."

"Fine," Timberlaine said. "Come on."

"I'm going too," Steve said.

Sanders frowned. "That won't be necessary."

"Maybe not for you," Steve said. "Mr. Timberlaine, if you insist on this course of action, I can't stop you. But I'm sure going with you."

"All right, all right," Timberlaine said impatiently. "Let's go."
He turned and started down the hall toward the far end.

"Where's your room?" Steve said.

"Over this wing on the second floor. From here the back stairs are quicker."

Steve frowned. "I didn't know there was a stairway here."

"Oh, sure."

At the end of the hall, Timberlaine turned left. There in an alcove was a staircase that couldn't be seen from the main hall. They went up the stairs to the second floor, then back down the hallway.

"My rooms are on the second floor back," Timberlaine said. He led the way to a door halfway down the hall. "Here we are." He turned the doorknob, pushed open the door.

"Unlocked?" Steve said.

"Of course, unlocked. Why would it be locked?" Timberlaine said.

They followed him in. It was a huge suite. The room they had entered was a living room/sitting room with desk, couch, table, chairs, TV. Through double doors was the bedroom, dominated by a massive, four-poster bed, with carved wooden end tables. On one of these was a hat and gun belt. The hat was sitting on the gun belt, covering the holster.

"There you are," Timberlaine said.

He started for the gun belt, but Sanders grabbed his arm. "You'll pardon me, I'm sure," he said. He reached in his pocket, pulled out a plastic evidence bag. "If you don't mind, *I'll* do that."

Sanders walked over to the end table.

Tracy Garvin, whose wildest fantasies were coming true and who was hanging on every move, half expected the gun belt to be empty, but when Sanders picked up the hat, there was a gun in the holster. Sanders took a pen out of his pocket, used it to ease the gun out of the belt. He held up the gun with the pen, sniffed the barrel.

"The gun's been fired recently."

"That's right," Timberlaine said.

"Did you fire it?"

"Yes, I did."

"When and where?"

"After the auction, I went out and fired it at the pistol range."

"Oh? And why did you do that?"

"That's hardly relevant," Steve said. "In the first place, Mr. Timberlaine, you're answering questions about this gun, and you haven't identified it. You barely looked at the gun downstairs and you stated that it is genuine. I don't think you know that. You're just assuming that. You barely looked at this gun at all, and you're claiming it's the copy and the gun you fired at the pistol range this afternoon."

"Well, it is," Timberlaine said irritably.

"Maybe so, but the point is, you don't know."

"And the point is well taken, counselor," Sanders said with a grin. He slipped the gun off the pen into the plastic evidence bag, zipped the bag shut. He crossed over to Timberlaine, held up the bag. "All right, Mr. Timberlaine. We now have a second Colt .45, also fully loaded with one shot fired. For the record, can you identify *this* gun?"

"Of course," Timberlaine said.

"Fine," Sanders said. "Please look at it carefully and tell me that you *can* recognize it as the gun you said it was."

Timberlaine took the evidence bag, held it up, looked closely at the gun.

Tracy Garvin squeezed Steve Winslow's arm. She knew this was when Timberlaine was going to notice the substitution.

But Timberlaine merely said, "Absolutely. This is the fake gun. The one I found substituted for the real gun. The one I wore today and fired at the pistol range."

14

STEVE WINSLOW LEANED BACK in his chair, inclined his head toward Tracy Garvin and said in a low voice, "Think you can get out of here long enough to use the phone?"

They were sitting at one of the dining room tables. The police had herded all the guests into the dining room and were holding them there while Lieutenant Sanders conducted the questioning. Steve and Tracy, by virtue of having found the body, had been among the first questioned. This had been brief, due to the fact that Steve had taken the position that Russ Timberlaine was a client, and therefore anything he had told them was a confidential communication. As a result, all he and Tracy could testify to was the actual finding of the body. Even then, they refused to discuss any *reasons* for being in the gun room and finding the body, but merely the fact they had done so. Their statements, both similar, were basically this: that they had gone to the gun room and found the body; that Steve had remained with it while Tracy went for help; that she had located Martin Kessington and brought him to the gun room; that he had left her and Steve there and gone to phone the police; and that he had rejoined them and waited with them until the police arrived. While that was somewhat less than Lieutenant Sanders might have wanted, he soon came to the realization it was all he was going to get, and Steve and Tracy were now confined to the dining room while Sanders finished with the other guests. Since he was taking them one at a time, and conducting all the examinations personally, they appeared to be in for a long stay.

"Piece of cake," Tracy said. "What do you need?"

"Call Mark. Tell him to get his ass out here."

"On a Saturday night? He's not going to like that."

"Tell him it's murder."

"He'll like that even less."

"Yeah. I don't care for it much myself. Can you swing it?"

"No sweat."

Steve jerked his thumb at the cop stationed at the dining room door. "What about him?"

"Hey, they're letting people out to go to the bathroom. It's not like we're being held as suspects."

"Not yet."

"What do you want me to tell Mark?"

"Spare him the details. Just tell him there's been a murder and I need him to investigate. If he's got a pipeline into the cops out here that would help."

"You really think Timberlaine's in trouble?"

"I know it."

"Why'd you jump in upstairs, make him identify the gun?"

Steve grimaced. "Because he wouldn't shut up. Sanders was asking him why he fired off the gun at the pistol range, and he was about to say because he was pissed off about the auction. Which is just about the worst admission he could make right now. It won't take much for Sanders to put it together. Timberlaine's pissed off about the auction, he thinks someone tipped off Burdett, the one he thinks did it is Potter and Potter winds up dead. Once Sanders cops to that, Timberlaine's apt to find himself assisting the police with their inquiries, as they say in British detective fiction."

"What's your obligation at this point?"

"What do you mean?"

"Well, you accepted a retainer from the man with regard to a stolen gun. Does that mean you have to represent him for murder?"

Steve looked at her. "You don't want me to?"

"I didn't say that. I'm just asking."

"Yeah, but why?"

"Because Timberlaine won't shut up and refuses to follow your advice. He's spilling his guts to the cops now, and we're cooling our heels here 'cause he didn't want you with him. I'm just wondering why you're not telling him to go to hell."

Steve took a breath. "There's a good chance I will. But not until after the cops I.D. the murder weapon."

"How come?"

"Because until they do, the other gun, the one Mark bought and I altered, is still evidence in the case. I need to keep my hand in to make sure that evidence doesn't come out."

"Great. You gonna tell Mark?"

"Tell him what?"

"What do you think? About the substituted gun."

"I've got to, Tracy. He's a friend. He's got a right to know."

"Don't you think he's gonna be a trifle pissed?"

Steve smiled slightly. "I think it would be safe to say that."

15

MARK TAYLOR'S EYES WERE BUGGING OUT of his head. "Run that by me again."

"Well, Mark, the bottom line is the gun you bought is being held in evidence in a murder case."

"Jesus Christ."

"But don't worry," Tracy said. "Steve filed the serial number off, so there's no way the cops can trace it back to you."

Mark Taylor blinked. "That's a felony."

"Yes, but you didn't commit it," Steve said. "I did. You're totally in the clear."

"I'm an accessory."

"No, you're an unwitting accomplice," Tracy said. "They hardly ever go to jail."

Taylor looked back and forth between the two of them. "O.K. the two of you rehearsed this pretty well. I'm gonna assume we're not really in trouble, or you wouldn't be kidding about it."

"Well, you're half-right, Mark," Steve said. "It's a mess, but it could be worse. The cops are holding our gun, yes, but only so it doesn't get mixed up with the murder weapon. It looks just like it, you see."

"Gee, what a surprise. And which gun is the murder weapon?"

"Apparently, the original gun we set out to copy. Now, wait a minute. That's confusing. Because the gun we set out to copy was not the original. It was the first substitute." Steve grinned. "Sounds like the Miss America Pageant. The First Alternate Gun. In the event the real Pistol Pete gun was unable to fulfil its duties, then—"

"Jesus Christ," Taylor said. "What the hell is with you?"

"We're punchy, Mark," Tracy said. "We've been living a murder mystery out of a storybook for two days and it just came true."

"Plus we snuck out on our police guards, so we feel like school kids getting away with something," Steve added.

Steve and Tracy had slipped out of the dining room just in time to intercept Mark Taylor and hustle him down to one of the gun examination rooms. Since that was at the opposite end of the building from the gun room, it seemed a place where they would have a good chance of not being found.

Taylor exhaled. "Great. I'm glad you're having so much fun. Would you mind telling me why you got me out here? Or was it just to have a good laugh at my expense?"

"Didn't Tracy ask you if you had any police ties out here?"

Taylor made a face. "This is Nassau County. I don't know from Nassau County. I'm trying to find out about Nassau County, but it happens to be the weekend and everybody's off. I reached my receptionist, and I got her callin' around trackin' down all my operatives asking them if they got any ties out here. But it's the weekend, reachin' 'em is gonna be a bitch, if she can I don't know. If I can get to a phone, I'll call in and find out."

"Hold up on that." Steve said. "You might get picked up looking for one."

"Get picked up for what?"

"You'll get mistaken for a witness and confined to the dining room."

"Fuck that," Taylor said. "In the meantime, what do you want me to do?"

"We'll get you a phone as soon as we can," Steve said. "In the meanwhile we're all kind of on hold. What we do depends on what the cops do. So far they haven't charged anyone. If they do, it only concerns us if it's Timberlaine."

"Will it be?"

"Sure looks like it. It was his gun. He can tell all the fancy stories he wants about it being stolen, the cops are only gonna half care.

Right now the cops are down the hall listening to fifty witnesses telling their stories. All of 'em are going to testify Timberlaine came to the auction this afternoon wearing a cowboy suit and a gun. At least half of 'em will testify Timberlaine stalked out of the auction in a huff. Some of 'em will testify later they heard a shot—that was nothing, that was down on the pistol range, but still it was Timberlaine firing off the gun."

Steve held up his hand. "Now, Mark, that is *not* the murder weapon. It's the substitute gun. The one you bought."

"Oh, shit."

"But it is *not* the murder weapon. Now, the cops may try to *claim* it's the murder weapon."

"How can they do that? Ballistics will prove it wasn't."

"Right," Steve said. "That's not what I mean. They won't claim *the gun you bought* was the murder weapon. They'll claim *the gun Timberlaine was wearing at the auction* was the murder weapon. See what I mean?"

"Right. Will they do that?"

"I don't know. But if they did, who could disprove it?" Steve waved it away. "Anyway, that's a side issue. The problem is a lot of people will be able to testify that Timberlaine was angry about the auction."

"Why?"

Steve gave Taylor a rundown of Timberlaine's attempt to fool Burdett by having Crumbly bid on the cavalry piece. "That's the motive," he said. "The cops will claim Timberlaine figured Potter was the one who tipped Burdett off, confronted him, made him confess and shot him."

Taylor frowned. "Is that sufficient motive for murder?"

"Not at all. It's thin as all hell. But if the cops can't come up with any other obvious suspect, what do you bet they go for it?"

"No takers."

"What makes the whole thing really stupid is the odds are no one tipped Burdett off at all."

"Whaddya mean?"

"I mean Burdett may be obnoxious, but the man is no dope. And Timberlaine's plan of having Crumbly bid for him was transparent as glass. In the second half of the auction, there was only one gun of any import, Timberlaine's a sucker for a gun with a history and this gun had one, and yet he sits on his hands and doesn't make a bid, but his buddy Crumbly does. Even without a tipoff, it wouldn't take a genius to see through that one."

"Which blows the cops' motive?"

"No, because Timberlaine was angry. Which means he was acting like *he* believed there was a tipoff. I can show it's stupid, but in the end it's really my client I'm showing who's stupid."

"Right," Taylor said. "So that's the worst case scenario? The cops grab Timberlaine and make a case he shot this guy out of spite?"

"Oh," Steve said.

Taylor looked at him sharply. "What the hell does that mean?"

"Well," Steve said. "Actually, there's a slightly worse scenario, Mark."

"Oh, yeah? What's that?"

"Well, Timberlaine's been shooting off his mouth a lot."

"Yeah. So?"

"And he's claiming the gun found next to the body was stolen from him a week ago."

"I don't think I wanna hear this," Taylor said.

"Probably not. Anyway, to back up his claim, Timberlaine whips out the test bullets you had your expert compare. The one he gave us matches the murder weapon just fine. But the one fired from the gun he gave us doesn't happen to match the gun he's got now, and the cops want to know why not."

Taylor thought that over. He nodded glumly. "I was right. I didn't wanna hear that."

16

MARK TAYLOR CONSULTED HIS NOTEBOOK, punched in a number. "Never seen such a big house with so few phones," he said.

His claim was justified. There were no phones in any of the guests rooms, hallways, or public rooms of the mansion. They were using the one Tracy had used to call him, which was located in a small office alcove on the first floor.

"Hello, it's me," Taylor said. "You got anything?" He listened a moment. "When'd you talk to him? . . . Uh-huh. Give me the number . . . O.K., good work." He broke the connection, punched in another number. "Got a lead," he said.

"Oh?" Steve said.

"Yeah. It's indirect. Operative who knows a reporter." Into the phone Taylor said, "Fred, it's me. What you got?" He listened a moment, said, "Aces, where's he now? . . . He gonna call you back? . . . How soon? . . . Fine, hang in there, I'll get back to you." Taylor hung up the phone, said, "That's a break."

"Oh?"

"We got a crime reporter for the *Daily News*, covers this county. Fred tipped him off to the murder. TV crews haven't got here yet, so it's still a hot tip, the guy's gotta be grateful. Even though he didn't need it."

Steve frowned. "What do you mean?"

"The guy already had the tip when Fred called. Guy's got a source, you see. Inside track."

Steve grinned. "No shit."

"None. The guy got the tip, was just fixin' to leave when my man caught him. Anyway, he promised to call back."

"Who is this guy?

"Reporter named Harold Coleman."

"You know him?"

"Never met him, but my man says he's all right." Taylor leaned back in the chair and stretched. "So what you wanna do now?"

At that moment the door was flung open by a uniformed officer. The officer was young, aggressive and not taking any chances. He had his gun out. "All right," he demanded. "Who the hell are you?"

"Unarmed civilians," Steve said. "At least I think we are." He turned to Tracy. "You aren't carrying a gun tonight, are you, dear?"

The officer flushed slightly, but was not about to be put off. "What are you people doing here?"

"Making a phone call," Steve said. "There's no phone in the dining room."

"You're not supposed to be making phone calls."

"Is that right?" Steve said. He smiled. "We're sorry. We didn't know that."

"You were told not to leave the dining room. Now come on. Let's go."

"Certainly," Steve said. "Mark. Tracy. Come on. Let's not argue with the man. After all, he has a gun."

They went out the door and walked down the long hallway to the dining room. Steve tried to lead Mark and Tracy inside, but the young officer wasn't falling for it. He stopped them at the door.

"Wait here," he said. To the officer at the door he said, "Keep an eye on these three."

He turned and walked off down the hallway in the direction of the gun-examining rooms. A few minutes later he was back with Lieutenant Sanders.

Sanders raised his eyebrows. "So," he said. "These are the people making the phone calls? What a surprise."

"You have no reason to hold us," Steve said.

"Material witnesses to a murder? I beg to differ." Sanders's eyes fixed on Mark Taylor. "And who, might I ask, are you?"

"Mark Taylor," Steve said. "Mark, let me introduce Lieutenant Sanders."

"This is hardly a social situation," Sanders said. "I wasn't asking for an introduction. I want an explanation. I haven't seen you before. Who are you? Are you one of the guests?"

"Mark Taylor happens to be my detective," Steve said.

"*Your* detective? You brought a detective along for the weekend?"

"Of course not."

"I didn't think so. You just arrived, didn't you, Mr. Taylor?"

Taylor frowned. "That depends what you mean by just."

"Yeah. Right," Sanders said. "Fulton," he barked.

The officer at the dining room door looked up. "Sir?"

"I don't mean to comment on the job you're doing," Sanders said sarcastically. "But we've got people arriving, people leaving, people making phone calls, people slipping out and having rendezvous—are you keeping track of all this?"

Fulton looked uncomfortable. "Sir," he said.

"How about the rest of the guests? You having any trouble keeping them in here?"

"As a matter of fact," Fulton said, "I believe the staff is about to serve dinner."

"Excellent idea," Sanders said. "You see these three people? I want you to notice them particularly. Remember their faces. Can you do that?"

"Yes, sir."

"Good. Now, these three people—you know what I think? I think they look hungry. Do me a favor and see that they have some dinner."

"Yes, sir."

Sanders turned on his heel and stalked off.

Fulton glowered at them.

Steve smiled and shrugged. "Well, gang. Let's eat."

17

MARK TAYLOR THREADED HIS WAY through the tables across the dining room to the far corner where Steve Winslow and Tracy Garvin stood. Steve had given him the high sign, otherwise Mark would have been perfectly happy to remain at his table and have dessert. Unable to resist, he had scooped up the rich wedge of chocolate layer cake, and was munching on it as he went.

Taylor walked up to them, chewed twice, swallowed and said, "What's up?"

"I hate to interrupt your dinner," Steve said, "but we have this murder on our hands."

"Don't be a grouse," Taylor said. "If we're stuck here, we should eat. Didn't you eat?"

"We've been interviewing witnesses," Tracy said.

"No excuse for not eating. I bet I interviewed more than both of you combined."

"Oh, yeah?" Steve said.

Taylor shrugged. "Hey, you said I could tell 'em who I am. I sat down at a crowded table, told 'em I was a private detective, and people fell all over themselves wanting to talk to me. I not only got those people, I had them runnin' around grabbin' people and bringin' 'em over. Didn't you see me?"

"I saw you stuffing your face."

"Hey, if you didn't eat, you got no one to blame but yourself."

70

Taylor shoved the last bit of cake in his mouth, licked his fingers, then reached in his jacket pocket and pulled out his notebook. "I got names, addresses, stories, what have you. I had dinner and I still talked to more people than you."

"So what'd you learn?"

"The prime rib is fabulous. Timberlaine may be a murderer, but the man sets a hell of a table."

"Mark."

"Sorry. Couldn't resist." Taylor flipped open his notebook. "I got two kinds of people here. People with the check are people who have already been interrogated by the police. People without the check haven't."

"What have you got?"

"Nothing helpful. At least, nothing *I know* that's helpful. When I get it all typed up you can go over it. For right now, there's nothing that jumps out and grabs you. I got everybody's alibi and they're all pretty much the same. After the auction, they either went out on the patio where there was a bar set up, or they went up to their room, or they just hung out in the grand ballroom. Usually a combination of the three.

"Now, as far as Timberlaine's concerned, practically everyone recalls seein' him stalk out of the auction. No one remembers seein' him between that time and the time you guys found the body." Taylor winced. "Gee, that sounds bad, doesn't it? Maybe I should just say, the time the body was found."

"Let's not get hung up on semantics, Mark."

"Right. Or legalities, technicalities, or whatever. Anyway, no one remembers seein' him.

"Now, Potter, it's a different story. Most people can't remember seein' him at the auction at all. Those that do remember, aren't that sure about it. And none of 'em saw him leave. So the bottom line is, I can't prove he was even there."

Steve frowned.

"What about you?" Taylor said. "You got a definite eyewitness?"

Tracy smiled. "We were just talking about it. We were hoping you would."

"Oh?"

"That's why we called you over," Steve said. "We can't find anyone either."

"Well, neither can I. Can I go back now? They're serving coffee."

"Jesus, Mark."

"Well, it's probably good coffee, not the lousy shit you get on the corner."

"You mind giving me the rest of your report first?"

"That's basically it. Everyone saw Timberlaine, no one saw Potter and no one went near the gun room at any time after the auction."

"How about before the auction?"

"Huh?"

"Well, if no one saw Potter at the auction, he could have been shot before it."

Taylor's face fell. "Shit, Steve. Give me a break. Besides, I got people *thought* they saw him at the auction."

"I know. Depending on when they fix the time of death, those people may or may not be important."

Melvin Burdett pushed his way past the officer at the door, looked around the dining room, spotted them and bustled over.

"They just interrogated me," Burdett said. "That lieutenant—what's his name?"

"Sanders."

"That's the one. I don't like him. The man is obnoxious."

Steve kept a straight face. "Oh?" he said.

"His manner's insulting. As if he didn't believe you."

"What did he ask you?"

"If I saw Potter, and if Potter tipped me off."

"Tipped you off?"

"To the gun. To the damn stupid gun. To the cavalry piece."

"He wanted to know if Potter tipped you off about the gun?"

"Yeah. To the fact Russ was going to bid."

"What did you tell him?"

"What do you think I told him? I said no way. Potter's a professional. No pro would do a thing like that."

"Potter didn't tip you off?"

"I just said he didn't."

"Then how'd you know Timberlaine was going to bid on the gun?"

Burdett made a face. "Give me a break. A child of four knew Russ was going to bid on the gun."

"Is that what you told Sanders?"

"Sure I did. And the son of a bitch doesn't believe me."

"What else did he ask you?"

"Did I see Potter at the auction."

"Did you?"

"No. And he doesn't believe that either. He says if I bought rare guns, I'd want Potter to check 'em out."

"What did you tell him?"

"The man's a moron. You don't check out guns *after* you bid on 'em. You check 'em out *before*. I mean, the guy may not know anything about guns, but he's a cop, he should know how to think. What, he thinks I buy a gun and then have someone check it out to see what I bought?"

"So you didn't see Potter at the auction?"

"No."

"You didn't notice if he was there?"

"Why should I? It's got nothing to do with me."

"But you didn't?"

"No."

"Did he ask you if you saw Timberlaine leave the auction?"

"Of course he did."

"And did you?"

"Of course I did. I just bought the gun, of course I'm going to look to see how he took it."

"You surprised when he stormed out?"

"Not at all. Russ has a temper. He hates to lose."

"What about you?"

"What?"

"Do you hate to lose?"

Burdett smiled. "Are you kidding? Everyone hates to lose. Now look, you gotta do something."

"What?" Steve said.

"You're Timberlaine's lawyer, right? Well, this cop, this lieutenant's all screwed up, thinks Russ did it. Ridiculous. Russ wouldn't hurt a fly. Now, I hate to say this about our host, but the man's a little naive, you know? Like thinking I wouldn't know he wanted that gun. Anyway, this cop's talking like he thinks Russ did it, and Russ isn't going to believe that could happen to him, and he's apt to walk into something, you know?"

"I sure do."

"So you gotta shut him up before he hurts himself."

"You like to suggest how?"

Burdett grinned. "That's a problem, isn't it? Russ doesn't take kindly to suggestions. So how the hell you gonna protect him?"

"Do you think Timberlaine killed Potter?"

"Of course not."

"Fine," Steve said. "Then someone else did. All I gotta do is find out who."

"How you gonna do that?"

"By asking questions. Tell me, what did *you* do from the time the auction was over to the time the body was found."

Burdett grinned. "Right, right. You mean I'm a suspect. O.K., let's see. I went up on stage, verified my purchases and wrote checks."

"You take possession of the guns you bought?"

Burdett shook his head. "Absolutely not."

"Why not?"

"Russ's rules. Dealers retain possession of the guns sold at auction until such time as the purchasers leave."

"Why is that?"

"Security reasons. Russ doesn't want to be liable for a guest having a gun stolen from his room. Dealers retain possession and the collections are locked in the safe."

"What safe?"

"This huge safe in Timberlaine's office. My guns are there now."

"O.K.," Steve said. "So you went up on stage, wrote checks for the guns and then what?"

"Went out on the patio and had a drink. They had a bar set up on one end, you know. So I had a drink. I looked around for Russ, didn't see him. So I stayed on the patio for a while, talking to people about the auction. Then I went to my room to freshen up and change for dinner. I was still there when I heard the commotion and the police cars arrived."

"I see," Steve said. "And you hadn't seen Timberlaine or Potter since the end of the auction?"

"That's right."

"And Potter never tipped you off about the gun?"

"That's right."

"And last night, when you came by Timberlaine's table, you told Potter you wanted to talk to him after dinner?"

"Yeah?"

"Did you?"

"Sure."

"What about?"

"What do you think? I had him check out some guns."

"Including the cavalry piece?"

"Of course."

"Was that the only gun you had him check out?"

"No, I had him do a whole bunch."

"But you did ask him about the cavalry piece?"

"Yes, of course."

"You asked him specifically to check out that gun?"

"Yes, I did."

"The lieutenant ask you that?"

"What?"

"About talking to Potter last night? Asking about the gun?"

"Yeah, he did. Why?"

"He bring it up, or you did?"

"He did, of course. I wasn't volunteering anything. Why?"

"If he asked about it, it means he heard it from someone else."

"Of course." Burdett said, impatiently. "That's obvious. All right, look. I've answered your questions. Now you answer mine. What are you going to do for Russ?"

Steve looked at Burdett, pursed his lips. "You want an honest answer?"

Burdett frowned. "What, are you nuts? Of course I do."

Steve shook his head. "Then, frankly, Mr. Burdett, I haven't the faintest idea."

18

MARK TAYLOR SLAMMED DOWN THE PHONE and stood up. It rang again. He cursed, sat down, snatched it up.

"Yeah," he growled. "Yeah, Frank, just a minute." He covered the mouthpiece, looked up at Steve Winslow who was standing near the door. "Another operative. I'll send him out."

Steve nodded, walked into the next room where Tracy Garvin was also on the phone.

It was Sunday morning. They were in a small motel just off the Long Island Expressway. They'd been held in the dining room Saturday night until just after midnight when the cops had finished their interrogation and finally allowed everyone to leave. Of course, most of the guests were staying over anyway. Steve and Tracy had stuck around looking for Timberlaine. Mark Taylor, desperate for phones, had gone out and found the motel. Unable to get what he wanted, a unit with two phones, he had settled for two adjoining units, and spent the night running back and forth between the two phones. It had been quite a relief when Steve and Tracy had showed up the next morning with coffee and doughnuts.

Tracy hung up the phone, shook her head, and said, "Nothing."

"Oh?" Steve said.

"That reporter again. Harold Coleman. He may be chummy with a cop, but the cop don't know shit. He's got nothing you can't read in the morning papers."

"And no sign of Timberlaine?"

"None."

"Shit."

"Yeah. What a bummer."

"This is the type of thing I thought they didn't do anymore."

"What?"

"Bury a suspect. No sign of Timberlaine, no sign of Sanders. They're not at the mansion and they're not at headquarters. They got lost somewhere along the way. The thing is, if they arrest him, even Timberlaine's smart enough to shut up and stop cooperating. At which point he has the right to an attorney and I step in. But as long as he's talking, they're not going to do that. They'll just hold him and let him keep talking and talking until he makes their case for them."

"How do you know they're doing that?"

"Because this reporter's got an in with a cop and the cop doesn't know where they are. Or says he doesn't. Which means what's going on is something extralegal the cops don't want to have appear in the press."

"What can you do about it?"

"Absolutely nothing. That's what's infuriating. Once he's arrested and charged with murder I can make a stink about it, but by then the cops will have an airtight case. Meanwhile I sit here twiddling my thumbs and there isn't a goddamn thing I can do."

"Steve," Mark Taylor yelled from the other room.

"Yeah," Steve said, heading for the door.

"Got something," Taylor yelled.

Tracy sprang up, followed Steve in.

"What you got?" Steve said.

Taylor, still on the phone, held up his hand. "O.K., good work," he said. "See what else you can get and call me back." He slammed down the phone. "Got the medical report."

"Oh, yeah?"

"Yeah. It's just preliminary, but my man swears it's accurate. O.K. Cause of death—gunshot wound to head. Big deal. We knew that. Time of death—yesterday afternoon between the hours of four and six."

Steve frowned. "Damn."

"What's the matter?"

"Can't they do any better than that? The cops were there by six. We found the body before then, for Christ's sake. And the medical examiner was there by at least six-thirty. He ought to be able to do better than that."

"Maybe he can, but the fact is he's not. Four to six is the best he'll do."

"Shit."

"What's so bad about that anyway?"

"The auction was over by four-thirty. Timberlaine slammed out of there around four o'clock. And no one's sure Potter was at the auction. If he wasn't, it sure makes a nice opportunity for Timberlaine to find him alone and kill him before the auction broke up."

Taylor frowned. "I see what you mean."

"What's a pain in the ass is most likely he didn't. What I mean is, if they put the time of death between four and six, it's likely the guy was killed around five. *After* the auction. So why can't the M.E. put the time of death after the auction broke up, so at that time anyone could be likely to do it? Instead of having a special time when everyone will testify *only Timberlaine* had left the room."

Taylor frowned and shrugged. "Hey, it's not so bad. This case must be really pissing you off. Because either way Timberlaine could have done it. It's no big deal."

Steve sighed. "I know. It's just, what do you do when your client's a big jerk who's shooting off his mouth and there's nothing you can do about it?"

"You tell him he's free to find another attorney."

"Which is *exactly* what I'd do if the son of a bitch hadn't handed the gun you bought over to the cops."

"I understand. Considering that, I'm very grateful you're not dropping him as a client. And I understand why you're pissed off. But the time of death's the time of death. The M.E. putting it between four and six is not really a major kick in the ass."

"It is in one respect. After Timberlaine stormed out of the auction, he fired the gun. A lot of people heard the shot, and can testify it was before the auction broke up."

Taylor frowned. "That's right."

"The stupid thing is, that shot is virtually irrelevant."

"Why?"

"Because they heard it. The way I understand it, the gun room is virtually soundproof, and there's no way anyone sitting in the auction room could have heard the shot that killed Potter. Assuming that's where it was fired." Steve yawned and stretched. "Tell me, how did you get the report anyway? Tracy just got through telling me the reporter had nothing."

"I'm sure he doesn't," Taylor said. "This came straight from the medical examiner's office."

"Oh?"

"Hey, sometimes you get lucky. I got a guy knows a girl got a boyfriend whose sister works for the medical examiner."

"You're kidding."

"No. So for once you get a break. You're getting your information ahead of the press."

The phone in the other room rang.

"I'll get it," Tracy said, and disappeared through the door.

Steve followed her into the next room. Taylor came and stood in the doorway.

"Hello," Tracy said. "Yes, he's here." She looked up at Steve. "Carrie Timberlaine."

Steve walked over, took the phone. "Yeah, Carrie?" He listened. "Where is he? . . . O.K., I'll be right there."

Steve hung up the phone. "O.K., gang. Shit's hit the fan. They just gave Timberlaine his one phone call."

"You're kidding," Taylor said.

"No. Brought him in, charged him with murder. Tracy, hang out with Mark, wait for my call. I'm going over there."

Steve turned and headed for the door.

The phone in the other unit rang.

"Shit," Taylor said. "Wanna hang on in case it's important?"

"Haven't got time."

Steve jerked the door open, went outside. He crossed the parking lot, got in the rental car and gunned the motor. He backed out of the space and was just pulling out of the lot when Tracy Garvin came flying out the door waving her arms.

Steve slammed the car to a stop, jerked open the door.

"What is it?" he yelled.

"I don't know. Mark just yelled to stop you."

"Shit," Steve said. He switched off the motor, jumped out of the car, ran back to the motel.

Mark Taylor was still on the phone.

"What is it?" Steve said.

"Just a second," Taylor said. "O.K., call me back." He slammed down the phone, turned to look at Steve. "The reporter finally got the news. They arrested Timberlaine."

"I know that," Steve said impatiently. "Shit, I was on my way over there."

"I know, but you don't know the half of it. They got the ballistics report. That's why they arrested him. They matched up the bullet with the gun."

"So what? We knew they would."

"Yeah, but it's the wrong gun."

"What?"

"It's the wrong fucking gun," Taylor said. "According to ballistics, the gun Potter was killed with was the gun Timberlaine gave them. The gun he was wearing at the auction." Taylor looked up at Steve and cocked his head. "You know. The gun I bought you."

19

Russ Timberlaine ran his hand over his face and looked at Steve Winslow through the wire-mesh screen in the lockup. "I'm sorry," he said.

"Hey," Steve said. "No reason to be sorry. You're the one charged with murder."

"I can't understand that."

"It's perfectly easy to understand," Steve said. "You disregard your lawyer's advice, shoot your mouth off to the cops. Of course they're gonna ask you everything they want to know until they get enough on you to charge you with murder."

"That's not the point," Timberlaine said irritably. "All right, in retrospect I shouldn't have talked. But how the hell was I to know?"

"Know what?"

Timberlaine's eyes blazed. "That that gun killed him. It's absolutely impossible. It can't have happened."

"According to ballistics—"

"Fuck ballistics. I know what I know."

"And what do you know?"

"What?"

"Tell me what you know," Steve said. "Do me a big favor, since I'm your lawyer, and catch me up with the cops."

"There's no reason to be sarcastic."

"No, of course not," Steve said. "You fuck everything up, hand me a hopeless murder case and say defend it. What the hell am I supposed to do?"

"Now hang on," Timberlaine said. "This is not my fault. Someone has framed me and framed me good. If that hadn't happened, nothing I said would have mattered. Now let's stop bellyaching and take a look at the facts."

"Fair enough," Steve said. "And what is your version of the facts?"

Timberlaine glared at him. "My version is the truth. If it doesn't make any sense, I can't help that. But that's the way it is."

"Fine," Steve aid. "Let me in on this truth."

Timberlaine took a breath. "All right," he said. "First off, Burdett outfoxed me on the auction. Outbid Crumbly for the gun I wanted."

"No shit," Steve said. "That was obvious to everybody there. You were furious because Burdett got a tip."

"Right," Timberlaine said. "Exactly."

"Did you tell that to the cops?"

"Of course I did."

"Christ," Steve said. "But there was no reason to think that. It was a gun you would have naturally wanted. Burdett could have come to that conclusion himself."

"I know that," Timberlaine said.

"So there was no reason to think he got a tip."

"Maybe not, but I think he did."

"He says he didn't."

"I don't care what he says. I *still* think he got a tip."

"Fine," Steve said, without enthusiasm. "Let's not argue about it. Anyway, what did you do?"

"I started out of the auction, I was angry. I went out the back door onto the patio. Of course, no one was there. Everyone was in the auction."

"So what did you do?"

"I felt like letting off steam. I went out to the pistol range to shoot the gun."

"Was that what you did?"

"No."

Steve frowned. "What?"

"I never got there. Halfway there it occurred to me I didn't give a shit about hitting the target, I just wanted to fire off the gun. So I did."

"What do you mean?"

"I just took out the gun and shot it."

"Where?"

"Right there. On the path."

Steve's eyes widened. "Jesus Christ."

"Hey, what's wrong with that?"

"Where were you aiming?"

"Nowhere in particular."

"What?"

"Relax. I shot up in the air, away from the house."

"Are you sure?"

"Sure, I'm sure. I know guns, for Christ's sakes."

"Yeah, but—"

"So there's no chance the shot I fired magically returned to the house, entered the gun room and killed Jack Potter."

"O.K. Say it didn't. After you shot, did you reload?"

"No. I just jammed the gun back in my holster."

"What did you do then?"

"Kept on walking."

"Where?"

"Actually, I went out past the pistol range."

"Did you stop?"

"No. I'd already shot the gun. I kept on going."

"Where?"

"I walked right on by it on the path. I actually made a big circle, wound up back at the house."

"At what time?"

"I don't know. But the auction wasn't out yet."

"Oh, yeah?"

"Yeah. There was no one on the patio. And I could actually hear the auctioneer over the loudspeaker as I went inside. I went in the back door up the stairs to my room."

"What did you do then?"

"Just like I told the cops. I changed my clothes."

"And what did you do with the gun?"

"It was right there in the holster. Hell, you were there. You saw when I gave it to the cops."

"Yeah. And that's where you left it?"

"Absolutely."

"O.K. You took off the gun and you left it there next to the bed. What time was that?"

Timberlaine shrugged. "I can't give it to you any better than I already have. Like I say, I went out, walked around and when I came back the auction wasn't over yet."

"The auction broke up at four-thirty."

"Then it had to be before that."

"How much before?"

"I don't know."

"You didn't hear it break up?"

"No, I wouldn't have. I was in the shower."

"You took a shower?"

"Yeah."

"Why'd you do that?"

"What do you mean, why'd I do that? I took a shower."

"In the middle of the afternoon?"

"So what? I can't take a shower in the middle of the afternoon?"

"Of course you can. But you need to say why."

"That's stupid."

"Not when you're charged with murder. Why'd you take a shower?"

"I don't know why, actually. It's not like I had to think about it. I was pissed off and I wanted to get out of the cowboy outfit. Because that was all associated with what I was pissed off about. So I wanted to change. And I was hot and sweaty from walking around and all. And getting all worked up. And I wasn't about to put on clean clothes without taking a shower. So that's what I did."

"Your hair wasn't wet."

"What?"

"When I saw you with the cops—your hair wasn't wet from the shower."

Timberlaine's eyes narrowed. "You saying you don't believe me?"

"No. I'm just saying your hair wasn't wet. I noticed it, so you can bet the cops noticed it. So when you say you took a shower the cops are going to want to know why your hair wasn't wet."

"I have long hair, it's a pain in the ass to dry. I don't always wash it. Particularly like that in the middle of the day. I took a shower from the neck down, kept my hair dry." Timberlaine looked at Steve. "You got long hair. Don't you ever do that?"

"Sure," Steve said. "But this isn't my alibi."

Timberlaine grimaced. "Alibi. Jesus."

"Yeah, well, that's what we're talking here. You finished the shower and you put on clean clothes, right?"

"Right. Except for the pants."

"Why not the pants?"

"Well, the pants aren't really dirty. They're part of the costume, yeah, but they're just jeans. I like jeans. Plus I got all my shit in the pockets—change, keys, wallet, what have you. It's a pain in the ass to have to change it to another pair of pants. So I put on all clean clothes except for the jeans."

"And where'd you go then?"

"Nowhere."

"Nowhere?"

"That's right. Nowhere. I was fed up, and I didn't feel like talking with anyone. I sat down and watched TV."

"You're kidding."

"Why should I kid about a thing like that?"

"You watched TV?"

"Yes."

"What did you watch?

"The baseball game."

"What game?"

"The Yankees."

Steve looked at him. "This was four-thirty in the afternoon?"

"Around then."

"And the game was still on?"

"They're in California. The game started four o'clock our time."

"How long did you watch the game?"

"Until the cops came."

"Oh?"

"In the sixth or seventh inning. I don't know. I was sittin' there watching the game, I heard a siren. Went to the window, looked out. That's when I saw the cop cars."

"What time was that?"

"I don't know. Sometime around six."

"What'd you do then?"

"You know what I did. You were there. I came downstairs, asked the cops what was going on."

"I didn't see you come downstairs."

"Right, right. I came to the gun room, I found you and the cops."

"How'd you get downstairs?"

"What do you mean?"

"Which stairs did you take?"

"The front stairs."

"Why not the back ones?"

"What the hell kind of question is that?"

"It's the kind of question you may be asked. If you go on the stand, you're gonna be grilled by a D.A. He's gonna throw questions at you, and you gotta have the answers. It'll be a damn sight better if you get used to answering them now. And stop trying to figure out why I'm asking and just concentrate on answering. Why the front stairs, why not the back stairs?"

"I looked out the window, saw the cop cars. They're pullin' up to the front door. Naturally, I'm going down the front stairs to meet 'em."

"But you didn't meet 'em there."

"No. Because by the time I get downstairs they've already gone to the gun room."

"And that's where you met 'em?"

"Yeah."

"Then why didn't you come down the back stairs? It's closer to the gun room."

"I didn't *know* they were going to the gun room," Timberlaine cried in exasperation.

Steve smiled. "I'm glad to hear it. You *shouldn't* have known they were going to the gun room. See, you're answering just fine. Now, that's when you came walking up and found the cops and saw me."

"That's right."

"You had just come from upstairs."

"That's right."

"Watching the ballgame, which was then in the sixth or seventh inning."

"Something like that."

"What was the score?"

"What?"

"The score of the game—what was the score?"

Timberlaine looked at him. "The Yankees were up three to two. California was batting, there were runners on first and third, and I think there were two fuckin' outs, for Christ's sake."

Steve held up his hand. "All right, take it easy," he said. "This is your alibi. It may seem stupid, but the more details the better.

"Now, correct me if I'm wrong. You stormed out of the auction; walked down the path; fired off the gun, shooting up in the air; put the gun back in your holster; walked around; went upstairs; took off the gun belt with the gun in it; took a shower; changed your clothes; watched the ballgame until you heard a siren; then came downstairs and saw the cops. Is that right?"

"Yes, it is."

"Fine. Let's talk about the gun."

"What about it?"

"When you came upstairs to give it to the cops, the gun was on the end table by the bed. Only I couldn't see it right away because it was covered up by your cowboy hat."

"Yeah. So?"

"Think about it. When you were getting undressed to take the shower—you took off your gun belt, you took off your cowboy hat—do you remember putting your cowboy hat down on top of the gun belt?"

"Why should I?"

"Because that's where it was when you went to get it for the cops."

Timberlaine's eyes widened. "You mean . . . ?"

"Hey," Steve said. "Ballistics says that gun killed Potter. The way I see it, that leaves only two possibilities. One, you're lying and you shot him. Or, two, you're telling the truth, and someone took that gun and shot him while you were taking a shower."

Timberlaine frowned. "I see."

"So?"

"So, I don't remember."

"Shit."

"Well, why should I? There was no reason for me to think about it at the time."

"I know that, but still."

"But still what? Either I remember or I don't."

"Sometimes you can jog your memory. Think about it. You come back from your walk, you fired the gun, you're pissed off. You walk across the patio, you don't see anybody. You go upstairs. Which stairs?"

"Front stairs."

"You go up the front stairs. You walk down the hall. You go into your apartment—is the door unlocked?"

"Yeah."

"You leave it unlocked?"

"Usually."

"When wouldn't you?"

"I don't know. If I'm away. If I go to town for the day."

"By town you mean New York?"

"Yeah."

"It was unlocked then?"

"Yeah."

"Did you lock it?"

"No. Of course not."

"So it was unlocked when you took the shower?"

"Right."

"So anyone could have come in and taken the gun?"

"Sure."

"Would you have seen 'em or heard 'em?"

"No."

"Was the bathroom door open or closed?"

"Closed."

"How long were you in the shower?"

"I don't know. Pretty long, I guess. I was pissed off, the water felt good, I didn't want to see anyone. There was no reason for me to get out. I guess I was in there a fairly long time."

"It would have to be."

"What?"

"Long enough for someone to have taken the gun, gone down-stairs, shot Potter, got back upstairs and replaced the gun."

Timberlaine frowned. "Right."

"That would take some time."

"Yeah."

"And, of course, Potter is not cooperating. I mean, it's not like he's standing there waiting to be shot."

Timberlaine frowned. "What are you talking about?"

"Well, the whole thing has to make sense. Either the killer brings Potter to the gun room, leaves him there, runs upstairs, gets your gun, comes back and shoots him. Or, the killer gets your gun, then finds Potter, brings him to the gun room and shoots him." Steve shrugged. "Either way, it's going to take time."

"I see that."

"And the killer would have to replace the bullet."

"Huh?"

"When you gave Lieutenant Sanders the gun, it was fully loaded with one empty shell. That was the shot you fired up in the air on the path. If the murderer took the gun and shot Jack Potter, he'd have to reload one bullet, or there would have been *two* empty shells in the gun."

Timberlaine frowned. "That's right."

"Which is why it makes much more sense the other way around."

"What do you mean?"

"We have two bullets fired, one into the air and one into Jack Potter. By rights, one gun fired one and one the other. We know the fake gun killed Potter. So the whole thing would be simple if the real Pistol Pete gun were the gun you fired up in the air."

"But it wasn't."

"Stick with me a moment. I know. That gun was stolen and the other substituted and the whole bit. But look. If the gun you wore at the auction were the real gun, you could shoot it in the air, go back to your room and leave it on your end table. And the murderer could kill Potter with the fake gun, then sneak upstairs and swap guns while you were in the shower. That would leave each gun with one bullet fired and you with the murder weapon. Simple, easy and possible."

"Yeah, but it's *not* possible," Timberlaine said. "I didn't have the gun."

"I know you *think* you didn't. But what if the murderer who swapped the guns swapped them *back*? Maybe just that afternoon? And you didn't notice and so you wore the real gun at the auction and shot it in the air? After all, there's no reason why you'd notice."

"But I *did*." Timberlaine said. "When I put the gun on, I looked at it particularly. And it was not the real gun. Believe me, I would know."

Steve took a breath, blew it out again. "All right, fine," he said. "But you see why it would be much better if it were?"

"Of course. But the facts are the facts."

Steve rubbed his head. "Great. O.K. We'll leave it. But whatever happened, one way or another, had to have happened while you were in the shower. Let's get back to that. Before I digressed, I was trying to jog your memory. You came upstairs, the door was unlocked, you opened the door, you closed the door, you walk over to the bed and you start getting undressed. You take off the gun belt first?"

"No, I take off the hat."

"You take off the hat first?"

"Yeah."

"Then how does it wind up on top of the gun belt?"

Timberlaine frowned. "Son of a bitch."

"You didn't put it there?"

"I'm trying to remember. Let's see. I took off my hat, I threw it down on the bed. Then I took off the gun belt, put it on the end table. Then I sat down on the bed to take off my boots and—" He broke off.

"What?"

"When I sat down I moved the hat off the bed."

"And set it on the end table over the gun?"

"Probably."

"Shit."

"Yeah. I know. But that's what I did."

"Do you *remember* putting it on the gun belt?"

"No, but that's what I must have done."

Steve took a breath, exhaled. "O.K. And when you came out of the shower—do you remember seeing the hat or the gun belt then?"

"Not particularly."

"Think. Was there anything that you noticed—doesn't have to be the gun belt, or the hat, or the cowboy outfit at all—but was there anything in the room you noticed *different* when you came out of the shower than when you went in?"

Timberlaine narrowed his eyes a few moments, then shook his head. "No, I can't remember."

"O.K. But if you think of anything, anything at all, no matter how trivial, let me know."

"Of course. Of course."

"You understand, if what you say is true, this is the *only time* someone could have taken the gun. The *only time* Potter could have been killed."

"I see that."

"That is a fact, though—from the time you went back to your room, you never left the room till the time you came down to find the cops—is that right?"

"Hey, I told you. I took a shower, watched the ball game."

"You did that because you were pissed off about the auction and you didn't want to see anybody."

"Right."

"Ordinarily, with a houseful of guests, and it being cocktail hour and all, you would have put in an appearance."

"Ordinarily."

"But you were pissed off, so you didn't."

"That's right."

"And the thing that pissed you off was Melvin Burdett buying that cavalry piece."

"Of course."

"And you still think he got a tip?"

"I *know* he got a tip."

"How do you know?"

"I don't know. I just do."

"Fine. That's what you thought then, and that's what you think now. O.K. Say he got a tip—where did he get it from?"

"I don't know."

"Where do you think?"

"I tell you, I don't know."

"You have no idea?"

"Not really."

"Not really? What does that mean?"

"I don't know what to think anymore."

"Why?"

"Because Potter's dead."

"I see. You thought it was Potter, now that he's dead you're not so sure?"

Timberlaine shrugged. "Something like that."

"At the time it happened, right after the auction—you're telling me you thought it was Potter?"

"It crossed my mind."

"You tell this to the cops?"

Timberlaine's eyes shifted.

Steve sighed. "Oh, Christ."

"Well, how the hell was I to know?"

"You weren't," Steve said. "There was no *way* to know. You couldn't know, and I couldn't know. That's why I told you to keep your fucking mouth shut until we found out what the facts were. But you didn't want to do that. You're smarter than your attorney, why should you listen to him?"

Timberlaine set his jaw. "I don't have to take this."

"No, you don't," Steve said. "You can fire me and hire other lawyers. If you do, I suggest you play fair with them and tell 'em as much as you told the cops. Now what about the bullets?"

Timberlaine blinked. "Bullets?"

"Yeah. The bullets, the bullets. What bullets do you think? You came to me about bullets. I identified them for you, put them in glass tubes."

"Oh, that," Timberlaine said.

"Yeah, that." Steve said. "Tell me, when you were shooting off your mouth, did you give the cops the bullets?"

"No."

"You didn't?"

"No, I didn't."

"You mean in all the time you were talking about that's not my gun, somebody stole my gun, I haven't seen that gun in weeks, you didn't say, I can prove it, I got bullets my attorney checked out for me?"

"No, I didn't."

"Really? Why not?"

Timberlaine shrugged helplessly. "I guess I just didn't think of it."

"Well, thank goodness for small favors," Steve said. "The cops have enough evidence to play with without that. All right, you didn't mention the bullets, that's fine. Now that I've reminded you, you're not going to mention 'em now."

"Why?"

"Because you're not going to mention *anything*. From now on, the cops ask you something, you say, see my lawyer. Any question at all, you say, see my lawyer. And you don't *volunteer* anything. You don't get some bright idea, suddenly come up with something you think, gee, the cops ought to know, and you run and tell them. From here on in, you don't give the cops the time of day."

Timberlaine blinked.

"You got that?" Steve said.

Timberlaine took a breath. "Yeah."

"Where are the bullets now?"

"In a safe-deposit box."

"That's the best news I've had all day. Just shut up about 'em and let 'em stay there."

Steve stood up, turned to go.

Timberlaine said, "Hey, I want to get out of here."

Steve turned back. He held up his finger. "Good thought." He pointed at Timberlaine. "Bet you wish you had it before you shot your mouth off to the cops."

20

STEVE WINSLOW WAS ON HIS WAY OUT the front door when a young cop stopped him.

"Mr. Winslow?"

"Yeah?"

"Mr. Vaulding wants to see you."

"Who?"

The young cop flushed slightly. "District Attorney Robert Vaulding."

"Oh, that Vaulding," Steve said.

The young cop gave him a look.

Steve shrugged. "Hey, I'm from Manhattan. What do I know? So where's Vaulding?"

The young cop led Steve to the D.A.'s outer office, parked him in the corner and conferred in low tones with the officer at the desk. The officer picked up the phone and spoke into it, and moments later the door to the inner office opened, and a tall thin man in a three-piece suit said, "Mr. Winslow?"

"Yes."

"Robert Vaulding. Please come in."

Steve sized the man up on his way in the door. Vaulding was young, probably no older than Steve himself. His jet black hair was cut short and carefully groomed. His appearance was impeccable if not fastidious. Even his nails looked manicured. The impression

94

Steve got was that, having gotten elected to the position of district attorney, Robert Vaulding had attempted to make up for his lack of years by disguising himself as a conservative old fart.

His smile, however, was still young, almost boyish. He grinned at Steve Winslow, said, "Sit down."

"I'll stand," Steve said. "You can skip the ceremony, Vaulding. Why am I here?"

Vaulding's smile became lopsided. "I heard you were direct."

"You heard right. Cut the shit. What's the story?"

"No story. I just thought we should talk."

"Why?"

Vaulding frowned. "There's no reason to be hostile."

"Oh, yeah?" Steve said. "I thought the habit of burying a suspect went out in the forties or fifties."

"Oh."

"Oh, indeed. The cops and my client got lost somewhere between his place and here. An accident, I'm sure. And I'm sure anything he might have told them in the meantime is entirely coincidental. But I guess you wouldn't know anything about that."

Vaulding spread his hands wide. "What can I say? I'm sorry about that. But I assure you, Mr. Timberlaine's rights were not violated in any way. He was perfectly aware of the fact he was under no obligation to speak, and anything he said was entirely of his own volition."

"I'm sure he was," Steve said, dryly. "That's not the point, and you know it. A man who didn't know any better was kept away from his attorney so the attorney couldn't advise him to keep his mouth shut."

Vaulding shrugged. "An unfortunate situation. But I happen to know Russ Timberlaine. Short of tying and gagging him, you think you could have kept him quiet?"

"Probably not."

"There you are."

"No, I'm not. Jesus Christ, you gonna argue like this in court, Vaulding? 'Yeah, the way we got the evidence was wrong, but what the hell, we'd have got it anyway, so what's the difference?' "

"I admit the situation is unfortunate. I'm wondering if we can get beyond it for the moment."

"Why?"

Vaulding took a breath. "I got a call this morning. From Harry Dirkson."

"Oh? And what has the Manhattan district attorney got to do with life out here?"

"Absolutely nothing. But he heard about the Timberlaine case."

"Oh?"

"And the fact you were his attorney."

"You mean he had opinions about that?"

"I'll say. Would it surprise you to learn Harry Dirkson does not hold you in the highest regard?"

"No. I would imagine he told you I was living poison, I was the kiss of death, you should have nothing to do with me."

"Or words to that effect," Vaulding said, grinning. "Well, without admitting he said anything like that, I think you get the picture."

"So?"

Vaulding, who had remained standing when Steve did, now sat down at his desk, leaned back in his chair and cocked his head. "So, that's all well and good, but I don't have to buy it. I've followed some of your cases." He grinned. "Not surprising. They're hard to miss. Anyway, the way I see it, Dirkson's got no beef coming. The people he was trying to prosecute happened to be innocent. Which is hardly your fault."

Steve eyed Vaulding narrowly. "What are you trying to say?"

"I'm trying to say you're gonna get a fair shake here. We're adversaries, yes, and I want to win. But not if it means convicting an innocent man."

"How noble of you."

Vaulding frowned. "You're not making this particularly easy."

"I'm pissed off and you know why. If you think a speech about your good intentions makes up for it, you're wrong. That's for starters. The clincher is, I *still* don't know why I'm here."

"I told you—"

"Bullshit. Cut the commercial, Vaulding. What do you want?"

Vaulding took a breath. "All right. For one thing, your client is a wealthy man. I hate to inconvenience him, and I want to do everything possible to expedite things and assure him a speedy trial. If that is also your intention, then we have no problem. If you were planning delays and postponements, we do."

Steve Winslow looked at Vaulding a moment. "Of course. Bail.

You got a jail full of minority defendants can't make bail on a whole bunch of chickenshit charges. You're a politician, you gotta keep the masses happy, the last thing you need is some rich white defendant walking around free on a murder charge."

Vaulding smiled. "Nice deduction. It's not the type of thing I'd tell the press, but since it's just you and me talking here, let's say you're right."

"That would piss me off," Steve said. "If it's in my client's interest to push for bail, I'll push for bail."

"Of course you would," Vaulding said. "In fact, the standard procedure would be to get him out on bail and stall like crazy. However, you have a reputation for the unorthodox. So I was thinking you might like to go right to court."

"Again, it would depend on what's in my client's best interests."

"Of course. I'm just telling you my preference so you know if you want to expedite matters you have that option."

"That's fine, but I know perfectly well what my options are and I'll do whatever's best for my client."

Steve turned to go.

"Hang on, hang on," Vaulding said. "That's a minor matter. That's not why I asked you in here. I want to discuss your participation in the case."

"I beg your pardon?"

"I mean your *direct* participation in the case. I'm referring to the fact you and your secretary found the body."

"Oh, that," Steve said.

"Yes, that. It may not be a first for you, but it's a first for me. Defense attorneys do not find the body of the victim. It just isn't done outside of story books."

"I'm sorry to disillusion you."

"It's not just that," Vaulding said. "It's a problem in terms of procedure. I guarantee you there isn't a judge in this county who's going to look kindly on me calling the defense attorney as a witness for the prosecution."

"Guess you have a problem," Steve said.

"It's your problem too, if the judge should rule you had to step down as counsel."

"I would resist such a ruling."

"Yeah, but would you win? Maybe on appeal, but even if you

eventually do, the case drags on. And it isn't going to please your client any if he's not on bail."

Steve's eyes narrowed. "So the bail issue *is* tied up in this."

"Not at all," Vaulding said. "I just mentioned the effect on your client. But, no, they're not related in the least."

"So what's your point?"

"If I call you as a witness, it's going to make trouble. It could even get you removed from the case. I don't want to do that. If you're agreeable, I'd like to expedite matters so neither you nor your secretary would have to testify."

"How would you do that?"

"As I understand it, after you found the body your secretary informed the butler—" Vaulding picked up a paper from his desk, glanced at it, "—that would be Martin Kessington—and he was the one who called the cops. Is that right?"

"Yeah. So?"

"I can use him instead. Him and Lieutenant Sanders. Between them I may not have to call you at all."

"My recollection may not coincide with theirs."

"Which you can bring out on cross-examination."

"If I couldn't, I might have to put myself on the stand."

"If you have to, you have to. I don't think you will. It's a chance I'm willing to take."

Steve looked at him. "Why, Vaulding? What's the catch? Is this tied up in the bail issue after all?"

"Absolutely not," Vaulding said. "I'm telling you straight out I know the judges here, and if you go on the stand there's a good chance you get disqualified as counsel. I don't want that to happen."

"Why not?"

Vaulding smiled. "You have to ask me that? You're good. In fact, you're very good. You got a reputation. Top gun. Young sensation." He jerked his thumb. "Dirkson hears you're on the case, he calls me to warn me."

"So?"

Vaulding cocked his head and grinned. "Well, guess what? I'm good too."

Vaulding looked Steve right in the eye. He smiled, but his eyes were hard.

"I'm gonna beat you."

21

BACK AT THE MOTEL things were really popping.

"Search warrant?" Steve said.

"Right," Tracy said. "Timberlaine's daughter called, all upset. The cops were there with a search warrant, what should she do?"

"What did you tell her?"

"What *could* I tell her? You were off talking to her father, and even if you weren't, what could you do anyway? If it's a search warrant, you gotta honor it."

"Yeah," Steve said. "But still."

"Hey, it's not like the cops were standing around waiting for you to give permission. She's on the phone, they're searching the place, she's practically hysterical wanting to know what she should do about it and frankly not making much sense. The bottom line is, whatever the cops were looking for, they found it and took off while she was on the phone. At which point she slammed down the receiver, was not there when I called back, and is probably on her way here."

"Shit. When was this?"

"When she left? Maybe ten minutes ago."

"Great," Steve said. He raised his head, bellowed, "Mark!"

Taylor yelled back from the other room, "I'm on the phone."

Steve strode to the door. "What you got on the warrant?"

Taylor was sitting on the bed with the phone tucked under his chin and a pad and pen in his hands. "Just a minute," he said irritably, then into the phone, "Hang on, willya?" He raised his chin, dropping the receiver into his lap, and looked up at Steve. "I got nothin' on the warrant except they served a warrant. That's what I'm doin' now, but with one stinkin' phone it ain't easy." Taylor snatched up the receiver again, then looked back up at Steve. "Now hold your horses and let me get on with it. I'll tell you as soon as I know."

"Just so you're happy," Steve said. He shook his head, went back into the other room.

Tracy, noting his expression, said, "Mark take your head off?"

"Oh? He been snappin' at you too?"

"Mark hasn't been quite himself since he heard the gun he bought was the murder weapon."

"That didn't really make my day, either. And now this damn warrant."

"You're really pissed off."

"Yeah. And it's not just what they may have found."

Tracy frowned. "Oh? Then what is it?"

"The timing."

"What?"

Steve pointed to the door. "I just got called into the D.A.'s office. Young guy named Vaulding. Slick son of a bitch."

"So? What did he want?"

"That's just it. On the surface he wanted to talk me out of pressing for bail in return for keeping us off the witness stand. Or so I thought. Now I just don't know."

"You mean?"

"Exactly. I show up to talk to Timberlaine, Vaulding says, 'Great, he's out of the way, serve the warrant.' Then, to make sure I *stay* out of the way, he calls me into his office."

"Isn't that being a little paranoid?"

"Maybe. But just between you and me, that gun turning out to be the murder weapon's got me spooked too. I feel like I'm walkin' through a mine field, just waiting to see what blows up next."

"Steve!" Taylor called from the other room.

Steve Winslow barreled through the door with Tracy right behind.

"You got it?" Steve said.

"On the warrant, no, but something's up. The reporter just checked in. He says Vaulding—that's the D.A. out here—"

"Yeah, I know."

"Oh, yeah? Well, he just called a press conference for this afternoon, so something must be up."

"Any idea what?"

"No, but odds are the warrant must have something to do with it."

"Yeah, but what? I mean, they already have the gun. What else is there?"

"You got me." Taylor shrugged. "Hell, maybe that's not it. Maybe the guy just wants to puff up his chest and say just 'cause Timberlaine's got money it cuts no ice with him, and he will prosecute him fearlessly to the full extent of the law."

"Could be. He already gave me the same spiel."

"Oh?"

"Trying to discourage me from pressing for bail. Timberlaine out on bail would be a political black eye for him. Vaulding intimates if I don't push for bail, he'll expedite everything and generally make life easy, including keeping me off the stand."

"Then what the hell's this press conference?"

"Well, I didn't say yes."

"Will you?"

"I don't know. It's in Timberlaine's best interests and it's probably the way I'd play it anyway." Steve chuckled mirthlessly, shook his head. "I just hate to do anything Vaulding wants."

There came a knock on the door in the other unit. Tracy disappeared through the connecting door, came back ushering in a rather harried-looking Carrie Timberlaine.

"So, what did they get?" Steve demanded.

That was too abrupt for Carrie. "What?"

"The cops. The search warrant. What did they get?"

"I don't know."

"Shit," Steve said, irritably. "It's like waiting for Christmas and you don't get a present. What *do* you know?"

"Hey, ease up," Tracy said, coming between them. "Don't mind him, murders make him grouchy. Just what happened with the cops? It must have been very confusing."

Carrie looked at Tracy gratefully. "That's just it. With so much going on and cops there all the time anyway, and suddenly there's more cops with a warrant, and they've shown it to me and started searching before it really registered that this was something different."

"Do you have the warrant?" Steve said.

"No. Should I have?"

"No, don't worry about it," Tracy said. "He's a lawyer, they like to read documents. Just tell us what the cops did."

"Just what I told you on the phone. They started searching. As soon as it dawned on me this was something different, I called."

"Right," Tracy prompted. "And then you heard them leaving and hung up to go see. Now what did you see?"

"I couldn't really tell."

"Then how do you know they found something?" Steve put in.

"That's just it. They were carrying something. I just couldn't tell what it was."

"Carrying what? Big, small, what shape was it?"

"Not that big. It was in a plastic bag. You know, like they put the gun in."

"*Was* it a gun?" Steve said sharply.

Carrie shook her head. "I don't think so."

"How could you tell? If you didn't see it."

"I know. But it was the wrong shape. Longer, thinner. And straight, you know. More like a pipe."

"Metallic?"

"Yeah. But it wasn't a gun."

"Damn. Where'd they find it?"

Carrie bit her lip. "I'm not sure, but I think it was Dad's room."

"Got it!" Taylor said, coming through the door from the other unit.

"What?" Steve said.

"The dope on the press conference. Now this is real hush-hush and we're lucky to get it, but the upshot is Vaulding's got new evidence."

"From the warrant?"

"I don't know about that. This has to do with the murder weapon."

"What about it?"

"Well, they matched the fatal bullet. But apparently it wasn't easy."

Steve frowned. "Jesus Christ, Mark. I don't want to play twenty fucking questions. Why the hell not?"

"Because someone scratched up the gun barrel."

Steve's mouth fell open. "You're kidding!"

Taylor shook his head. "Nope."

"Of the gun Timberlaine was wearing?"

"Yeah," Taylor said. With a significant look at Carrie Timberlaine he added, "*That* gun."

"Good lord," Steve said. "So Vaulding's going to claim Timberlaine tried to protect himself by altering the barrel of the gun. With what? What do they think he used?"

Taylor shrugged. "I don't know. Most likely a rattailed file."

"Oh!"

At this low exclamation Steve, Mark and Tracy all turned to see Carrie Timberlaine, eyes wide, face registering startled comprehension.

22

Russ Timberlaine looked utterly baffled. "I don't know what you're talking about."

"It's perfectly simple," Steve said. "The district attorney just held a press conference to release the information that the barrel of the gun had been tampered with."

"That makes no sense."

"It does and it doesn't. If a murderer were going to hang onto the murder weapon, he'd naturally want to rough up the barrel so ballistics couldn't match up the bullets."

"Yeah, but why keep it at all?"

"Why, indeed?" Steve said dryly. "Don't think I won't be arguing that. I'm just telling you what the prosecution's going to claim."

"It's absurd."

"I'm glad to hear it. The point is the cops found a rattailed file in your room."

"I can explain that."

Steve stopped dead, stared at him. "You *know* about that?"

"Of course I do. Why?"

Steve closed his eyes, mentally shot himself. "Why? Why, you ask. Well, when I heard the cops found the file in your room, I said, fine, someone framed him with the gun, it follows someone would frame him by planting the file. But you *know* about it?"

"Yeah. I found it in my room."

"Don't tell me. Right after the murder. In fact, right after you took the shower. You found it while you were watching the baseball game and before the cops came."

Timberlaine shook his head. "No. Before."

Steve frowned. "Before what?"

"Before that. Well, anything you said, really. I found it a couple of days ago."

Steve blinked. "What?"

"That's right."

"Let me get this straight. You found the file *before* the murder?"

Timberlaine nodded. "Oh, sure."

"That doesn't make any sense."

"That's what *I* said."

"Hold on. Let's pin this down. Just when did you find the file?"

"I'm not sure. Either yesterday or the day before."

"The murder was yesterday."

"Right."

"And the day before was Friday. The day your guests arrived."

"Yeah. So?"

"So which was it?"

"I'm not sure."

"Well, if it was Friday, was it early Friday, or late Friday, after your guests arrived?"

"I don't know. Why should I? It wasn't important. I just looked on top of my dresser and there it was."

"Your dresser?"

"Yeah."

"You were getting dressed then?"

"I don't remember *what* I was doing."

"Try."

"Hey. I've tried. I just don't remember."

"You understand why this is important?"

"Hey, I'm not stupid."

Steve let that pass. "Fine. Then help me out. Concentrate. Think. Jog your memory. You think I'm asking you if you were getting dressed because I give a damn what clothes you were wearing? I'm trying to reconstruct the scene of you finding the file to jog your memory as to what time of day it might have been. A good clue would be, were you putting clothes on or taking them off?"

"I realize that," Timberlaine said. "I also realize the significance of whether I found the file before or after my guests arrived in trying to figure out who could have planted it."

"That's wonderful," Steve said, "but slightly incidental. Did you happen to catch the bigger picture, by any chance?"

Timberlaine frowned. "Huh?"

"You found the file before the murder. The actual time doesn't matter, the fact is it was *before* the murder. That's the killer. I gotta argue someone roughed up the barrel of the gun and then planted the file on you. That's tough enough. It's a hell of a stretch, but it's still an argument.

"But once you're in possession of the file *before* the murder, what the hell do I argue then? Someone stole the gun from you. Someone stole the file from you. Then they killed Potter with the gun, roughed up the gun with the file, planted the gun back in your holster and hid the file back in your room, and all while you were conveniently taking a fucking shower." Steve blew out a breath. "Now, I may not be a bad attorney, but if I can get a jury to believe that, I should make Lawyer of the Year."

Timberlaine frowned. "So what are you going to do now?"

"There's a saving grace."

"What?"

"The cops don't know it."

"Know what?"

"When you found the file. They got the file, they can prove it was found in your possession, but they *can't* prove you had it in your possession before the murder. So I don't have to explain why you did."

Timberlaine's eyes faltered.

Steve groaned. "Oh, Jesus Christ. Don't tell me."

Timberlaine shook his head ruefully. "Well, the cops came to me with this file."

"When?"

"Just now. Just before you got here."

"And?"

"Well, they told me that things looked bad, they just found this file in my room and—"

"Right," Steve said sarcastically, "and they said if you could just explain how it got there they'd let you go."

"How'd you know?"

"Give me a break. You told them you found it there?"

"Right."

"Before the murder?"

"Well . . ."

"Well what?"

"I told 'em I wasn't sure when."

"That's what you told me. But it *was* before the murder."

"Yeah."

"And you told 'em that?"

Timberlaine sighed. "Yeah."

"Great," Steve said. "You remember me telling you not to talk?"

"Damn it—"

"I hope you remember it. It was just this morning."

Timberlaine's eyes blazed. "I don't have to take this."

Steve shook his head. "No, that's the problem. The fact is, you do." He got up, headed for the door.

"Hey," Timberlaine said. "Where are you going?"

Steve stopped in the doorway. "I'm going to hunt up the D.A., tell him we're not going to press for bail, and let's start the trial."

23

ROBERT VAULDING'S OPENING WAS SHOWY. Vaulding was young, handsome and personable, and he knew it and he used it. Most prosecutors would have been solemn and ponderous, emphasizing the gravity of the charge of murder. Vaulding kept it light. He actually smiled during his opening statement, played to the jury, and implied without actually saying it that they were in for a show. Yeah, it's murder, Vaulding's attitude seemed to say, and it's a serious charge. But I didn't do it and you didn't do it, and I'm here to tell ya, we're gonna get a kick out of pinning it on the guy who did.

"So you see," Vaulding said, "this is a very simple crime." He shrugged his shoulders. "Elemental. It almost insults my intelligence to have to argue it.

"But at the same time, it is absolutely fascinating and it has elements that merit our attention.

"What are they? Well, let's start with the two guns. There was a gun found next to the body. A Colt .45 with the initial R carved in the handle. A gun that experts will testify was the original, genuine article once owned by Pistol Pete Robbins, a notorious gunslinger from the Old West. A gun we can show was owned by Russ Timberlaine. There it was, right next to the dead body."

Vaulding turned, shrugged his shoulders and smiled. "Simple

crime, yes? But ballistics will show that this was *not* the murder weapon.

"And what *was* the murder weapon?" Vaulding shrugged again. "What else? An identical gun, a Colt .45 with the letter R carved in the handle, obviously a duplicate of the original gun, but one that experts will testify was not authentic and was mocked up only recently to resemble the original gun."

Vaulding paused, looked around the courtroom again. "And where was this gun found? In Russ Timberlaine's bedroom. On Russ Timberlaine's night stand. In Russ Timberlaine's holster."

Vaulding paused, let that sink in. "And how did it get there?" Vaulding turned and pointed. "According to Russ Timberlaine himself, he put that gun and holster there. He took it off after he came upstairs after the auction that afternoon and after, by his own admission, firing the gun. A gun numerous witnesses will testify he was wearing after the auction."

Vaulding paused, pursed his lips. "I've already laid out the events leading up to the murder, but let me summarize them briefly. Russ Timberlaine went to the auction with the express purpose of buying a gun. A gun he knew Melvin Burdett would bid on if he knew he wanted it. Therefore, he enlisted the aid of Henry Crumbly to bid on the gun for him. Nonetheless, Burdett outbid Crumbly. In Russ Timberlaine's opinion, the only way Burdett could have known Crumbly was actually bidding on the gun for him was if his expert, Potter, who had appraised the gun for him, had tipped him off."

Vaulding held up his hand. "The merits of this contention are irrelevant. The defense may argue, and quite rightly so, that Burdett could have learned this information from another source, or could have surmised it himself from the way events transpired. That's wholly irrelevant. The fact is, whatever the merit of the contention, Russ Timberlaine believed it to be true. And because he believed it to be true, he was incensed. His own expert, Jack Potter, had betrayed him. He stormed out of the auction at that point in full cowboy regalia. Including the holster and the gun. By his own admission, he fired that gun. And the next time we see that gun, it is discovered in Timberlaine's holster on Timberlaine's night table in Timberlaine's bedroom by the police immediately after the murder."

Vaulding held up his finger. "Our ballistics expert will testify that gun was the murder weapon. The gun Timberlaine was wearing at the auction. The gun Timberlaine claims he fired off after the auction. The gun that was found immediately after the murder on Timberlaine's night table."

Vaulding paused, smiled again. "Now then, this is a murder trial. The judge will instruct you that in a murder trial, the burden of proof is on the prosecution. It is up to us to prove the defendant guilty beyond a reasonable doubt."

Vaulding turned, gestured to the defense table where Steve Winslow sat next to Russ Timberlaine. "The defense attorney may argue that this is a case of circumstantial evidence. In other words, there is no eyewitness. No one saw Russ Timberlaine shoot a bullet into the head of Jack Potter. You are required to deduce that happened from the evidence that we are going to lay before you. We, the prosecution, are going to show that the circumstances lead to the inescapable conclusion that Russ Timberlaine killed Jack Potter. That is what is meant by circumstantial evidence. Now, as I'm sure you are aware, it is necessary to prove Russ Timberlaine guilty beyond a reasonable doubt. Now, in a case involving circumstantial evidence, as I am sure counsel for the defense will point out, it is necessary that the circumstances that we lay out for you are not open to any interpretation other than the guilt of the defendant. If the defense can come up with a reasonable explanation for these circumstances, then you must find the defendant not guilty."

Vaulding stopped, looked around, and this time actually grinned broadly. "To which I say, be my guest. As prosecutor, I intend to lay out the circumstances surrounding this crime. When I am done, if the attorney for the defense can come up with a reasonable explanation other than the guilt of the defendant, well, ladies and gentlemen of the jury, you won't have to return a verdict of not guilty, because at that moment, I, myself, will personally move for a dismissal of the case."

Vaulding shook his head. "But I assure you, that is not going to happen. He is guilty, he can be shown to be guilty, he can be proven to be guilty beyond a reasonable doubt. I would even say beyond a shadow of a doubt. And if any other explanation exists, I for one am the first one to want to hear it. But I am confident that I am not going to. Just as I am confident that when I am done, you are going to return a verdict of guilty as charged.

"I thank you."

Vaulding bowed to the jurors, walked back to his table and sat down.

Judge Hendrick leaned forward on the bench. Elderly, bald and bespectacled, Hendrick provided a nice counterpoint to the young Vaulding. "Does the defense wish to make an opening statement?" Judge Hendrick asked.

All eyes in the courtroom turned to Steve Winslow. The jurors, in particular, looked at him expectantly. His reputation, or at least his flair for the dramatic had preceded him. This was where he was supposed to shine.

In the back of the courtroom, Tracy Garvin bit her lip. Steve had gone over his opening statement with her, so Tracy was the one person in that courtroom who knew what had just happened. She took a breath, scrunched forward on the edge of her seat. What the hell was Steve going to do now?

The problem was, Vaulding had stolen his thunder. That whole speech about circumstantial evidence and a hypothesis other than that of guilt—that was the defense attorney's speech to make. But Vaulding had made it for him. By doing so, he had undermined him and cut the legs out from under him. Steve Winslow couldn't go over the same ground again.

And Vaulding had challenged him to come up with a reasonable explanation. Almost dared him. Steve couldn't meet that challenge, couldn't accept that dare. Even if he *had* a reasonable explanation, which he didn't, if he tried it now, it would be like taking the dare. It would be like two schoolboys fighting.

That was it, Tracy realized. That was the real problem. Vaulding was young. Young, dramatic and unconventional. In short, Vaulding was just a better dressed, straighter version of Steve Winslow. As a result, there was no real contrast between Vaulding and Winslow as there was between Vaulding and the judge.

And as a result, Tracy realized, there was nothing Steve could do. He'd just have to grit his teeth, smile and announce that the defense would reserve its argument until it began putting on its case.

In the front of the courtroom, Steve Winslow paused, took a breath.

Judge Hendrick had a reputation for being rather crotchety, brusk and generally moving things along. He frowned now, said, "Well? Does the defense wish to make a statement or not?"

Steve Winslow looked up and smiled. "The defense does, Your Honor."

24

"YOU EVER BUY A USED CAR?"

Steve Winslow raised his eyebrows, looked at the jury. He shrugged. "It doesn't matter if you have or not, you know what I mean. The spiel. I'm talking about the spiel. The used car salesman's spiel. 'Cause you know and I know, even if we're talking about some clunker with four bald tires, the guy selling you that car's gonna make it sound pretty good.

"Now, I just heard Mr. Vaulding's opening statement, and I must say, it sounded pretty good. And if it sounded pretty good to me, I bet it sounded pretty good to you.

"But you have to remember something. It's *supposed* to sound good. Otherwise you wouldn't buy the car. But if the salesman is nice and bright and young and personable and talks real fast, you're gonna have that sucker home before you notice it's leaking oil."

Steve paused and looked at the jurors. He had their attention, yes, but that was it. It was obvious no one had the faintest idea what he was talking about.

Steve plunged ahead. "Of all the things Mr. Vaulding told you, there was one thing he got right. The burden of proof is on the prosecution. He only said it because he knew I was going to say it and he wanted to say it first. But be that as it may, the fact is he is absolutely right. The burden of proof is on the prosecution. I don't have to prove a thing.

"But you wouldn't know that from the *rest* of Mr. Vaulding's statement. He talks about a reasonable hypothesis other than that of guilt. As if he's going to lay out the facts for you, and then if I can explain them in a way that doesn't implicate my client, then my client can go free.

"Well, that's mighty nice, but that's not the way it happens to work. I don't have to explain the evidence Mr. Vaulding brings out." Steve turned and pointed his finger. "*He* does. If the facts that the prosecution brings out do not make sense, that's not my fault. That's not my client's fault. And we have no responsibility to sort those facts out for you." Again, Steve pointed his finger. "*He* does. And if he *can't* sort 'em out for you, if he *can't* explain the facts in a way that they make sense—then he doesn't have a case. And *that* is when the charge should be dismissed. Right then and there."

In the back of the courtroom, Tracy Garvin nudged Mark Taylor who was seated next to her and whispered, "What the hell's he doing?"

From the side of his mouth, Taylor whispered back, "You got me."

Steve took a breath, settled himself. He looked over at the prosecution table, saw Vaulding smiling. And in that split second, Steve knew why. He'd played right into Vaulding's hands. He was losing it. He'd gotten himself all worked up, but he was leaving the jurors cold. He was making a perfectly sound legal argument, and Vaulding understood it perfectly well. But as far as the jurors were concerned, it was dry lawyer doubletalk.

Steve smiled, shook his head, and chuckled. He looked sideways up at the jury with an impish grin. "Not buyin' it, huh? A bunch of lawyers spewing out their theories, big deal, what does it all mean?"

Steve clapped his hands together. "O.K. Let's look at the facts of this case. During his opening statement, Mr. Vaulding told you time and time again that my client, Russ Timberlaine, was seen wearing the murder weapon at the auction on the afternoon of the murder." Steve held up his finger. "He states this as fact. Again and again and again. Russ Timberlaine was seen wearing the murder weapon. Russ Timberlaine admits firing the murder weapon.

The murder weapon that Russ Timberlaine was wearing at the time of the auction was found on Russ Timberlaine's night table."

Steve shrugged. "Pretty damning, right?" He shook his head. "Wrong. It's the spiel sounding good, but when you get the car home it's a lemon." Steve held up his finger. "The reason Mr. Vaulding keeps stating that Russ Timberlaine was seen wearing the murder weapon is because he can't prove it. He has no proof whatsoever. Now, I am sure there are witnesses who saw Russ Timberlaine wearing *a* gun at the auction. But he doesn't have one *single* witness who can testify Russ Timberlaine was wearing *the murder weapon* at the time of the auction." Steve shook his head. "No, Mr. Vaulding states it as fact, but it's just part of the spiel. There is *no* witness to identify that gun, and there is *no other means* of identifying that gun.

"Now, Vaulding didn't mention this during his opening statement, but the murder weapon has no serial number. The serial number on that gun has been ground off. As was the serial number on the other gun, the gun that was found next to the body, the gun Mr. Vaulding assures us will be identified as the real Pistol Pete Robbins gun. Vaulding says he has experts who can testify to that. And he has witnesses who can testify to the fact that Russ Timberlaine was known to have owned that gun."

Steve grinned, raised his hand. "Keep your eyes on the gun, ladies and gentlemen. Forget the used car salesman. Let's talk about a magician. Yeah, I had it wrong. That's what Mr. Vaulding was during his opening statement. A magician. Keep your eyes on the gun.

"There are witnesses who will testify that the gun found next to the body was owned by Russ Timberlaine. Big deal, since that gun had absolutely nothing to do with the murder. But there are no witnesses whatsoever who can testify that the murder weapon was owned by Mr. Timberlaine, or was ever in Mr. Timberlaine's possession. At most, the prosecution can show that the murder weapon was eventually found on a night table in Russ Timberlaine's bedroom. And when was it found? After the cops arrived. And how was it found? The cops asked Russ Timberlaine for his gun and he said oh sure, here it is, and showed them the gun on the night table.

"Does that sound like the action of a guilty man? Does that sound like the action of a man who had any reason to believe that gun might be involved in a murder? Absolutely not. That sounds like the action of a man with absolutely nothing to hide. A man who was absolutely astounded to find out the gun in his possession was the murder weapon.

"And why is that?" Steve smiled. "Because Russ Timberlaine is innocent. Because the gun found in his gun belt on his night table is not the gun he was wearing at the auction, much as the prosecutor would like you to believe it was. No, the gun found in Russ Timberlaine's gun belt in Russ Timberlaine's bedroom—a room that was unlocked and could have been entered by anyone at any time—that gun was planted there after the murder by the murderer to make it look like Russ Timberlaine was guilty."

Steve smiled. "Hey! There's a reasonable hypothesis other than that of guilt. We got there after all.

"And you know what? There is absolutely nothing to contradict that hypothesis. There's no evidence that the gun on that night table was the gun worn by Russ Timberlaine at the auction. No witnesses whatsoever. The only assertion that is true is the unsubstantiated word of the prosecutor, District Attorney Robert Vaulding. And how much credence may we place in that? Well, the man is not omniscient, he's not a psychic, and he's not a witness. He's expressing his opinion. What he'd *like* to have be true. But for a real assessment of how much his opinion's worth, consider this: if the gun found next to the body had turned out to be the murder weapon, Mr. Vaulding would now be claiming *that* was the gun Russ Timberlaine was wearing at the auction."

Steve paused and let that sink in. He shrugged. "He'd like that much better. See, *that* gun he can tie to Timberlaine. *That* gun, he can prove Timberlaine owned. But the murder weapon he can't."

Steve tugged open the cuffs of his jacket one at a time, a nothing-up-my-sleeves gesture. He smiled. "Keep your eyes on the gun, ladies and gentlemen." He held up his hand. "Mr. Vaulding says, I hold in my hand the murder weapon." Steve snapped his fingers. "He snaps his fingers, poof, the gun disappears. He walks across the stage to the table where he's left his top hat, reaches in and, voilà, pulls out a gun. This is where you the audience are supposed to clap because it's the same gun."

Steve shrugged. "Wanna bet if it is? Keep your eyes on the gun, ladies and gentlemen. As I said, the prosecution is going to put on a host of witnesses to testify about the gun. Well, consider this: if I were to introduce evidence that any one of them had purchased a Colt .45 at some time before the murder, the prosecution would have no way whatsoever to prove that gun was not the murder weapon."

In the back of the courtroom, Mark Taylor coughed and nearly gagged.

Steve Winslow took no notice. He smiled at the jury. "So keep your eyes on the gun, ladies and gentlemen. Keep your eyes on the case."

Steve rubbed his hands together, then suddenly broke them apart and spread them wide, palms out.

Steve smiled.

"Poof."

25

Mark Taylor was fit to be tied.

"Jesus Christ, what the fuck do you think you're doing?"

Steve smiled. "Don't pull your punches, Mark. If you're upset with me, just say so."

"Keep it down, guys," Tracy said, looking around apprehensively.

Steve, Mark and Tracy were catching lunch at a small sandwich shop near the courthouse. They'd chosen a table in the far corner, but the place was fairly crowded, and in a place like that there was no telling who might be listening.

"Fine," Taylor said. "I'll keep it down. I'll talk low. I'll even fucking whisper. Just tell me what the hell you think you're trying to pull."

"You mean about the gun?" Steve said.

Taylor stared at him in exasperation. "Yes, I mean about the gun. I'm sitting there in the back row, I almost had a heart attack. I mean, you practically out-and-out suggested to Vaulding that he start checking on who bought Colt .45s in the last few days."

"I had to."

"Why? You got a death wish? You wanna be killed by a really pissed off private detective? Or you wanna go to jail? I tell you, I sure don't. I go out and buy a gun for you, the next thing I know you're sicking the district attorney on my case."

118

"Not on your case, Mark. I didn't mean you."

"So fucking what! What do you wanna do, tap Vaulding on the shoulder, say, 'Excuse me, when I told you to check out who bought guns before the murder, I meant everybody except Mark Taylor?' "

"I admit that part of it's unfortunate."

"Unfortunate? You scared the shit out of me. Why the hell'd you do it?"

"I'm fighting for my client, Mark, and I had to do something."

"Why?"

Steve picked up his cup of coffee, took a sip. He shook his head, exhaled. "Because, frankly, Vaulding's good. He's much better than I expected. His opening statement caught me by surprise, I felt I had to do something to get back. I started making my opening statement, it was going nowhere, I found myself up in the air, I had to say something. I'm just sorry it was that."

"You and me both."

"But come on, Mark. Checking up on gun purchases is not such an original idea. You think Vaulding hadn't already thought of it?"

"Yeah, I know. But you don't have to throw it in his lap. I mean, you practically challenged him with it, for Christ's sake."

"I know."

"So what's the bottom line?" Tracy said.

Taylor looked at her. "Huh?"

Tracy shrugged. "I mean, come on, boys, we can squabble over who did what to whom. What's done is done. Now how much did it hurt, and what's going to happen next?"

They both looked at her. Taylor shrugged. "O.K. You're right, as usual. But will you grant me cause for bein' pissed?"

"All day long, Mark," Tracy said. "Now how bad does it hurt?"

"Right," Steve said. "What *is* the bottom line? If Vaulding starts looking, what's he going to find?"

Mark Taylor took a sip of coffee. If it agreed with him, Steve and Tracy couldn't have told from his expression. He sighed. "Hopefully, not that much."

"You buy from a dealer?"

"Yes and no."

"What's that mean?"

"I bought from a collector."

"What's the difference?"

"Big difference. Collector doesn't run a gun shop. Doesn't keep an arms register. The gun's registered, yeah, but it's registered at the shop where he bought it."

"And where's that?"

"I don't know," Taylor said irritably. "That's what's killing me. That's what's pissing me off. I mean, I try to be discreet, sure. I take precautions. But Jesus Christ. I mean, how the hell am I supposed to know there's gonna be a murder?"

"No way you could know, Mark. But just what are you saying?"

Mark Taylor looked around the coffee shop, grimaced, lowered his voice. "All right. You show me a Colt .45, tell me you want a duplicate of the gun. I got an operative knows a dealer. So I pass along the word. No problem, made the buy. Gives me the identical gun I gave you." Taylor grimaced again. "You know. The murder weapon. The one you filed the serial number off of."

"Yeah, Mark. What's the point?"

"The point is, I don't know. I should know, but I don't. It just wasn't that important at the time. The gun came from the collector. But did the collector have it in stock, or did the collector have to buy it for us?"

"Wouldn't the operative know?"

"Sure."

"So why don't you ask him?"

"You're a sexist pig."

"Huh?"

"The operative's a woman."

"Fine. Why don't you ask *her*?"

"Because she's on vacation and I can't *find* her."

Steve looked at him. "And you don't know what collector she bought from, only she knows that?"

"Bingo," Taylor said. "Right on the button. See why I'm goin' nuts?"

"Yeah, I do. But there's a saving grace."

"What's that?"

"If she's on vacation and you can't find her, the cops can't either."

"Right. So instead I just gotta sit here peein' in my pants wondering if they're gonna stumble over the collector."

"Why should they?"

"Because some collectors are dealers too, and who's to say this collector isn't."

Steve frowned. "I see."

"Do you? Good. Then you know why I'm going nuts. So tell me, what's the point? I mean, aside from wanting to compete with Vaulding, what are you trying to prove?"

"Basically, that my client didn't buy the gun. I mean, of course, assuming we hadn't made the substitution. I mean, here's the murder weapon with the number ground off. Nothing to tie it to my client except the fact it was found in his room. No, if Vaulding had any way of showing Timberlaine could have purchased that gun, he would. My play is to dare him to do it and taunt him when he can't. Now, if that runs the risk of him tripping over our back trail, that's too bad, but I can't back off because of that."

"Yeah, I know," Taylor said moodily.

"Fine," Tracy said. "Now, if we've exhausted that subject, tell me about the file."

Taylor frowned. "What about it?"

"That's what I want to know," Tracy said. "Vaulding serves a search warrant, finds the file, holds a press conference to announce it. Then he makes his opening statement and he doesn't even mention it once."

"Exactly," Steve said. "That's when I knew the guy was good."

"Wait a minute," Taylor said. "That's right. He didn't mention it. How come?"

Steve shrugged. "I imagine he figures he's got enough on Timberlaine without it. So he leaves it out, so when it comes up later it's yet another damning item on top of all the rest of the evidence."

"Shit," Taylor said. "Can he do that?"

"Moot point, Mark. He's already done it."

"I mean, is it legal?"

"There's no law says you gotta say everything in the world in your opening statement. Hell, there's no law says you gotta *make* an opening statement. Vaulding could have waived his opening statement and started calling witnesses for that matter. He made his opening statement, it was a good one, he just chose to leave that out.

"Which is one of the things that set me off. One of the reasons maybe I said more than I should've."

"Then you think it's a good tactic?"

"Hell, yes. It also anticipates the moron factor."

"The what?" Taylor said.

Steve made a face. "One of my big problems in this case is my defendant's not very bright. Be that as it may, I still gotta argue the guy couldn't be so dumb as to do such and such. The main thing, of course, is hold on to the murder gun.

"Of course, Vaulding knows that. And he anticipates the argument and this is his response."

"Timberlaine used the file so he could keep the murder weapon?"

"Exactly."

"But then he goes ahead and keeps the file."

"I told you it's the moron factor, Mark."

"Jesus."

"Hey, it's in our favor. Vaulding's the one's gotta argue the guy had to be that dumb."

"Well, just between you and me, maybe he is."

"No takers."

"So how you gonna play it?"

Steve grimaced. "That's the problem with this case. I haven't the faintest idea. Vaulding's unconventional, which makes it hard to plan. So I'm not acting, I'm reacting. Basically I gotta sit back and see what Vaulding does next." Steve shrugged. "And there, Mark," he said, "your guess is as good as mine."

26

VAULDING LED OFF with Lieutenant Sanders, who testified to responding to a report of a homicide at the Timberlaine mansion.

"And what did you find when you arrived?" Vaulding asked.

"Two officers were already on the scene. There was a body on the floor, and it was indeed an apparent homicide."

"And had the officers taken any action?"

"Only to secure the premises and hold it until the Crime Scene Unit arrived."

"And what happened when you arrived?"

"I took charge from the officers and inspected the crime scene."

"You inspected it personally?"

"Yes, I did. I instructed the Crime Scene Unit to process it, but I naturally inspected it myself. I always do."

"Could you please describe the crime scene and tell us what you found?"

"Yes, sir. The crime scene was the gun room in the Timberlaine mansion. If I may explain, Russ Timberlaine, the defendant, is a gun collector. What I refer to as the gun room was a room with shelves and cases where his collection was displayed."

"Similar to a museum exhibit?" Vaulding asked.

Sanders nodded. "Good analogy. There were glass-enclosed cases, glass-topped tables with guns on display in them. Very similar to a museum exhibit."

"And where was the body?"

"It was lying face up on the floor, in the middle of the room. Right next to one of the gun cases. The glass-enclosed table-top cases, I mean. And he was bleeding from the forehead, from what I presumed to be the wound of a bullet."

"But you don't know that for a fact?"

"No, sir, I do not. I only know that I saw blood coming from a wound in the forehead."

"I see," Vaulding said. "Now, in addition to the police officers you have already testified to, was there anybody else present at the scene of the crime when you got there?"

Sanders nodded. "Yes, sir. There were several guests staying at the mansion over the weekend, and by the time I got there, many of them had heard of it and gathered around to find out what was going on. In fact, the main job of the two officers on the scene was keeping them away."

"Did you have dealings with any of these guests in particular?"

"Yes, sir."

"And who would that be?"

"Mr. Steve Winslow and Miss Tracy Garvin."

"Steve Winslow?" Vaulding said. "Are you referring to Mr. Steve Winslow, the attorney for the defense?"

"That's right."

"I see. And who is Miss Tracy Garvin?"

"She is Mr. Winslow's confidential secretary."

Vaulding smiled. "Thank you," he said. He turned to the judge. "Your Honor, at this point I have a motion that had best be made outside the presence of the jury."

Judge Hendrick frowned. "Very well. Bailiff, if you would show the jury out."

The jurors looked at each other as the court officer opened the doors and led them out. There was a low buzz of conversation in the courtroom while this was happening, and Steve was sure he heard his name mentioned.

When the jurors had been led out, Judge Hendrick said, "Yes, Mr. Vaulding, what is your motion?"

"Your Honor," Vaulding said. "You will note that Lieutenant Sanders has just testified in response to my question that two weekend guests he paid particular attention to were Steve Winslow and Tracy Garvin. Steve Winslow is the attorney for the defense. Tracy Garvin is his confidential secretary. Mr. Winslow and Miss Garvin were guests of Mr. Timberlaine at the time of the murder, and actually happened to be the first ones to discover the body. I have no wish to embarrass Mr. Winslow or Miss Garvin in this manner, or run the risk of tainting these proceedings by having the attorney for the defense testify as a witness for the prosecution. Therefore, I am attempting to avoid calling Mr. Winslow or Miss Garvin. Frankly, I don't think their testimony is necessary. Nor do I think undue importance should be attached to the fact that they were the ones who found the body. It is not my intention to imply, for instance," Vaulding said, "that the reason they found the body was because their client told them it was there."

Steve Winslow sprang to his feet. "Oh, Your Honor!"

"Exactly," Judge Hendrick snapped. "Mr. Vaulding, you must understand why that remark is extremely objectionable. In fact, with the jury present, that alone could be enough for a mistrial."

Vaulding smiled. "I'm sorry, Your Honor. I was just pointing out why I don't feel that their testimony is necessary. But to the point at hand. As it is my stated intention to avoid putting Mr. Winslow and Miss Garvin on the stand, it becomes necessary to refer to their finding of the body in a manner that otherwise might technically be regarded as hearsay."

Judge Hendrick frowned. "You intend to ask Lieutenant Sanders why in particular he questioned Mr. Winslow and Miss Garvin, and expect him to answer that it was because they were the ones who found the body?"

Vaulding nodded. "Exactly, Your Honor. Which is of course hearsay, because how could Sanders know that except from something they or some third party told him."

"I see," Judge Hendrick said. "And what, specifically, is your motion?"

"I am willing to stipulate that Mr. Winslow and Miss Garvin need not be called to testify about finding the body, if Mr. Winslow will stipulate that I may ask questions regarding the finding of the body that might technically be considered hearsay."

Judge Hendrick turned to Steve Winslow. "Mr. Winslow?"

"Yes, Your Honor."

"You've heard what Mr. Vaulding has in mind. In light of the stipulation that he intends to avoid calling you and Miss Garvin to the stand, are you willing to stipulate that he be allowed the latitude to ask questions that might technically be considered hearsay?"

"No, Your Honor."

There came a surprised murmur from the spectators in the courtroom. Obviously, all of them had expected Steve to agree.

Apparently, Judge Hendrick had too. He frowned. "You're not willing, Mr. Winslow?"

"Absolutely not, Your Honor," Steve said. "I'd be a fine attorney if I stipulated away my client's rights to avoid embarrassing myself.

"I'll go this far, however. Mr. Vaulding can ask Lieutenant Sanders whatever questions he wants, and I'll try not to object unless I feel an answer might tend to violate the rights of my client. But to make a blanket statement that I don't intend to object—that's just ludicrous. Frankly, Your Honor, I don't know what questions he's going to ask or how the witness is going to answer. And I'm certainly not willing to let Lieutenant Sanders speak for me. If it works out, fine. But as far as being a witness in the case, let me tell you this. If Lieutenant Sanders's recollection differs from mine, I'll not only cross-examine him on it, when I start putting on my case, I'll put myself on the stand to contradict him and try to impeach his testimony."

Judge Hendrick frowned. "In that event, it might be necessary for you to step down as counsel."

"I think not, Your Honor," Steve said. He gestured to a stack of law books on the defense table. "And I have the precedents to back it up."

"We'll cross that bridge when we come to it," Judge Hendrick said. He turned back to Vaulding. "Mr. Vaulding, let's proceed. While the defense counsel does not wish to make a stipulation, he has assured us he does not intend to object unless he has to. Now let's proceed on that basis and go as far as we can until we hit an objection. And if we don't, the matter becomes moot. Bring in the jury."

When the jurors had been brought in and seated, Vaulding said, "Now then, lieutenant, you stated two of the guests you questioned particularly were Mr. Winslow and Miss Garvin?"

"Yes, sir."

"And why was that?"

"Because they were the ones who found the body."

"The first ones to find the body?"

"That is correct."

"How do you know that?"

"Actually, only by hearsay. I was told that by the officers on duty when I got there. It was later confirmed by Mr. Winslow and Miss Garvin themselves."

"You questioned them at the scene of the crime?"

"That is correct."

"Do you know what time they found the body?"

"Only indirectly. From what they told me. And by what I was able to confirm from other sources."

"What other sources?"

"When they found the body, Mr. Winslow stayed with it and Miss Garvin went to inform the butler, Martin Kessington, who then called the police. I have his statement, as well as the officer who logged the phone call."

"What time did the call come in?"

Sanders hesitated. "Again, I only know from what I've been told."

Vaulding smiled. "Unless there's an objection, you can tell us. When was that, lieutenant?"

"Approximately five forty-five."

"Does that coincide with the time Mr. Winslow and Miss Garvin told you they found the body?"

"Yes, sir, it does."

"According to your interviews with them, was anyone else present when they found the body?"

"No, sir. They were alone when they found it. Then Miss Garvin went and got Mr. Kessington, and he called the cops."

"And did they indicate what led them to find the body?"

"Objection," Steve said.

Judge Hendrick frowned. "Let's have a sidebar."

When the attorneys and court reporter had assembled at the sidebar, Judge Hendrick said, "Now, Mr. Winslow, as to your objection. You are objecting to that question as hearsay?"

"No, Your Honor."

"No?" Judge Hendrick said. "But it does call for hearsay. If you objected on that grounds, I would have to sustain it."

"I don't want to object on those grounds, Your Honor."

Judge Hendrick frowned. "You what?"

"Begging Your Honor's pardon," Steve said. "But while I didn't stipulate, I certainly agreed to let Mr. Vaulding attempt to present this technically hearsay testimony. And I have no wish to renege on it.

"But this question is something else. I object on the grounds that it is leading and suggestive."

Judge Hendrick frowned again. "Leading and suggestive? Mr. Winslow, are you anticipating what Lieutenant Sanders answer will be?"

"Yes, Your Honor. I anticipate his answer will be no."

"Then how can that be leading and suggestive?"

"Not for Lieutenant Sanders, Your Honor, but to the jury." Steve jerked his thumb at Vaulding. "It's the same thing he tried to pull during his motion. If you let him get away with it, Your Honor, his follow-up question will be to ask Lieutenant Sanders if I found the body as a result of anything anybody told me."

"Yes, I see. And yet that would be a perfectly legitimate question. Mr. Vaulding is attempting to avoid putting you on the stand, but if you *were* on the stand, and testified to finding the body, he would have every right to ask you why. Including whether your finding it there was a direct result of something someone had told you."

"Exactly."

"So it's really the same thing."

"No, it isn't, Your Honor. And that's why I didn't want to stipulate. If I were on the stand and he asked me that question I could say, 'Absolutely not, no one told me anything.' If he asks that question of *Lieutenant Sanders*, he will respond that he asked me that question and in response I claimed that no one had told me anything. Even worse, he may state that I *denied* that anyone had told me anything.

"See the difference, Your Honor? Even though the answer is essentially the same, there is a huge difference in the spin one can put on it, and the implications one can make in the manner in which one happens to give it."

Judge Hendrick's face was beginning to take on a perpetual frown. After all, here it was, the first witness, and the attorneys were already at odds over a relatively unimportant point. He looked at Steve Winslow. "You could do me a big favor, you know, just by objecting to the question on the grounds that it's hearsay."

"In that case, Your Honor," Steve said, "I would have to object to this entire *line* of questioning on the grounds that it's hearsay. In which case Mr. Vaulding would have to put me on the stand. I personally have no objection to that, but I don't think Your Honor would like it much.

"But it's up to you. I'm objecting to that question on the grounds that it's leading and suggestive."

Judge Hendrick took a breath. "The objection is sustained." He turned to Vaulding. "Mr. Vaulding, I don't want to tell you how to run your case, but I suggest you make every effort to get beyond this."

"Yes, Your Honor."

When they had all returned to their positions Judge Hendrick said, "The objection is sustained. Mr. Vaulding, please rephrase your question."

Vaulding smiled as if perfectly satisfied with the judge's ruling. "I'll withdraw it, Your Honor, and ask something else. Lieutenant Sanders, were you personally present at the crime scene until the medical examiner arrived?"

"Yes, I was."

"What time was that?"

"That would be approximately six-fifteen P.M."

"At six-fifteen that evening the medical examiner arrived and examined the body?"

"That's correct."

Vaulding nodded. "Thank you. Your Honor, I have no further questions at this time. I may wish to recall the witness later."

Judge Hendrick nodded. "Very well. The witness may step down."

Steve Winslow stood up. "One moment, Your Honor. I have a few questions of the witness."

Judge Hendrick frowned, hesitated a moment, then announced, "Let's have a sidebar."

When the attorneys and court reporter had once again assembled at the sidebar, Judge Hendrick said, "Mr. Winslow. In light of what we discussed, I had not anticipated that you would attempt to cross-examine this witness."

"I certainly never stipulated that I wouldn't, Your Honor."

"I'm aware of that," Judge Hendrick said testily. "But you must be aware we are treading on dangerous ground here. Just as I would not allow Mr. Vaulding to ask the witness questions that you deemed leading and suggestive, I do not want to get into a similar situation of your leading the witness with regard to your version of finding the body."

"I have no intention of doing so, Your Honor. And I am indeed sorry if your opinion of me is such that you would assume that is something I would naturally do."

Judge Hendrick's wits were obviously becoming frayed. "I assume nothing of the sort," he snapped. "I am merely trying to head off a situation before it develops. I do not wish to spend this entire trial at the sidebar. It's only natural to assume you intend to question him about finding the body, since he didn't really testify to anything else."

Steve nodded. "Your Honor is certainly entitled to your opinion. But I am entitled to my cross-examination. I certainly hope it won't be objectionable."

Judge Hendrick bit his lip. He was not happy with the situation, but he was stymied by the fact Steve Winslow was absolutely in the right.

When they had all resumed their positions, Steve Winslow said, "Now, lieutenant, you testified to arriving at the scene of the murder and finding the body of a man lying on the floor, is that right?"

"Yes, sir."

"In what position was the body lying?"

"On its back."

"I believe you testified that the body was bleeding from a wound in the forehead?"

"That's right."

"Was the body alive or dead?"

"Objection, Your Honor."

"Overruled. Witness may answer."

"Was the man alive or dead?"

"He was dead."

"Really?" Steve said. "Tell me. Do you have any medical training, lieutenant?"

"No, I do not."

"Ever take any medical courses?"

"Objection. Already asked and answered."

"Sustained."

"Lieutenant, how did you determine that the man was dead?"

Lieutenant Sanders took a breath. "Let me make something clear. *I* did not determine that the man was dead. I left that to the medical examiner. Who, as I testified, arrived shortly after I did.

"But if you ask me if the man was dead, in my opinion the man was dead. But that is admittedly not a medical opinion, and does not have the same evidentiary value as the opinion you are going to get from the medical examiner."

Steve smiled. "Thank you. But whatever weight you may wish to attach to it, your personal opinion is that the man was dead?"

"Yes, it is."

"Fine," Steve said. "Now I think you testified that the man was bleeding from a wound in his forehead?"

"That's right."

"Is it?" Steve said. "But there are certain instances, are there not, where the simple act of bleeding would in itself be a sign of life? An indication that the heart was still functioning, pumping blood from the body. So I ask you again, lieutenant, are you certain the body was bleeding when you found it?"

Lieutenant Sanders hesitated. "There was blood on the face that had come from a wound on the forehead."

"I understand," Steve said. "But was that blood still flowing? In other words, lieutenant, I see three possibilities. Blood was *flowing* from the wound, indicating the heart was pumping blood from the body; blood was *seeping* from the wound, indicating the heart had stopped but blood was still draining from the body; and blood was no longer flowing, draining or seeping at all, and the blood on the face was merely an indication that the body *had been* bleeding."

Steve paused, looked over at Lieutenant Sanders, who was practically glowering on the witness stand. Steve smiled. "Now, which would you say that was?"

Lieutenant Sanders took a breath. His effort to keep the irritation out of his voice was only partly successful. "The blood was not flowing and the heart was not pumping," he said. "The blood was either seeping very slowly from a dead body, or had very recently stopped seeping from a dead body. You can split hairs any way you like, but I can't give it to you any better than that."

Steve smiled. "That will do quite nicely, lieutenant. And what time was it when you found the body?"

"Approximately six o'clock."

"Would that be approximately fifteen minutes before the medical examiner arrived?"

"That's right."

"Thank you, lieutenant. That's all."

When Vaulding announced he had no questions on redirect, Judge Hendrick took note of the time and adjourned court for the afternoon.

27

WHEN COURT RECONVENED the next morning, Vaulding called Fred Blessing, a chubby man with twinkling eyes who looked like a vaudeville comedian, but who turned out to be the medical examiner. Blessing testified to arriving at the Timberlaine mansion and examining the body of the deceased.

"And what time was it when you arrived?"

"Six-fifteen."

"Exactly?"

"I arrived at the mansion at six-thirteen. I was at the scene of the crime by six-fifteen."

"And what did you find?"

"I found the body of a man lying face up on the floor."

"What did you do?"

"I immediately examined the body for signs of life."

"Were there any?"

"There were none."

"The man was dead?"

"Yes, he was."

"Could you tell how long he had been dead?"

"Obviously, not for very long. The body was still warm."

"Did you make any attempt to pin down the time of death?"

"Naturally. What I just gave you was my initial impression based on a preliminary examination of the body. Of course I made a more detailed inspection later on."

"How much later on?"

"If I could consult my notes?"

"Please do."

Dr. Blessing reached into his jacket pocket, took out a notebook. He thumbed through it. "Actually, not that much later. I have a note here that I took the body temperature at six twenty-one."

"Before the body was removed to the morgue for your autopsy?"

"Absolutely. Body temperature is generally the most accurate means of determining time of death. It should always be taken as soon as possible."

"And your records indicate you took it at six twenty-one on the evening of the murder?"

"That is correct."

"From this were you able to more accurately determine the time of death?"

"Yes, I was. I would put the time of death between four o'clock and five-thirty on the afternoon of the murder."

Vaulding nodded. "Very good, doctor. And did you also determine the cause of death?"

"Not at the time. My preliminary indication was that the man had met his death due to a wound in the forehead, but I could not verify that until I did my autopsy."

"I understand," Vaulding said. "But when you did, what was the result?"

"I found that the man had died from a bullet wound to the head."

"A single bullet?"

"That is correct."

"The bullet was the sole cause of death?"

"To the best I could determine."

"Was the bullet wound sufficient to have caused death?"

"Oh, yes. The bullet had penetrated the forehead and lodged in the brain, causing extensive cerebral damage. It would be extraordinary to find any sign of life under those circumstances."

"And there was none?"

"No. As I've stated before, the man was dead."

"And death was caused by the bullet you found lodged in the brain?"

"That is correct."

"Did you remove that bullet from the brain, doctor?"

"Yes, I did."

With a flourish Vaulding strode back to the prosecution table, opened his briefcase, pulled out a plastic bag and held it up. "Your Honor, I ask that this be marked for identification as People's Exhibit Number One."

After the court reporter had marked the exhibit, Vaulding took the plastic bag and handed it to Dr. Blessing. "Doctor, I hand you this plastic bag marked for identification People's Exhibit Number One and ask you if you recognize the contents."

"Yes, I do."

"What is it?"

"It is the bullet I removed from the head of the victim."

"How do you recognize it?"

Dr. Blessing pointed. "By my initials, which I scratched on the base of the bullet."

"And this is the bullet that your examination determined to be the sole cause of death?"

"That is correct."

Vaulding smiled. "Thank you. Your witness."

Steve Winslow stood up. "Six twenty-one, doctor?"

"I beg your pardon?"

"You took the body temperature at six twenty-one?"

Dr. Blessing referred to his notes. "That is correct."

"And what was it?"

"I beg your pardon?"

"What was the body temperature at six twenty-one?"

Again Blessing consulted his notes. "Ninety-six point six."

"Ninety-six point six? That's two degrees cooler than normal, isn't it?"

"Yes, it is."

"Now, tell me, doctor, what is the normal rate of cooling of a body after death?"

"It's approximately one and a half degrees Fahrenheit per hour."

"Let's do the math. You say the body had cooled two degrees. One and a half degrees would be one hour. Half a degree would be twenty minutes. So the body had cooled approximately an hour and twenty minutes. You took the temperature at six twenty-one.

An hour and a half earlier would be five oh-one, say approximately five o'clock. Is that right?"

"Yes, it is."

Steve smiled. "Well, that's mighty strange, doctor. Didn't you put the time of death between four o'clock and five-thirty?"

"Yes, I did."

"I thought you did. That's why I had expected the median time of death, the most likely time of death, the time of death we would mathematically come out with, to be four forty-five. Because that's halfway between those times. Or in other words, when you said death took place between the hours of four o'clock and five-thirty, I assumed you meant it was because you were indicating death could have taken place within forty-five minutes *before* the median time of death, or within forty-five minutes *after* the median time of death."

Dr. Blessing said nothing. His lips were set in a firm line.

"Is that not the case?" Steve said.

"No, it is not the case," Dr. Blessing snapped.

"It isn't? But didn't you testify that a body cools at one and a half degrees Fahrenheit per hour? Didn't you testify that when you took the body temperature it was two degrees below normal, or ninety-six point six? Didn't you testify that you took the body temperature at six twenty-one?"

"Yes, I did," Dr. Blessing said. "And those are very good indications of when the man met his death. But no determination of the time of death could be that exact. You can't say it had to be five o'clock any more than you can say it had to be four forty-five."

"Granted," Steve said. "But don't your findings indicate death was *more likely* to have been at five o'clock than four forty-five?"

"Not necessarily," Dr. Blessing said.

"Really?" Steve said. "Well, maybe we should do the math again."

"Objection," Vaulding said.

"Overruled," Judge Hendrick said. "Witness may answer."

"Answer what?" Vaulding said irritably. "That's not even a question."

"What's that?" Judge Hendrick said. He turned to the court reporter. "Read back that last exchange."

The court reporter shuffled through her notes, read back, "Answer: 'Not necessarily.' Question: 'Then maybe we should do the math again.'"

"It was not a question," Judge Hendrick ruled. "Mr. Winslow, would you please rephrase your remark and put it in the form of a question?"

"Certainly, Your Honor. Dr. Blessing, would you please explain to me why the math we have just done in court comes up with the median time of five o'clock, whereas your estimation of the time of death gives us the median time of four forty-five?"

Dr. Blessing was somewhat red in the face. He took a breath. "As I've already stated, while body temperature is generally the most accurate method of determining the time of death, no method can be that precise. In coming up with a reasonable estimate of the time of death, it is necessary for me to consider all the factors involved."

"That's very interesting," Steve said. "What other factors were there?"

"I beg your pardon?"

"What other medical factors were there that you used in determining the time of death?"

Dr. Blessing paused, frowned.

"Rigor mortis hadn't begun to set in, had it?" Steve asked.

"No, it had not."

"No, I wouldn't think so, that soon after death. So that wasn't a factor. And post mortem lividity wasn't a factor either, was it?"

"No, it was not."

"The stomach contents—were they useful?"

Dr. Blessing hesitated again. "Not particularly. The decedent had had a late brunch of bacon and eggs and sweet rolls. However, brunch was served that morning from nine till one, and no one has been able to supply me with the time they believe the decedent ate."

"I see. So the stomach contents do not help you pin down the time of death, do they, doctor?"

"No, they do not."

"Then what other medical factors did you rely on in determining the time of death?"

"There were no other medical factors."

Steve frowned. "Is that right, doctor? You mean the only medical factor you relied on was the body temperature?"

"That is basically correct."

"Basically?" Steve said. "Why do you qualify your answer with the word basically? Is it correct, or is it not correct?"

Dr. Blessing hesitated.

Vaulding sprang to his aid. "Objection, Your Honor."

"Overruled," Judge Hendrick snapped.

"Is it correct, or is it not correct?" Steve repeated.

"It's correct," Dr. Blessing said grudgingly.

"Thank you, doctor. I thought it was. Then your use of the word basically is incorrect, is it not?"

"Objection."

"Overruled."

"Was your use of the word basically incorrect?"

"Not, it was not," Dr. Blessing snapped. "I said it was basically correct, and it *is* basically correct."

"It is also basically misleading, doctor. Isn't it true that what I said was *entirely* correct, and you used the word basically because you were reluctant to admit this? Because you are the prosecution's witness and you are biased in their favor. And you used the word basically because you were reluctant to admit anything that might hurt the prosecution's case. And your use of the word basically is an indication of your bias."

"Objection."

"Overruled. The witness may answer."

"Absolutely not," Dr. Blessing sputtered. "I used the word casually, not expecting it to be picked apart in this manner. If anything, I misspoke myself."

Steve smiled. "Then you were wrong, doctor?"

"I was not wrong. I regret the use of the word basically. I retract it. I withdraw it."

"I'm glad to hear it," Steve said. "Then there *were* no other medical factors, were there, doctor?"

"No, there were not."

"Then why do you compute the median time of death at four forty-five rather than five o'clock?"

"Now there you're putting words in my mouth. I never said I

did that. You said that. All I did was put the times death could have occurred between four o'clock and five-thirty."

"Of which the median time is four forty-five, is it not?"

"Yes, but that is *not* how I arrived at those outside limits," Dr. Blessing said. "While there were no other medical factors involved, there were factors to consider. The median time *is* five o'clock. Medically speaking, it would be possible for the man to have been killed between the hours of four and six. But the man couldn't have been killed at six, because by that time there were already police on the scene. And as I understand it, you yourself found the body at five forty-five. And while it is still possible the man met his death as early as four o'clock, it is *not* possible he met his death as late as six. So I have tried to give the time of death in a means that takes into account both the medical circumstances and the physical circumstances surrounding the crime as we know them. And that is why the median time, as you attempt to compute it, is meaningless. Yes, five o'clock would have been the median time from those figures—the man still could have been killed as early as four or as late as five-thirty."

"I see, doctor," Steve said. "So you are now testifying that your medical opinion of the time of death is based on nonmedical factors?"

"No, I'm not!" Dr. Blessing snapped. "You can twist my words around any way you want, but I think I've given a fair and accurate appraisal of the situation."

"After a certain amount of prompting," Steve said dryly.

"Objection!" Vaulding snapped.

"Sustained. Mr. Winslow, please refrain from such asides."

"I'm sorry, Your Honor. Doctor, let's take a look at this fair and impartial appraisal. You say death could have occurred as early as four or as late as five-thirty?"

"That is correct."

"But you also say according to your *medical* evidence, death could have occurred as late as six o'clock. You discount that on the grounds that by that time officers were on the scene."

"That is correct."

"Tell me, was one of those officers Lieutenant Sanders?"

"Yes, he was."

"Now, I don't want to mislead you, but Lieutenant Sanders who has already testified in this case, mentioned observing blood on the face of the decedent. He first testified that when he arrived on the scene he saw blood *flowing* from the wound, but when I cross-examined him on it he said the blood was not flowing but was either seeping from the wound or had recently stopped seeping from the wound.

"With regard to that, I wonder if *you* observed the blood coming from the wound of the decedent?"

"Of course I did."

"And when you first examined the body, was that blood flowing?"

"It was not."

"Was it seeping?"

"If so, it was very slow. So slow as to be indistinguishable from the fact it had stopped."

Steve nodded. "I see, doctor. And it was then that you determined that the man was dead?"

"Or immediately thereafter."

"Yes, doctor," Steve said. "While Lieutenant Sanders *presumed* the man was dead, it was you as medical examiner who *pronounced* him dead, who made that official determination?"

"That is correct."

"Well, doctor, let me ask you this: if what Lieutenant Sanders observed was indeed blood coming from the wound of the decedent, is it possible that the decedent was alive when Lieutenant Sanders and the police got there, but died before you examined him?"

Dr. Blessing stared at him in exasperation. "How could I answer that?"

"You could say yes, you could say no, or you could say I don't know."

"Objection, Your Honor," Vaulding said. "Badgering the witness."

Judge Hendrick smiled. "I believe the witness asked him the question. The objection is overruled."

"Is that possible?" Steve Winslow said.

Dr. Blessing shifted his position on the stand. "What do you mean, possible?"

"I mean physically possible. In terms of your medical findings. In other words, is there anything you discovered in your autopsy that would indicate that could not have happened?"

Dr. Blessing hesitated a moment. "No."

Steve smiled. "I didn't think so, doctor. So when you say to me the medical findings indicate the time of death could have been between four and six, but you altered that time because six was out of the question because the police were already on the scene, that is not entirely correct, is it? For all you know he could have been still alive when the police arrived, and expired before you examined him."

"That's highly unlikely," Dr. Blessing said.

"I agree. I think it's highly unlikely death occurred between five-thirty and six. But is it not a fact, doctor, that it is also highly unlikely death occurred between four and four-thirty? Is it not a fact that your medical findings regarding body temperature indicate that the victim probably met his death between the hours of four-thirty and five-thirty, with five o'clock as the median time? And while it is highly unlikely, there is an outside chance he met his death between four o'clock and four-thirty? And the only reason you include that half-hour in giving the probable time of death is because the police indicated to you that they would like to be able to show that the victim could have been killed around four o'clock when only Russ Timberlaine had left the auction. Is that not a fact?"

"No, it is not," Dr. Blessing said. "I have answered that question to the best of my ability, taking all factors into consideration."

"And you say the victim could have been killed between the hours of four and five-thirty?"

"That is correct."

"And in lopping off the last half-hour you cite the fact that I, myself, found the body at five forty-five?"

"It is a factor. It is not a medical factor, but it is indeed a factor."

"Yes, it is, doctor. But you picked a cutoff point of five-thirty. Couldn't the victim actually have met his death at five forty-four? Couldn't I have walked in the very minute after he died?"

Dr. Blessing said nothing. He glowered at Steve Winslow.

"Well, doctor?"

"It's possible, but highly unlikely."

Steve nodded. "I agree, doctor. I would say most likely he died between four-thirty and five-thirty. Wouldn't you?"

"Objection."

"Sustained."

"When did the decedent meet his death?"

"Objection. Already asked and answered."

"Sustained."

Steve frowned. He shot a glance at the jurors, smiled slightly and shook his head to give the impression he was being hampered by Vaulding being overly technical. Then he turned back to the witness. "Very well, doctor. Regardless of when the decedent met his death, the fact is he was killed by a single bullet that pierced the forehead and entered the brain, is that right?"

"Yes, it is."

"I believe you stated that was the sole cause of death."

"Yes, it was."

"There were no contributing or secondary causes?"

Dr. Blessing hesitated a moment. "I would say no."

Steve smiled. "You would, doctor? Is that because the answer is no, or because you feel the prosecution would like that answer?"

"Objection."

"Sustained."

"May I be heard, Your Honor?" Steve said.

Judge Hendrick shook his head. "The objection is sustained. You may rephrase the question."

"Thank you, Your Honor. Dr. Blessing, when I asked if there were any contributing factors in the death of the decedent, you hesitated, then said you would say no. I wonder what you were considering when you hesitated, and why you qualified your answer in that fashion. Therefore I ask you, were there other factors that you considered, which you determined were *not* a direct cause of death, but which were still significant enough to have been under consideration?"

Dr. Blessing took a breath. He clamped his lips together, puffed out his cheeks for a second before he exhaled. "Well," he said. "There was evidence of a possible concussion."

"Concussion?" Steve said. "You mean a blow to the head?"

"That's right."

Steve gawked at the doctor, blinked twice. He turned, stared open-mouthed at the jury, then turned back to the doctor. "I beg your pardon, doctor, but I'm a little confused. I asked you if you found any contributing factors besides the bullet wound and you said no. Did you not?"

"Yes, I did."

"You don't consider a blow to the head a contributing factor?"

Dr. Blessing clamped his lips together, shook his head. "I was asked for the cause of death. A blow to the head, if indeed there was one, is absolutely insignificant in terms of the cause of death. It was not severe, could not have caused death, could not have even contributed. The bullet was the sole, necessary and sufficient cause of death."

"I'm sure it was, doctor," Steve said. "Let's talk about this blow to the head. Where was it?"

"On the back of the skull. Just above and behind the right ear."

"What form did it take?"

"There was a bruise and slight swelling."

"Really?" Steve said. "Was there any indication when this blow was delivered?"

"I didn't say a blow was delivered," Dr. Blessing snapped.

"No, you didn't, doctor. Are you now saying the blow to the head appeared of its own accord?"

"Certainly not. We've been using the term blow to the head to refer to the concussion. Which is misleading. The concussion is as likely to have occurred from the head striking something as from something striking the head."

Steve frowned. "What are you saying, doctor?"

"Simply this. If the man was shot, fell down and the back of his head hit the floor, that would be entirely consistent with what I found in my autopsy."

"Are you saying such is the case?"

"No, I'm just saying it's possible. More than possible, it's likely. Therefore I would tend to minimize the blow to the head."

"I see. Tell me, doctor. Did you discuss your testimony with District Attorney Robert Vaulding?"

"Objection."

"Overruled."

"Of course I did," Dr. Blessing said. "He's not going to put me on the stand without knowing what I'm going to say."

"Of course not, doctor. But did he *tell* you what to say?"

"Objection!"

"Overruled."

"Absolutely not," Dr. Blessing said. "And I resent the implication."

"I'm sorry about that, doctor, but I have to ask you this: did he tell you what *not* to say?"

"I beg your pardon?"

"Specifically, did District Attorney Robert Vaulding tell you *not* to mention the blow to the head unless you were specifically asked?"

Dr. Blessing shifted his position on the witness stand. "I don't believe he said that."

"You don't *believe* he said that?"

"No, I'm sure he didn't say that."

"What *did* he say?"

"Objection."

"Sustained."

Steve Winslow smiled. "Doctor, you just testified that because the blow to the back of the head could have been caused by the decedent falling after he was shot, you tended to minimize the importance of that concussion. Do you recall that?"

"Yes, I do."

"Was that the *only* reason you chose to minimize the importance of the concussion? Or did District Attorney Robert Vaulding make any suggestion to you that led you to believe it would be best to minimize that concussion?"

"He did not," Dr. Blessing said. "He merely said I should give my testimony as clearly as possible and not let a lot of extraneous testimony cloud the issue."

Steve smiled. "Well, I'm sorry if I clouded the issue with this extraneous blow to the head." Steve chuckled, shot a look at the jury. "Now, I believe you said this concussion took the form of a bruise and a slight swelling, is that right?"

"Yes, it is."

"Did you photograph it?"

"Yes, I did."

"Do you have those photographs in court?"

"No, I do not."

"What about photographs of the entrance wound of the bullet. Surely you took some of those."

"Yes, I did."

"Are those photographs here in court?"

"No, they're not."

"You have no photographs from your autopsy here in court?"

"No, I do not."

"Why not?"

"I wasn't asked to bring them."

"Were you asked *not* to bring them?"

"No, I simply wasn't asked for them."

"The matter never came up?"

"I think we mentioned the photographs and decided it would not be necessary."

"I see," Steve Winslow said. He turned to Judge Hendrick. "At this time I would like to conclude my cross-examination, but ask that this witness be instructed to return to court tomorrow and bring with him the photographs he took during his autopsy."

"So ordered," Judge Hendrick said. "You say that concludes your cross-examination at this time?"

"Yes it does, Your Honor."

"Mr. Vaulding, do you have any redirect?"

"Not at this time, Your Honor."

"Very well. The witness is excused. You will return tomorrow with the photographs."

As Judge Hendrick said that, Steve looked over at Robert Vaulding. The district attorney did not seem particularly concerned. If anything, there was a slight smile on his lips.

28

WHEN COURT RECONVENED the next morning, Vaulding recalled Dr. Blessing, who introduced a series of photographs taken during his autopsy. The photographs were marked for identification and introduced into evidence. Then they were shown to the jury.

As the jurors passed the pictures along their faces became hard, a natural consequence of looking at a bloody dead body.

Seeing this, Timberlaine stirred restlessly, looked at Steve in exasperation. Twice he seemed on the verge of speaking, but under Steve's stony gaze he held his tongue.

Vaulding sat quite placidly through all this. If anything, his attitude was bemused.

When the jurors were finally finished with the pictures, Vaulding turned to Steve Winslow and said with a bit of a smirk, "Your witness."

Steve leafed through the photographs, frowned. He selected one, stood up and approached the witness.

"Dr. Blessing, I hand you a photograph marked for identification as People's Exhibit Two-G and ask you to describe what it shows."

Dr. Blessing took the photograph and looked at it. "That is a closeup of the back of the head of the decedent showing the concussion."

"Can you describe the concussion?"

"It is a raised discoloration on the back of the skull."

"Could you describe the hair in that area?"

"I beg your pardon?"

"Or lack of it?"

"Oh. Yes, I shaved the hair away from the head in that area so that I could photograph the bruise."

"How large an area did you shave, doctor?"

"That appears to be approximately a three-inch square."

"You did this so that you could photograph the bruise?"

"That's right."

"Well, doctor, if I understand your testimony, you found this blow to the back of the head to be important enough to shave away a three-inch-square section of the hair on the back of the head, considered it important enough to photograph that bruise, and you considered it important enough to blow those photographs up to eight-by-tens, but you did not consider it important enough to mention on the stand in your direct examination yesterday."

Dr. Blessing smiled. "As I've already stated, I was asked to describe the cause of death. The blow to the head was not the cause of death."

Steve took a breath. Things weren't going as planned. He wanted to do something, anything, to rip the smug look off the doctor's face. But with the doctor calmly conceding everything he wanted to prove, and Vaulding raising no objection, Steve had nothing to push against. The end result was, all Steve had accomplished was the introduction of a bunch of photos destined to prejudice the jury against his own client.

Steve stole a look at Vaulding, saw him watching the proceedings with a superior smirk. But there was nothing he could do about it.

Steve took another breath, blew it out again. "No further questions."

When Dr. Blessing had been excused from the stand, Robert Vaulding stood up and said, "Your Honor, I now wish to call a witness for a limited purpose only. This is a gentleman who will be a main witness for us later on, but right now I am attempting to establish orderly proof, and at the moment I am concerned with the corpus delicti, specifically the identification of the body. I am now calling the witness for that limited purpose. I apologize in advance for this witness giving his testimony piecemeal."

"So noted," Judge Hendrick said. "Call your witness."

"Call Melvin Burdett."

Melvin Burdett gave every indication of being a hostile witness. He took the stand reluctantly, smiled encouragingly at Russ Timberlaine, then glared at the prosecutor.

"What is your name?" Vaulding asked.

"Melvin Burdett."

"Are you familiar with the defendant, Russ Timberlaine?"

"Yes, I am."

"Where you familiar with a man by the name of Jack Potter?"

"Yes, I was."

"You had met Jack Potter?"

"I just said so, didn't I?"

Judge Hendrick held up his hand before Vaulding could ask another question. "That will do," he snapped. "Mr. Burdett?"

"Yes?"

"Call me Your Honor."

Burdett glared at the judge a moment, then said, "Yes, Your Honor."

"This is a court of law. You have been called as a witness and you are required to answer questions. Please do so in a civil manner or I will hold you in contempt of court. Is that clear?"

After a moment's pause, Burdett said, "Yes, Your Honor."

"Thank you. Proceed, Mr. Vaulding."

Vaulding looked up at the judge. "I trust Your Honor recognizes this as a hostile witness and will allow leading questions?"

"Ask away. You have your ruling."

"Thank you, Your Honor. Mr. Burdett, on how many occasions had you met Jack Potter?"

"I don't know."

"Was it more than once?"

"Yes, it was."

"More than a dozen times?"

"I don't think so."

"More than six?"

Burdett hesitated a moment. "I don't know."

"I see. Mr. Burdett. Directing your attention to the night of the murder, were you asked by police officers to look at the body of a man?"

"Yes, I was."

"Did you look at that body?"

"Yes, I did."

"Did you recognize the man whose body you saw?"

"Yes, I did."

"Could you tell us who that was, please?"

"Jack Potter."

"Thank you. No further questions."

As Burdett rose to leave the stand, Steve Winslow stood up. "One moment, Mr. Burdett. I have a few questions."

"Objection, Your Honor," Vaulding said. "This witness was called for a limited purpose only."

Judge Hendrick raised his eyebrows. "Mr. Vaulding, you can't object to a witness being cross-examined."

"May I have a sidebar, Your Honor?"

Rather reluctantly Judge Hendrick said, "Very well."

At the sidebar Vaulding said, "Your Honor, I think the situation is clear. This witness is hostile to the prosecution and favorable to the defense. As such, he can logically be expected to repeat any words the defense attorney wishes to put in his mouth. Given any latitude in my direct examination, that might be permissible. We could at least debate the points. But he was called for the limited purpose of identifying the body. And that should not allow counsel to go on a fishing expedition for the express purpose of getting me to put my case on out of order."

"I understand your contention," Judge Hendrick said. "Still, counsel has the right to cross-examine. If his questions go afield, you can object, and those objections will be sustained."

"Giving the jury the impression that the prosecution is hamstringing the defense and that I have something to hide," Vaulding said in exasperation.

Judge Hendrick's eyes narrowed. "Mr. Vaulding," he said with just an edge in his voice. "Give me some credit for being able to run my courtroom. If counsel's questions are irregular, he will be told so and instructed by the court not to ask them. Now could we please get on with it? It is somewhat extraordinary to have an objection before a single question has been asked."

When they had resumed their positions, Steve Winslow said, "Mr. Burdett, you stated you met Jack Potter several times?"

"That is correct."

"Tell me, where did those meetings take place?"

"At Russ Timberlaine's mansion."

"And all the occasions when you met Jack Potter were at Russ Timberlaine's mansion?"

"That is correct."

"Tell me, on the weekend of the murder, did you meet Jack Potter at that time?"

"Absolutely."

"And in the course of the weekend, did you have occasion to speak to him personally?"

"Yes, I did."

"And on or before the day of the murder, did you have a conversation with Jack Potter, asking him to tell you what gun Russ Timberlaine intended to bid on in the auction?"

"Objection, Your Honor!"

"Absolutely not!" Burdett snapped angrily.

Judge Hendrick's gavel smacked down. "That will do," he growled. He turned to the witness. "Mr. Burdett, you have been warned before. You are now warned again. In the event of an objection, you will wait for the judge's ruling before answering the question. Is that clear?"

"It's clear, Your Honor. But I'm not going to sit here and let my reputation be smeared."

"Your reputation is not on trial here, Mr. Burdett. And I'll thank you to heed the court's instructions."

"Yes, Your Honor," Burdett mumbled.

"Now then, the objection is sustained. That question and answer may go out. Mr. Winslow, please confine your questions to any specific meetings and not what was discussed in them."

Steve Winslow smiled. "No further questions, Your Honor."

When Burdett had been excused from the stand, Vaulding recalled Lieutenant Sanders.

"Lieutenant," Vaulding said. "Directing your attention once again to the scene of the murder at Russ Timberlaine's mansion, you arrived at the scene and discovered the body on the floor. The body that we have now identified as Jack Potter. Now then, was there any weapon in sight?"

Lieutenant Sanders hesitated, then smiled. "I think you'd better rephrase that, counselor," he said. "You'll recall this was Russ Timberlaine's gun room."

The remark produced a laugh in the courtroom.

Vaulding smiled good-naturedly. "Well-said, lieutenant. Then let me ask you this: was there any weapon in particular that you took notice of?"

"Yes, there was."

"And what would that be?"

"A Colt .45 lying on the floor next to the body."

"Was there anything in particular you noticed about this Colt .45?"

"Yes. There was the initial R carved in the handle."

"That was readily apparent?"

"Yes. That side of the handle was facing up."

"Did you notice anything else in particular about this gun?"

"Yes, I did."

"What was that?"

"The serial number had been filed off."

"The serial number?"

"That's right."

"How had that been done?"

"Someone had taken a file or other rough grinding implement and ground the number off the gun."

"The serial number was metal then?"

"Yes. The serial number was stamped in metal on the underside of the gun, just back of the trigger guard, between the cylinder and the handle."

"And the serial number had been ground off?"

"That is correct."

"Is that the only serial number on the gun?"

"Yes, it is."

"Lieutenant, would you know this gun if you saw it again?"

"Yes, I would."

"How, if the serial number has been ground off?"

"I scratched my initials on the underside of the handle."

Vaulding nodded. He took a gun, had it marked for identification, and handed it to Lieutenant Sanders. "Lieutenant, I hand you a gun marked for identification People's Exhibit Number Three and ask you if you recognize it."

"Yes, sir," Lieutenant Sanders said. "This is the gun I described. The one I found on the floor of Russ Timberlaine's gun room, next to the body of Jack Potter."

"There is no question in your mind?"

"None whatsoever."

"This is the gun you found that evening and scratched your initials on?"

"That's right."

"Did you take possession of that gun at that time?"

"Yes, I did."

"Then let me ask you this: did you take possession of any other gun on that particular evening?"

"Yes, I did."

"Can you tell us how that happened?"

"I showed this gun—the one we've just identified—to Russ Timberlaine and asked him if it was his gun, and, more specifically, if it was the gun he'd been seen wearing that day."

"You asked this of the defendant, Russ Timberlaine?"

"Yes, I did."

"Let me ask you this: was Mr. Timberlaine's attorney present?"

"Yes, he was."

"I am referring to Mr. Steve Winslow, the attorney for the defense—you say he was present at the time?"

"Yes, he was."

"And was Russ Timberlaine advised that he did not have to answer your questions?"

"Yes, he was. I gave him that advice, and his attorney gave him that advice."

"Despite that, he answered your questions?"

"Yes, he did."

"And what did he say at the time?"

"He said—referring to this gun—People's Exhibit Three, is it?—he kept saying it's the wrong gun."

"The wrong gun?"

"Yes."

"Did he tell you what he meant by that?"

"Yes, he did. He stated that this was not the gun he was seen wearing at the time of the auction."

"I see. And what did you do then?"

"I said if this was not the gun he'd been seen wearing at the auction, would he please produce that gun."

"What did the defendant do then?

"He led me upstairs to his bedroom and proceeded to point out a gun."

"Where was this gun?"

"In his holster on an end table next to his bed."

"The defendant pointed this gun out to you?"

"Yes, he did."

"And said it was the gun he had been wearing at the time of the auction?"

"That's right."

"Lieutenant, can you describe this second weapon?"

"Yes, I can. It was a Colt .45, apparently similar in every way to the one found next to the body."

"You say in every way?"

"Yes, I do."

"Does that include the R carved into the handle?"

"Yes, it does. The gun I took from Russ Timberlaine's gunbelt had an R carved in the handle as well."

"What about the serial number?"

"It had also been ground off."

"What was the condition of the gun—with regard to being loaded?"

"The gun was fully loaded, with one shot fired. That is, there was one empty shell under the hammer of the gun."

"I see. And what was the condition of the other gun, the one found next to the body?"

"That gun was also fully loaded with one shot fired."

Vaulding nodded. "So the guns were identical in this regard also?"

"Yes, they were."

"And did Mr. Timberlaine make any statement at the time, explaining why there were two identical guns?"

"Yes, sir. He said the gun found next to the body was a valuable gun from his collection—a gun that had once been owned by a Wild West gunslinger named Pistol Pete Robbins. He claimed that the gun had been stolen from his collection, and a fake gun left in its place. He claimed the gun in his gunbelt, the gun he had been wearing during the auction, the gun he pointed out on his bedside table, was that substitute gun."

"I see. And did you take possession of this gun at this time?"

"Yes, I did."

"What steps did you take to identify this gun?"

"I scratched my initials and the numeral two on the handle."

"Two?"

"That is correct."

"To indicate this was the second gun you had recovered?"

"That's right."

Vaulding nodded, marked another exhibit for identification and took it over to the witness. "Lieutenant, I hand you a gun marked for identification as People's Exhibit Number Four and ask you if you've seen it before?"

"Yes, I have."

"What do you recognize it to be?"

"It is the gun I recovered that evening from Russ Timberlaine's holster."

"Thank you, lieutenant. No further questions."

Steve Winslow stood up. "People's Exhibit Three was found next to the body?"

"That's right."

"People's Exhibit Four was taken from the holster of the gun belt on Russ Timberlaine's night stand?"

"That's right."

"You took possession of both guns on the evening of the murder?"

"Yes, I did."

"Lieutenant, is there any chance whatsoever that you confused these two guns?" As Lieutenant Sanders started to answer, Steve Winslow held up his hand. "Let me finish. That is to say, that the gun, People's Exhibit Three is actually the gun from Russ Timberlaine's holster, and the gun People's Exhibit Four is actually the gun that you found next to the body? Is there any chance, however slight, that that is the case?"

"Absolutely not," Lieutenant Sanders said.

"How can you be certain?"

"I told you. Because of my initials, which I marked on the gun."

Steve Winslow nodded. He walked over to the court reporter's

table, picked up the two guns and looked at them. He set them
down, turned back to Lieutenant Sanders.

"Tell me, lieutenant. *When* did you mark your initials on the
guns."

"I beg your pardon?"

"When did you do it? Relative to the time you found the guns.
When did you mark your initials?"

"I did it there at the scene of the crime."

"The scene of the crime?"

"That's right."

Steve smiled. "But the gun, People's Exhibit Four, wasn't found
at the scene of the crime. At least, according to your testimony."

"By the scene of the crime I am referring to the Timberlaine
mansion."

"I see," Steve said. "Well, that alters the time frame, lieutenant.
You were at the Timberlaine mansion most of the night. I'm wondering when you marked your initials on the guns. By your testimony, it could have been as late as six A.M. the morning after the
murder."

"It was not," Lieutenant Sanders said. "It was early in the evening, shortly after I arrived at the mansion."

"Shortly after? And how short might that be?"

"Within a reasonable amount of time."

"Our definitions of reasonable may differ, lieutenant. Let's be
specific. Referring to the gun, People's Exhibit Three. How soon
after you found that gun did you mark your initials on it?"

"I can't give it to you in minutes."

"I didn't think you could, lieutenant. But let's get at it another
way. I notice you marked this gun, L.S. dash one. Is that right?"

"Yes, I did."

"Well, obviously there would be no need to do that, lieutenant,
unless there was an L.S. dash two. Am I correct in assuming you
did not mark the gun, People's Exhibit Three, until after you had
found the gun, People's Exhibit Four?"

Lieutenant Sanders took a breath. "That is correct."

"Really? And why is that, lieutenant?"

"It was only after the second gun came into the picture that
marking the first gun became particularly important. Also, it was

not possible to mark the first gun, People's Exhibit Three, until after the Crime Scene Unit had finished examining it for finger-prints."

"I see," Steve said. "So it was after you had taken possession of the second gun that you returned and marked your initials on the first gun. Is that right?"

"Yes, it is."

"You marked the second gun first?"

"I beg your pardon?"

"Well, lieutenant. It was after you found the second gun that you decided to mark the first. I wonder if before you returned to mark the first gun that the Crime Scene Unit was processing for fingerprints, you first marked the initials L.S. dash two on the second gun that you had recovered?"

"No, I did not."

"You did not?"

"No."

"And why is that?"

"For one thing, the second gun had to be processed for finger-prints."

"I see. So what did you do with it?"

"I placed it in an evidence bag, marked and labeled it and turned it over to the Crime Scene Unit."

"The same Crime Scene Unit that processed the first gun?"

"That's right."

"It was this Crime Scene Unit that returned to you a gun that you subsequently marked L.S. dash one?"

"That is correct."

Steve smiled. "Well, lieutenant. If I understand your testimony correctly, you turned two guns over to the Crime Scene Unit, they gave one of them back to you and you marked that L.S. dash one?"

"Objection."

"Sustained."

Steve smiled again. "Lieutenant, how many guns did you give to the Crime Scene Unit?"

"Two."

"Did the Crime Scene Unit give one of those guns back to you?"

"They gave both of them back to me."

"At the same time?"

"No."

"They gave one gun back to you first?"

"That's correct."

"Was this after you had given them both guns?"

Lieutenant Sanders took a breath. "It was at approximately the same time. In other words, I delivered to the Crime Scene Unit the second weapon, which I had recovered from Russ Timberlaine's bedroom. I gave it to them in a sealed evidence bag with my name on it. At the same time I got back from them the first weapon that I had given them—the gun that was found next to the body."

"You say at the same time, but the fact is you gave them the second weapon first?"

"As I recall, I gave them the second weapon first. But it was within a matter of minutes."

"Minutes, seconds or days, the fact is you gave it to them first?"

"Yes, I did."

"Thank you, lieutenant. Now let me ask you this: when the Crime Scene Unit gave you this gun—the one that you have marked with the initials L.S. dash one—how did you know it was the same gun that you had given them earlier that evening, the gun that you had found next to the body of the deceased Jack Potter?"

Lieutenant Sanders took a breath. "If you insist that we reconstruct the chain of custody with regard to that gun, I am sure it can be done. I am testifying to the best of my ability and my testimony is based on allegation and belief. The gun appeared in every aspect to be the gun that I gave to the Crime Scene Unit, down to the filed off serial number and the R carved in the handle."

"How do you distinguish it from the other gun, the one you found on Russ Timberlaine's bedside table, the other gun you had given to the Crime Scene Unit?"

"I had just given them that gun. It was still in the bag. They had not even begun to process it for fingerprints yet."

"I understand your contention, lieutenant. But if the Crime Scene Unit had made a mistake and given you back the wrong gun, you would have no way to tell the difference, would you?"

"Objection, Your Honor."

"Overruled."

"Would you, lieutenant?"

Lieutenant Sanders took a breath, blew it out again. "No, I would not."

Steve smiled. "Thank you, lieutenant. That's all."

There was no redirect, and Lieutenant Sanders left the stand. As he did, Steve smiled in satisfaction and under his breath he murmured, "Keep your eyes on the gun."

29

WHEN COURT RECONVENED after lunch, Vaulding called
Philip Manning, a ballistics expert with fifteen years experience on
the force. Vaulding took his time qualifying him as an expert,
taking pains to lay out the man's credentials, which were impressive. When he was finally finished, he turned to the exhibits.

"Now, Mr. Manning," Vaulding said. "I hand you a gun marked
People's Exhibit Four and ask you if you've ever seen it before?"

"Yes, I have."

"And how do you recognize it?"

"By the initials L.S. dash two scratched on the handle."

"What kind of a gun is it?"

"It is a Colt .45 revolver. The initial R has been carved in the
handle and the serial number has been filed off."

"Thank you. Tell me, Mr. Manning, did you ever fire test bullets
through this gun?"

"Yes, I did."

"I hand you a bullet marked for identification People's Exhibit
One and ask you if you recognize it?"

"Yes, I do."

"What do you recognize it to be?"

"That is a bullet with which I compared test bullets that I fired
from this gun."

"You compared the bullet, People's Exhibit One, with bullets fired from the gun, People's Exhibit Four?"

"Yes, I did."

"With what result?"

"The bullets matched."

"Can you tell us what you mean by matched?"

"Yes. By that I mean in my professional opinion as a ballistics expert, the bullets came from the same gun."

"It is your professional opinion that the gun, People's Exhibit Four, fired the bullet, People's Exhibit One?"

"Yes. That is correct."

Vaulding smiled. "Thank you. No further questions."

Steve Winslow frowned. As he stood up to cross-examine, he was aware of Vaulding's eyes on him. He hesitated a moment.

"Does the defense wish to cross-examine?" Judge Hendrick prompted.

Steve Winslow took a breath. "Frankly, Your Honor, I'm not sure."

That produced a murmur of surprise in the courtroom.

Judge Hendrick frowned. "Mr. Winslow?"

"I'm sorry, Your Honor," Steve said. "But the fact is, the trial has progressed rather rapidly to this point. Some of the testimony that we have taken today I have not yet sorted out in my mind. For that reason, with regard to Mr. Manning's ballistics testimony I am not certain that I am fully prepared to cross-examine at this moment. I would like some time to think it over and prepare. I am therefore requesting an adjournment until tomorrow."

"I see," Judge Hendrick said. "That is a frank statement, and the trial has progressed rapidly. I'd be inclined to grant that request. Unless the prosecutor has some objection. Mr. Vaulding?"

As Vaulding hesitated, his dilemma was clear. An adjournment clearly did not fit in with his plans, but with Judge Hendrick deeming the request reasonable, Vaulding didn't want to seem unreasonable in objecting to it. Instead, he smiled and put on a good face. "No objection, Your Honor," he said. "I quite understand counsel's need to prepare."

"Very well," Judge Hendrick said. "Court's adjourned until tomorrow morning at ten o'clock."

30

"Double-think."

"What?"

Steve and Tracy had driven back to the office to pick up the mail and check the answering machine. At least, ostensively to do that. Actually the answering-machine messages could be picked up from any touch-tone phone and there was never any mail. Steve just needed to touch base. He was sitting tilted back in his desk chair with his feet up and his eyes closed, a position he often assumed during a case when he needed to think something out.

"Double-think," he repeated. He opened his eyes, shook his head. "That's the problem with this damn case. I keep second-guessing myself."

"Why?"

"Vaulding. Vaulding, of course. He's young, he's smart, he's aggressive. He's not going to make any stupid moves."

"So?"

"So everything he does I'm second-guessing him. Which means I'm second-guessing myself. And the result is I drive myself crazy."

"Be specific," Tracy said. She was having a hard time containing herself. Steve had refused to discuss anything during the car ride, and she was bursting to know what was up.

"O.K.," Steve said. "Take the witness. Manning. The ballistics expert. I stood up in court and said I didn't know if I wanted to cross-examine him. Did you think that was a ploy?"

"I didn't know what to think."

"That's the problem. Neither do I. It's no ploy. It's the straight goods. Frankly, I don't know."

"Why?"

"I told you why. Vaulding. Now, Dirkson I could handle. I know him, and I know what to expect. But this guy. I don't know what his game is and I don't know what's what."

Tracy nodded. "The thing with the doctor got you spooked."

Steve looked at her, then nodded too. "A little. I make a big stink, recall the doctor, get him to bring his photographs. What do I prove? Nothing. The jury gets an eyeful of gore and yours truly strikes out. I got to admit, that got me rattled.

"The kicker is Vaulding. I don't know if he did it on purpose. If he's really that good. I don't know if he said to himself, 'I'm not gonna have the doctor introduce the pictures, I'll make Winslow ask for 'em so he's the one who brings 'em out and hangs his own client.' "

"You think he did?"

"I don't know. It's double-think. First I think that, then I think, no. He left out the pictures because he didn't want me to see the blow on the head."

"But was the blow that important?"

Steve threw up his hands. "That's the thing. This doctor says it isn't. Vaulding acts as if it isn't. How the hell should I know? Is Vaulding playing it straight or not? On the other hand, is Vaulding double-thinking me? Is he saying, 'This blow to the head is totally unimportant, but let that son of a bitch Winslow get a hold of it, he'll blow it out of all proportion and make a federal case out of it. So I gotta keep the pictures out.' " Steve looked at Tracy, shook his head. "You see what I mean? I think the thing around in a big circle and come back to where I started."

"Right," Tracy said. "So the ballistics expert?"

"Same thing. Vaulding doesn't bring out the evidence. All he does is have the guy give his opinion as an expert that the bullet came from that gun. He leaves it to me to bring out the evidence. And I have to ask why? Is it because the evidence is conclusive so he wants me to bring it out so I'll crucify my own client? Or is it because there's a defect in the evidence that he wants to cover up? Or if not a defect, at least a side issue, something he thinks I'll pick up on and make a big deal about like the blow on the head."

"And there again, is it because *he* thinks it's important, or because he thinks I'll try to *make it* important?"

Tracy shook her head. "Jesus Christ."

"Yeah, and it gets worse. There's this goddamned file. That's the other pitfall here. The minute I start cross-examining this guy on his identification of the bullet, he's going to tell me how hard it was to get a match because someone had tampered with the gun barrel. There I'll be, schmuck-of-the-month again, because as soon as that happens, for his next witness Vaulding will call the police officer who searched Timberlaine's room and found the file."

"Right," Tracy said. "But you know that's going to happen sooner or later."

"Yeah, but in the eyes of the jury it hurts us ten times worse if I'm the one who brings it out."

"Shit."

"Yeah. So that's what's hanging me up," Steve said. "The simple fact is, I don't know how to play it."

There was a pause.

"Bullshit," Tracy said.

Steve's head snapped up. He turned, looked at her.

Tracy had taken off her large round-framed glasses and folded them up. She stood there, tapping them into her other hand. She shook her head. "Sorry," she said, "but I can't buy it. The way I see it, the simple fact is you hate to lose."

"What?"

"Come on," Tracy said. "Give me a break. All this double-think, and should you cross-examine this guy or not, and what's Vaulding pulling on you, and does Vaulding want you to do it or not, and the bottom line is who gives a shit? The simple fact is, you don't like to lose. You stood up in court this morning and you took a beating. You had the doctor bring in his pictures and that should have been a victory for you, but it wasn't, it was a defeat. And you sit back and rationalize and try to figure out why that happened, and then you say it's because it wasn't Dirkson it was Vaulding and you're not sure what Vaulding's doing so you don't know how to play it. But the simple fact is you lost one, and you hate to lose. What's more you're not used to losing. So you start second-guessing yourself and the whole bit."

Steve looked at Tracy a moment. Then he smiled. "Wow," he said. "Do I really do all that?"

"It's not funny," Tracy said. "You got a duty to your client. Now you may think all this agonizing you're going through is trying to figure out what your duty to your client is, but it's not. It's counterproductive."

"Say you're right," Steve said. "So what should I do?"

"First off, stop second-guessing Vaulding. The hell with him. Who the hell cares what Vaulding wants you to do?"

"That's the first thing? What's the second?"

"This ballistics expert?"

"Yeah. What about him?"

"Rip his can off."

31

JUDGE HENDRICK PEERED DOWN from the bench. "Ladies and gentlemen of the jury, when we left off yesterday the witness, Mr. Manning, was on the stand and had just completed his direct examination. We adjourned so the defense could consider if it wished to cross-examine. Mr. Winslow, are you prepared to proceed?"

"Yes, Your Honor."

"Do you intend to cross-examine the witness?"

"I have one or two questions, Your Honor," Steve said. He approached the witness stand. "Mr. Manning, you testified yesterday that the bullet, People's Exhibit One, came from the gun, People's Exhibit Four, is that correct?"

"Yes, it is."

"Correct me if I'm wrong, but you reached that opinion by comparing the bullet, People's Exhibit One, with test bullets fired from the gun, People's Exhibit Four?"

"That is correct."

"Could you describe that procedure for us?"

"Certainly," Manning said. "I examined the bullets under a comparison microscope."

"For the benefit of the jurors, just what is that?"

"It is a microscope on which two bullets can be magnified and compared at the same time."

Steve smiled. "As one might expect, Mr. Manning. Can you give us a bit more information than that? For instance, just what is it that you are comparing on these bullets?"

"The rifling marks."

"Rifling marks?"

"Yes. The scratches on the bullet made from the barrel of the gun."

"Now we're coming to it, Mr. Manning. Would you tell us please about these rifling marks?"

"Certainly." Manning turned to the jury. "The barrel of each gun has its own individual scratches and imperfections. As the bullet travels through the gun barrel, these markings are etched onto the surface of the bullet. And each barrel is unique—that is to say, the markings on no two gun barrels are exactly the same. So by observing the markings on a bullet, it is possible to tell what gun it was fired from."

"But not by comparing the bullet directly to the barrel of the gun?"

"No, of course not. That would be incredibly awkward. What you do is compare a bullet that you suspect was fired by a gun with a bullet *known* to be fired by that gun."

"How do you obtain this known bullet? How do you make sure it has been fired by that gun?"

"You fire it yourself, of course."

"And that is what you did in this case?"

"Yes. Of course."

"You took the gun, People's Exhibit Four, fired a bullet through it, and compared that bullet to the bullet, People's Exhibit One?"

"Yes, I did."

"With a comparison microscope?"

"That's right."

"And if I understand your testimony correctly, what you were doing was attempting to line up the scratches on the bullet made by the gun barrel, establishing an exact correspondence that would allow you to conclude that both bullets had been fired from the same gun?"

"That is correct."

"You compared the bullets side by side?"

"Yes and no."

"What do you mean by that?"

"The bullets are side by side. The image I'm looking at is not."

"Then what is it?"

"The alignment is the same as if the bullets were superimposed one over the other. Although that is not the image I'm seeing. What I'm seeing is the top half of one bullet and the bottom half of the other bullet. In other words, if you think of the picture I am seeing as the image on a movie screen, you could draw a horizontal line halfway across the screen. The top half of the screen would show the image of one bullet. The bottom half of the screen would show the image of the other bullet. That is, in each case, half the bullet. The top half of the screen would show the front half of the bullet and the bottom half of the screen would show the back half of the bullet."

"And how does this enable you to make your comparison?"

"The bullets are round, of course, and can be rotated. If the bullets were fired from the same gun, it is possible to rotate one bullet until it lines up exactly with the other bullet. In other words, so all of the scratches and indentations line up. So for all intents and purposes, it appears as if you were looking at one bullet."

"I see," Steve said. "And that is what you did in this case?"

"Yes, I did."

"I see," Steve repeated.

Steve paused a moment, looked around. In the back of the courtroom Tracy Garvin caught his eye. She raised her hand, gave him the thumbs up sign.

Steve took a breath, turned back to the witness. "All right, Mr. Manning," he said. "Let's refer to the bullet, People's Exhibit One, as the fatal bullet, and the bullet you fired from the gun, People's Exhibit Four, as the test bullet. Are you saying you were able to line these two bullets up on the comparison microscope so that each and every scratch on the fatal bullet lined up with each and every scratch on the test bullet?"

"No, I'm not," Manning said.

"You're not? Are you telling me the scratches *did not* line up?"

"Not each and every one."

"Didn't you just get through saying that that would happen if the bullets had been fired from the same gun?"

"Under ordinary conditions, yes. But these were not ordinary conditions. See, the barrel of the gun, People's Exhibit Four, had been defaced."

"Defaced?"

"Yes, it had been altered. Someone had taken a tool such as a rasp or file and scratched deep grooves onto the inside of the gun barrel. These grooves of course resulted in additional scratches on the test bullet that do not show up on the fatal bullet."

Steve frowned. "Let me be sure I understand this. You're saying the gun barrel was defaced after it had fired the fatal bullet?"

"Exactly."

"In other words, sometime between the time the gun fired the fatal bullet and the time the gun came into your possession, the gun barrel had been altered?"

"That's right."

"Is there any way for you to tell when that was done?"

"No. Only within the time frames you just described."

"I see. Now, can you tell me, in your opinion as an expert, why would someone deface a gun barrel? What would be the purpose of it?"

Vaulding started to stand up, thought better of it, sat back down again.

Manning smiled. "Obviously, so the gun could not be matched with the fatal bullet. It's not that uncommon for criminals to alter the barrel of their guns after the guns have been used in the commission of a crime. It's certainly not the first instance I've seen."

"And you say the purpose of this is so the gun cannot be matched with the bullet?"

"That's right."

"However, in this case you *were* able to match the gun with the bullet."

"Not without some difficulty."

"Oh? You say you had some difficulty?"

"Objection, Your Honor."

"Overruled. That's exactly what he said. If he wants to clarify it, he can. Proceed, Mr. Winslow."

"What do you mean, you had difficulty?"

"Just that. The fresh scratches on the gun barrel made it more difficult to line up the scratches that were already in existence when the fatal bullet was fired."

"But you were able to line them up?"

"Yes, I was."

"I see. And once you had achieved this alignment, did you photograph the result?"

"Yes, I did."

"It's standard practice to photograph the bullets on a comparison microscope?"

"Yes, it is."

"You do it in every instance?"

Manning hesitated.

"Or rather in every instance when you are preparing evidence for court?"

"Yes, I do."

"You have pictures of the fatal bullet and the test bullet in the comparison microscope?"

"Yes, I do."

"And these pictures show the scratches on the bullets lining up?"

"Yes, they do."

"And they also show the marks from the fresh scratches on the gun barrel, which you claim were made by a rasp or file?"

"Yes, they do."

"I see. And do you have those pictures here in court?"

"No, I do not."

"Why not?"

"Objection."

"Overruled."

"I wasn't asked to bring them."

"Were you asked *not* to bring them?"

"Objection."

"Overruled."

"I was told there was no need."

"Who told you that?"

"Mr. Vaulding."

"Mr. Vaulding told you there was no need to bring these pictures into court?"

"Objection. Already asked and answered."

"Sustained."

"Your Honor, I ask that this witness be instructed to return to court and bring with him the pictures he has just testified about. The pictures of the fatal bullet and the test bullet on the comparison microscope."

"So ordered," Judge Hendrick said. "Mr. Winslow. Does that mean you have completed your cross-examination at this time?"

"Actually, I have a few more questions, Your Honor."

"Very well. Then I'll withhold instructing Mr. Manning when he is to return until such time as this phase of his examination is complete. Proceed, Mr. Winslow."

"Thank you, Your Honor. Mr. Manning, you have already testified to comparing the fatal bullet with the test bullet?"

"Objection. Already asked and answered."

"It is preliminary, Your Honor."

"I should think so," Judge Hendrick said. "I'll allow it on that assurance. Could we try, gentlemen, to dispense if possible with overly technical objections? Proceed."

"You have testified to comparing the fatal bullet with the test bullet from the gun, People's Exhibit Four?"

"Yes, I have."

"Let me ask you this: did you compare the fatal bullet with test bullets fired from any other gun?"

"Objection. Irrelevant and immaterial."

"Overruled."

"Yes, I did," Manning said.

"You did? And what gun would that be?"

Manning cleared his throat. "That would be the gun, People's Exhibit Three.

"Really? The gun that was found next to the body?"

"I have no knowledge as to that," Manning said. "I wasn't there when the gun was found."

"No, you weren't," Steve said. "Nor were you there when the other gun, People's Exhibit Four, was found, were you?"

"No, I was not."

"When you say you don't know that this gun, People's Exhibit Three, was the gun found next to the body, you also don't know that the gun, People's Exhibit Four, was the gun found in Russ Timberlaine's bedroom, do you?"

"Objection."

"Overruled."

"No, I do not."

"Thank you, Mr. Manning. I didn't think you did."

"Oh, Your Honor," Vaulding said.

"Exactly," Judge Hendrick snapped. "Mr. Winslow, I've warned you about such side remarks."

"Sorry, Your Honor. Mr. Manning, you have testified to comparing the fatal bullet with test bullets fired from the gun, People's Exhibit Three, is that right?"

"Yes, it is."

"Can you tell us the results of that comparison?"

"Yes. The bullets didn't match."

"They didn't?"

"No."

"Was that readily apparent?"

Manning hesitated a moment. "Actually, it was not."

"And why was that?"

"Because the gun in question, People's Exhibit Three, is a Colt .45. As is the murder weapon, People's Exhibit Four. Therefore the class characteristics were the same."

"Class characteristics?"

"Yes. The markings that the barrel of a gun leaves on a bullet can be broken down into what we call class characteristics and individual characteristics. Class characteristics are the markings that are common to a particular make and model of gun. In this case we have the Colt .45. Since the guns are of similar manufacture, the barrels of all Colt .45s will leave some similar markings on bullets fired through them. Due to the similarity in structure. These similar markings are known as the class characteristics. By comparing them, it is possible to tell what make and model of gun a bullet was fired from.

"On the other hand, the individual characteristics are the markings on a bullet that are unique in terms of a particular gun. In other words, they are marks that will only appear on bullets fired from that gun."

"Thank you," Steve said. "So what you're saying is, when you compared the fatal bullet with a bullet fired from the gun, People's Exhibit Three, you found similarities?"

"Due to the class characteristics. As I've just explained."

"I understand. But the fact is you found them. And because you found them, you continued trying to match up the bullets."

"Which I could not do," Manning said. "I attempted to do so to the best of my ability, but it was not possible. I now realize it was because the bullet did not indeed come from that gun."

Steve Winslow's head came up. He raised one hand. "Just a minute, Mr. Manning. You say you *now* realize it was because that wasn't the gun?"

"Yes, of course."

"Then when you were attempting to align the bullets, you were acting on the assumption that it might be the gun?"

"Yes, of course. That's the whole point of doing the alignment."

"I understand," Steve said. "But if you had already matched the fatal bullet with the gun, People's Exhibit Four, you would have *known* it couldn't match with a bullet fired by the gun, People's Exhibit Three. Isn't that right?"

"Yes, it is."

"Are you saying now that you're not entirely sure that you have a match with People's Exhibit Four?"

"Not at all," Manning said.

"You do have a match?"

"Yes, we do."

"Well, if you're certain, why would you be comparing the bullet with another gun and looking for a match?"

"Well," Manning said. "As to that . . ." He hesitated, pursed his lips.

Steve Winslow smiled. "Am I to assume you compared the fatal bullet with a test bullet fired from the gun, People's Exhibit Three, *before* you compared it with a bullet fired from the gun, People's Exhibit Four."

Manning took a breath. "Yes. That is correct."

Steve Winslow's smile widened into a grin. "Gee, Mr. Manning," he said. "Let me be sure I understand your testimony. The police first came to you with a gun. The gun found next to the body. The gun, People's Exhibit Three. And you tried to match it up with the fatal bullet. When you couldn't get a match, they said, 'Try this one,' and gave you another gun, People's Exhibit Four, the gun taken from Timberlaine's bedside table, and asked you to try to match that up."

"As I said before," Manning said, "I have no personal knowledge as to where those guns came from."

"All you know is the cops gave you one gun, and when that wouldn't match with the fatal bullet they gave you another?"

"That's a gross oversimplification."

"Perhaps it is. Tell me, did you take pictures of the test bullet fired from the gun, People's Exhibit Three, on the comparison microscope?"

"Yes, I did."

"You took pictures showing that bullet in alignment with the fatal bullet on the comparison microscope?"

"Now, that's misleading," Manning said. "I did take pictures of the two bullets in those positions. But they are *not* in alignment. They are *aligned* in as much as it was possible to do so from the class characteristics. But there is no way they could be *in alignment*, because they were not fired from the same gun."

"I understand your contention, Mr. Manning," Steve said. "But the fact is, you took the photos?"

"Yes, I did."

"And this was done before you examined bullets from the gun, People's Exhibit Four?"

"Yes, it was."

"Thank you, Mr. Manning." Steve turned to the judge. "Your Honor, at this time I would like to suspend my cross-examination until such time as the witness shall have brought into court photographs of the fatal bullet shown on the comparison microscope with the test bullet fired from the gun, People's Exhibit Four.

"At this time, I also ask that the witness be instructed to bring into court any photographs he has taken showing the comparison of the fatal bullet with test bullets fired from the gun, People's Exhibit Three."

"I object, Your Honor," Vaulding said.

Judge Hendrick held up his hand. "Overruled. You may object to the introduction of these photographs, but this witness is going to bring them.

"Mr. Manning, you are temporarily excused from the stand. You are directed to return here tomorrow morning at ten o'clock and bring with you any and all photographs you have taken comparing the fatal bullet to bullets fired from the gun, People's Exhibit Four, to bullets fired from the gun, People's Exhibit Three, and any other bullets to which you may have compared it.

"Mr. Vaulding. Mr. Winslow. We will go into the individual merits of such evidence at that time. But for the time being, the witness is excused.

"Mr. Vaulding, do you have another witness available to call?"

"I will momentarily, Your Honor."

"Very well. Court will stand in recess for half an hour."

32

MARK TAYLOR CAUGHT UP with Steve and Tracy in the corridor on their way back into court.

"Vaulding's gonna drop a bombshell," Taylor said.

"I know that," Steve said.

"Oh, yeah?" Taylor said. "Then why am I getting it like it's a hot tip?"

"What's your source?"

"That reporter. He got the tip. Vaulding put out the word during recess to expect fireworks when court reconvenes."

"I know that too," Steve said. "It's what Tracy and I were just talking about. I did a number on the ballistics expert. Which ordinarily would have been great. Except for the bit about roughing up the gun barrel. That's where he turns around and kicks us in the teeth. But it's no surprise, it's just what we were expecting."

"Yeah, well the word is the shit's hitting the fan. And how does that add up? The press already has the scoop on the file. You know he's gonna club you with it. The press knows he's gonna club you with it. What's the big deal?"

"There's one possibility, Mark, and it's just what we were discussing."

"What's that?"

"Timberlaine swears he found the file in his room. He has no idea how it got there. If that's true, the worst Vaulding can do is call the cop who served the warrant and show the file was found in his room. Big deal. It's incriminating, but old hat. No, the kick in the teeth, the hold-the-phone bombshell, is if Timberlaine is lying about finding the file in his room. And, instead of the cop who served the warrant, Vaulding's next witness is some shopkeeper who will testify Timberlaine *bought* the file."

"Oh, shit," Taylor said.

"Right," Tracy said. "Or maybe even asked him to recommend what to use to rough up a gun barrel."

"Oh, come on," Taylor said. "He couldn't be that dumb."

"Yeah," Steve said dryly.

They pushed their way into the courtroom. Whatever word Vaulding had put out, people must have believed him, because the place was packed. Mark and Tracy couldn't get their usual seats and wound up standing in the back.

Steve pushed his way through the crowd up to the defense table, where court officers had already brought in Timberlaine.

"What's this all about?" he demanded as Steve sat down.

"I was hoping you could tell me. Vaulding's got some sort of surprise. I don't know what it is."

"Hell."

"You said it. You sure you told me everything about the file?"

"Sure. What else is there to tell?"

"That's what I'm asking you."

"Nothing. I found it in my room, I don't know where it came from."

"Great," Steve said.

The jury was led in. Judge Hendrick took his place on the bench. When they were all in position, Vaulding made a star's entrance, walking in from the back of the courtroom, pushing his way through the reporters and photographers gathered there. He strode up to the prosecution table and stood there, almost striking a pose.

Judge Hendrick regarded him with some irritation. "Well, call your next witness," he said.

"Call Frederick Henson," Vaulding said.

A middle-aged man with a sad-eyed, droopy sort of face made his way to the witness stand.

Confirming Steve Winslow's worst fears. Not a cop. A shop-keeper.

As Henson passed by the defense table, Steve heard a sharp intake of breath. He turned to see that Timberlaine had gone white as a sheet. "Smile," Steve said out of the corner of his mouth.

Timberlaine gawked at him. His lips trembled. His eyes blinked.

"No matter how bad it is, there's nothing we can do about it now," Steve said. "Just grin and bear it."

When the witness had been installed on the stand, Vaulding said, "State your name."

"Frederick Henson."

"Mr. Henson, I ask you to look around the courtroom and tell me if you see anyone you recognize."

"Yes, sir. Him."

"Let the record show that the witness is pointing at the defendant, Russ Timberlaine. That is correct, is it not, Mr. Henson? It is the defendant, Russ Timberlaine, whom you recognize?"

"Yes, sir. That's him all right."

"Where do you know him from?"

"He was in my shop."

"He was a customer in you shop?"

"That's right."

"When was this?"

"On July 16th."

"Are you sure of that date?"

"Yes, I am."

"How can you be so sure?"

"When you asked me, I looked it up."

"I see. And just what was it the defendant bought from you on that occasion?"

"A Colt .45 revolver."

33

"Why the hell did you buy the gun?"

"Take it easy," Timberlaine said.

"Easy, hell," Steve said. "You lie to me, you hold out on me. I prepare my whole defense on the basis of the fact there's no way in hell the cops can prove you bought that gun. And what happens? The whole thing blows up in my face because you *did* buy that gun."

"No, I didn't."

"Oh? You mean the witness is lying?"

"No. He's not lying."

"How can that be?"

"Well, I bought *that* gun, but it's not the one I showed you."

"What?"

"The gun I brought you in your office—the one I said I found substituted for the real gun—well, I didn't buy it, and everything I told you was true. I found that gun just like I said."

"And the one you bought?"

Timberlaine grimaced. "Like I said, I was afraid someone was trying to frame me with the gun. So I pulled a switch."

Steve looked at him. "*You* pulled a switch?"

"Yeah."

"When?"

"After."

"After what?"

"After I gave you the gun. To test the bullets. When you gave it back to me I substituted it for my gun."

"Wait a minute. By that you mean—?"

"The gun I bought. The one the witness just testified about."

"You bought that gun and substituted it for the one you found?"

"That's right."

"You bought that gun before you came to my office?"

"That's right. The day before."

"You filed the serial number off it and carved the initial R in the handle?"

"Yes, I did."

"What did you use to file off the serial number?"

"Why?"

"Why do you think?"

"Oh. No, it wasn't the file found in my room. There's a grindstone in the tool shed. I used that."

"The day before you came to my office?"

"That's right."

"But the gun you brought me in my office was—?"

"The other gun. The one I found."

"You had me test the bullets and then you switched guns?"

"That's right."

"There's no chance you switched the guns first?"

"No. I didn't."

"There's no chance the gun you gave me and had me test bullets in was the gun you bought?"

"Not at all."

"And the bullets I tested are in a safe-deposit box?"

"That's right."

"Where's the gun?"

"In a safe-deposit box."

"The same safe-deposit box?"

"No, a different one."

"You rented a different box just for the gun?"

"Sure."

"So the gun and the bullets are in separate boxes?"

"Hell, they're in separate *banks*."

Steve sighed. "Well, thank God for that."

"Why's that?"

"We may have to produce the gun. If so, we may not necessarily want to produce the bullets."

"Why do we have to produce the gun?"

"Why do you think? Look, here's the way it's gonna go. Vaulding's probably gonna serve a subpoena *duces tecum* on us, ordering us to produce the gun you bought. Of course, he won't expect us to do it."

"Why not?"

"Because he thinks he already has it. People's Exhibit Four. The subpoena will be just to embarrass us. He orders us to produce the gun. We can't do it. He smiles and points out to the jury that the gun you bought is identical to the gun that's been introduced in court as the murder weapon. As far as the jury's concerned, that will be enough to convince 'em the gun in court is the gun you bought."

"It *is* the gun I bought.

"I know," Steve said. "But only because you switched guns. The jury doesn't know that. As far as they're concerned, there's only two guns in the case, the real gun and the fake gun, and they're both here in court. They don't know about your substituting a fake gun you bought for a fake gun you found. As far as they're concerned, there's only one fake gun. And it's the murder weapon, and it's here in court, and the witness on the stand just testified to the fact that you bought it."

Timberlaine thought that over. "Shit," he said. "So what do we do now?"

"We wait and see if they try to subpoena the gun."

"You think they will?"

Steve shrugged. "It's a tossup. As I say, Vaulding can try to embarrass us with it. On the other hand, he may not make an issue of it at all. He's got the murder weapon in court; as far as he, the jury and everyone else in the courtroom are concerned, the murder weapon is the gun you bought, and if we'd like to dispute that, it's going to be up to us to prove differently." Steve nodded. "No, the more I think of it, he's more likely to let it go at that."

"Is that good?"

"In a way."

"Why?"

"Because it gives us time to figure out what the fuck to do about the damn gun. And the damn bullets."

"What about 'em?"

"Well," Steve said, "if you're telling me the truth—and frankly right now that's a big if—but if you are, then those test bullets were fired before any gun was defaced. So if you hadn't swapped guns, those test bullets would now be significant in that they could be compared to the fatal bullet. Since you *did* swap guns, that is no longer true."

Timberlaine's face lit up. "But those bullets prove the guns were swapped."

Steve frowned. "Yes and no."

"They *do*," Timberlaine said. "Those bullets didn't come from the gun I bought, they came from the gun I found. The one in my safe-deposit box. If we produce that gun and we produce the bullets—still in the glass tubes, all marked and dated so we can prove when they were fired—we can prove that that's the gun I brought you that day."

"Yeah," Steve said, "but so what?"

"What do you mean, so what?" Timberlaine said. "It substantiates my story."

"Yeah," Steve said. "Well, that's like 'I shot a deer by a big oak tree, and if you don't believe me I'll show you the tree.' "

"What?"

"The bullet and the gun prove nothing except that you had them on that day. They prove the existence of the other gun and that's it. They don't prove your story that you found a gun substituted for your real gun. See what I mean?"

"Not really."

"Trust me on this. Yeah, it's good, but it's not hold-the-phone-you're-suddenly-free type good. We've still gotta figure out how we want to play it."

"And how is that?"

"The way it looks now, we probably withhold all of this stuff until we get you on the stand. Then you tell your story, and then we start introducing this evidence so fast it makes their heads spin. That's how it looks right now, but it really depends on how things go. We got a bunch more body blows to take. So far they haven't even hit you with the file." Steve gave him a look. "You sure you didn't buy that file?"

"Swear to God."

"You found it in your room?"

"Yeah."

"Just like you found the gun?"

"Absolutely."

"You didn't happen to go out and buy *another* file any time recently, did you?"

"No."

Steve stood up. He exhaled, shook his head. "Christ, I hope not."

34

"I'M NOT SURE I WANNA HEAR THIS," Mark Taylor said when Steve and Tracy got back to the office later that afternoon and called him down to fill him in.

"You have a bad attitude, you know it?" Tracy said.

"Oh, yeah? Well, I'm sure it has nothing to do with this case. My life's been living hell ever since I bought that gun."

"I haven't been too happy myself," Steve said.

"Yeah, well lay it on me," Taylor said. "I wanna get back to the office so I can coordinate the stuff that's coming in."

Steve leaned back in his desk chair and exhaled. "The stuff that's coming in is basically irrelevant. Just wait'll you get a load of this."

"Of what?" Taylor said. "Come on. Give."

"O.K. Well, it's good news/bad news time again. The good news is the gun in court is *not* the gun you bought me."

"What?" Taylor said.

"That's right. Timberlaine switched guns."

Mark Taylor blinked. He looked at Steve. "Time out. Flag on the play. Let me be sure I understand this. You're saying the cops got the wrong gun?"

"That depends on how you look at it. They got the murder weapon. It just isn't the gun we thought it was."

Taylor blinked again. "There's another gun?"

"I know," Steve said. "It's a fucking nightmare."

"Wait a minute. You mean the gun the witness says Timberlaine bought really exists and it's the gun in court?"

"How would you feel about that?"

"Well," Taylor said. "I'll be really happy if the gun in court isn't my gun. But how the hell am I gonna prove that?" His eyes widened. "No, wait a minute. I can prove it with the bullet."

"What bullet?" Tracy said.

"The test bullets you had me fire. You got 'em in the safe, right. All marked, nice and legal. The bullet can prove the murder weapon wasn't that gun."

Steve frowned. "Well, that's a 'maybe' there, Mark. You gotta remember the barrel of that gun was tampered with."

"Right," Taylor said.

"Yeah, but after the murder," Tracy said. "The fatal bullet itself wasn't affected."

"That's true," Steve said.

"So if the fatal bullet doesn't match the test bullet from the gun Mark bought, it proves his gun wasn't the fatal gun."

"That's right," Taylor said.

"That's true," Steve said. "If we ever get that far. But hang on a minute. Can you seriously imagine me explaining all this to Vaulding? Let alone the jury?"

Taylor frowned. "I see your point."

"Exactly, Mark," Steve said. "It's not like we want to prove the gun you bought had nothing to do with the murder. We're not at the point here where we want to concede you bought a gun."

Taylor nodded. "I'm with you there." He scratched his head. "So what the fuck does this mean? I mean, Jesus Christ. You're sayin' the gun they claim Timberlaine bought he admits he bought and claims he substituted for mine. Is that right?"

"That's it in a nutshell."

"Then where's mine? Pardon me for asking, but where the hell's my fucking gun?"

"Well, Mark, right now there are two possibilities."

"I don't want to hear this, do I?"

"One, Timberlaine's telling the truth and your gun is in a safe-deposit box Timberlaine rented and we can produce it at any time."

"That's not so bad. What's the one I don't wanna hear?"

"Two, Timberlaine is lying. In which case there never *was* any other gun. The gun he bought from that witness is it. He bought it, filed the numbers off it, carved the initial R in the handle and brought it to my office to have you fire test bullets through it. If that is true, then that gun is *not* in a safe-deposit box, it's in my safe right here in the office. Which means Timberlaine *didn't* switch guns after he left here. And the gun in court *is* the gun you bought. And not only does the fatal bullet match up with test bullets fired through it, but the fatal bullet will match up with our test bullets. Which incidentally, Mark, would elevate our test bullets to the position of prime evidentiary value, since they would have been fired from the fatal gun *before* the barrel was altered and therefore would match up with the fatal bullet absolutely, thereby clinching the identification of the gun."

Mark Taylor looked sick. "Oh, Jesus Christ."

"Exactly," Steve said. "And that's not the half of it. Right now, the worst of it is Timberlaine doesn't know I switched guns. I'm sure as hell not gonna tell him. It's not that I don't want him to know—well, actually it is—but more than that, the son of a bitch just can't keep his mouth shut, and I sure as hell don't want Vaulding to know. Anyway, Timberlaine doesn't know I switched guns. So he thinks—assuming he's telling the truth—he thinks that the gun he gave me, that I fired the test bullets through, is the gun in his safe-deposit box, and will therefore match the test bullets. So all we have to do is give all of that to the cops. He's not bright enough to figure out why, even from his perspective, that wouldn't be that smooth a move, and he's already pushing me to do exactly that. I'm resisting to the best of my power without actually telling him why."

Mark Taylor ran his hand through his hair. "Good lord."

"Yeah. So I'm stalling the issue as long as I can. Vaulding can force it by subpoenaing the gun."

"Shit. Will he do that?"

"I'm hoping not. There's a good chance he won't, since he thinks he already has it. If he does, then I gotta deal with it. Right now, I don't. This is becoming one of those cases where stalling is the best tactic."

"You gonna ask for a continuance?"

Steve grimaced. "Well, there's stalling and then there's stalling. I'm stalling on specific points. The gun, for instance. But the case, no. I want to rush the case along before they start *finding* all these fucking guns."

"Yeah, right."

"And there's another thing."

"What's that?"

"Right now Vaulding's just happy to be hitting us with the shit. The file, the gun Timberlaine bought, the whole bit. Shock after shock, embarrassment after embarrassment. He's so happy springing the witnesses and piling on the evidence, I'm not sure he's stopped to figure out what it all means."

Taylor frowned. "I don't get you."

"I do," Tracy said. "You mean he hasn't explained any of it."

"Exactly," Steve said. "None of this stuff was in his opening statement. The jury's getting it fresh, just like we are. They don't know what it means any more than we know what it means. Even less, because they don't know what we know. Vaulding hasn't explained any of it, and he's got to 'cause it's his case." Steve spread his hands. "I mean, look at this shit. There's another gun just came down the pike. Now, Vaulding doesn't *know* it's another gun. He's gonna claim Timberlaine bought it and used it in the murder. If that's true, Jesus Christ. Timberlaine buys a gun, substitutes it for his own gun and claims somebody else did. He gets pissed off over Burdett's bid at the auction, so he kills Jack Potter thinking Potter tipped him off. Kills him with a gun that he bought and substituted for his own gun, the genuine Pistol Pete gun. And he leaves that genuine gun that he's claimed was stolen next to the body. Then he takes the murder weapon, roughs it up with a file and leaves it on his bedside table. He leaves the file somewhere in his apartment for the police to find it."

"Right," Taylor said. "It's the moron factor. It's the how-could-he-be-that-stupid."

Steve held up his hand and shook his head. "No. No, that's true, but besides that. There's a huge problem with all that. A huge glaring flaw in the theory that Vaulding's gonna have to deal with."

Tracy's eyes widened. "Son of a bitch."

"What?" Taylor said.

Tracy snapped her fingers. "Motivation. That's it, isn't it? Vaulding's laid out the motivation that Timberlaine killed Potter for giving Burdett the tip. That doesn't jibe with this new gun."

"Why not?" Taylor said.

"Premeditation," Tracy said. "Timberlaine bought this gun days before the auction. How was he to know he was going to get pissed off at Potter and shoot him?"

"Exactly," Steve said. "The way Vaulding's laid out the case, when Timberlaine bought the gun there was no way in hell he knew he was going to use it to kill Potter. The question is, why did he buy it? We know he bought it to switch with the other gun, the one he found substituted for the real one. Vaulding doesn't concede the existence of the other gun, so his theory can't be Timberlaine bought it for that. His theory has to be Timberlaine bought it to switch with the *original* gun. And why in the name of God would Timberlaine want to do that?"

"You got me," Taylor said. "I can't explain it."

"Yeah, well you don't have to, Mark. At least until Vaulding finds out you bought that gun."

"Shit." Taylor heaved himself out of the chair. "Can I get back to the office now?"

"I suppose so. What are you working on?"

"That's embarrassing."

"Oh?"

"My operative isn't back yet. I'm trying to find out who sold her the gun."

Steve grinned. "Are you telling me I'm paying you to investigate your own actions?"

"I told you it was embarrassing."

"Any luck yet?"

Taylor shook his head. "Not a thing."

"That's good. If you can't find out, it's a cinch Vaulding can't either."

"Yeah. Unless he trips over the back trail I'm leaving now."

"Yeah, right. Except he wouldn't know what you were after. That's where this is so bad it's good. If Vaulding finds out you're asking about guns he'll think that's perfectly logical. There's no way in hell he's going to figure you're trying to find out who sold a gun *to you.*"

"One would hope. So can I get back to the office?"

"I suppose so. I—" Steve broke off at the sound of the outer office door opening. "Hang on. We got company."

Tracy went out and came back moments later with Carrie Timberlaine and her fiancé, Donald Walcott.

The young man was quite upset. He had a paper in his hand, which he held up in front of him. "They subpoenaed me," he said disgustedly. "Can you believe that? Right in our own house. Just rang the bell and nailed me. Now I gotta testify for the prosecution."

"Can they do that?" Carrie Timberlaine said. "Can they make him testify if he doesn't want to?"

Steve frowned. "Let me see the subpoena."

Donald passed it over.

Steve took it, looked at it. "I'm afraid they got you," he said.

"Yeah, but for what? I don't know anything."

"Except what Timberlaine told you."

"Isn't that hearsay?"

Steve shook his head. "Anything anybody else told you is hearsay. Anything the defendant told you can be considered an admission against interest and you can testify to it."

"Yeah, but what? I mean, it's not like Russ took me aside and said, 'By the way, I'm going to kill Jack Potter tomorrow.'"

"Of course not. Most likely it's about the gun."

Donald frowned. "What about it?"

"Well, look. You knew why I was there that weekend, didn't you?"

"Yeah. Sure. Why?"

"Well, there's that. You knew it was because Timberlaine had found a gun substituted, right?"

"Yeah, right. But how does that hurt him? That's been his story all along."

"You didn't also happen to know anything about Timberlaine buying a gun and pulling a little substitution of his own?"

"Is that what he says he did?"

Steve grimaced. "Look. I'm not giving out any information, and you're better off not getting any. I'm trying to figure out why the prosecution would subpoena you. After what went on in court today, I figure it had to be something that confirmed that Timberlaine bought the gun."

"Well, it isn't."

"I'm glad to hear it. But what the hell is it?"

"I have no idea."

"Well," Steve said. "There's one way to find out."

"What's that."

Steve jerked his thumb. "Obey that subpoena."

35

Judge Hendrick looked down from his bench. "Once again we have matters to take care of before we begin. Mr. Vaulding, I understand you served a subpoena yesterday."

"That's right, Your Honor."

Judge Hendrick frowned. "Mr. Vaulding, yesterday we listened to the testimony of Mr. Henson, who was not on your original list of witnesses."

"We just found him, Your Honor."

"So I understand. Judging by the service of this subpoena, I gather we are about to be treated to the testimony of another witness not on your list."

"Again, the information just became known to us, Your Honor."

"I'm sure that it did. But I must say it's quite a coincidence for it to happen with such amazing regularity."

"I assure you it's not by design, Your Honor."

"I didn't say it was. I just remarked on the coincidence. You may take the statement I am about to make as entirely coincidental, also. This is a courtroom, not a sideshow. I intend to see that evidence is presented in an orderly manner. And that it is presented for the benefit of the jury, not for the benefit of the press."

"Oh, Your Honor," Vaulding said.

Judge Hendrick held up his hand. "One moment, Mr. Vaulding.

I'm not through." He lifted a newspaper from the top of his bench, turned it around and held it up.

It was a copy of the *Daily News* with the headline, PISTOL PETE: SURPRISE WITNESS.

Judge Hendrick held up another newspaper.

It was the *Post* with the headline, PISTOL PETE: HE BOUGHT THE GUN.

"I do not intend to have this case tried in the newspapers," Judge Hendrick said.

"Your Honor, I'm not responsible for the press."

"Surprise witnesses make news."

"I've already explained that was not my intention."

"Maybe not, but this is deplorable. I would like to point out that the jury has not been sequestered."

"They've been instructed not to read the papers."

"Not to read them, yes. But these are front-page scare headlines. You can't miss them."

"They are not my work."

"That's not the point. The point is, surprise witnesses and surprise testimony are the type of theatrics that *create* front page news. And if I found this was being done deliberately, I would not like it. Is that clear?"

"Yes, Your Honor."

"Good. Now, what with all the surprise witnesses and early adjournments it seems a long time ago, but I believe yesterday morning Mr. Manning was on the stand. His cross-examination was interrupted until he could bring some photos into court. May I ask if he has done so?"

"Yes, Your Honor."

"He's present and ready to proceed?"

"Yes, he is."

"Very well. Let's bring in the jury and return Mr. Manning to the stand."

When that had been accomplished, Judge Hendrick turned to Steve Winslow and said, "You may proceed."

Steve crossed in to the witness. "Mr. Manning, yesterday you were asked to bring into court photographs of the fatal bullet photographed in a comparison microscope with test bullets from the gun, People's Exhibit Four. Have you done so?"

"Yes, I have."

"You have those photographs with you?"

"Yes, I do."

"How many are there?"

"Referring only to the photographs showing the comparison of the fatal bullet to bullets fired from the gun, People's Exhibit Four?"

"Yes, that's right."

"There are five."

"Five pictures showing that comparison?"

"That's right."

"I ask that they be marked for identification as Defendant's Exhibits A-One-through-Five."

"Your Honor," Vaulding said. "I believe those are a prosecution exhibit."

"Well, the defense is producing them. You chose not to," Judge Hendrick said. "Mark them Defendant's Exhibits A-One-through-Five."

When the exhibits had been marked, Steve picked up the pictures, riffled through them. He selected one, approached the witness.

"Mr. Manning, I hand you the picture marked for identification Defendant's Exhibit A-Three and ask you what it shows?"

"It shows the comparison of the fatal bullet and the test bullet on the comparison microscope."

"Which is which?"

"The fatal bullet is the top half, the bullet from People's Exhibit Four is the bottom half."

"The bullets are in alignment?"

"Yes, they are."

"Mr. Manning, I notice scratches on the bottom half not present on the top half."

"Yes. As I said, those are the scratches made when someone used some sort of etching tool to deface the barrel of the gun."

"Then these scratches represent marks that do *not* line up?"

"Naturally."

"I count four scratches of that nature, is that right?"

"I'm not sure."

"Then take a look."

Manning studied the photograph. "Yes. There are four."

"How many marks do you find that *do* line up?"

Again Manning studied the photograph. "I count three."

"Four that don't, three that do?"

Manning frowned. "That is an unfair way of presenting the evidence."

"Oh? Why is that?"

Manning hesitated a moment, then blurted out, "You make it sound like a ball score, with my side losing."

Laughter rocked the courtroom. Everyone broke up, spectators and jurors alike.

Judge Hendrick, sensing everyone needed relief from the tension of the case, gave it a few moments before banging the gavel. "That will do," he said. "Proceed, Mr. Winslow."

Steve smiled. "Well-said, Mr. Manning. I'm sorry if I gave that impression. But four to three, that's what we just counted up, isn't it?"

"You can't go by that," Manning said. "The two things are in no way equivalent. There are four scratches where someone marked the barrel of the gun that *prevent* us from seeing the scratches that would line up. Despite this, we're still able to line up three. That does not yield a score of four to three. If the murderer had only scratched the gun barrel twice, would we then have a score of three to two and say the identification won? Not at all. The two things are unrelated. Except, if there were only two scratches made by the file, we could see even more scratches that matched. You see what I'm saying?"

Steve smiled, "Yes, I do, Mr. Manning, but the fact remains you have only three scratches in this photograph that line up."

"I've explained that."

"Yes, you have. What I want to know is, is that sufficient to make the identification?"

"Yes, it is."

"Is it, Mr. Manning? Didn't you testify yesterday that there were individual characteristics and class characteristics?"

"Yes, I did."

"Well, couldn't these be class characteristics, common to *all* Colt .45s?"

Manning hesitated a moment.

Steve's eyes widened. "Is that right, Mr. Manning? Is that what they are?"

"No, it is not," Manning said angrily. "And I resent the suggestion. If I hesitated for a moment, it is because I wanted to be absolutely fair. You mentioned class characteristics. There is *one* of the scratches in the photograph that is consistent with being a class characteristic. I would go so far as to say it is indeed a class characteristic. But there is only one of which I would say that."

"One of the three?" Steve asked.

"Yes. One of the three."

"You're saying now you think that *is* a class characteristic?"

"Yes, I do."

"Then that leaves *two* scratches that are *not* class characteristics?"

"That's right."

"You are now saying two scratches are sufficient for making the identification."

"No, I'm not," Manning said. "I'm merely saying the bullets match."

"But you must have some basis for saying so."

"I'm saying so on the basis of my examination. If you want to break that down and say I'm going on the basis of two scratches, I suppose you can do so, but that's not an accurate assessment of the situation. Aside from the scratch we call the class characteristic, there are two scratches that are a definite match. And there is every indication there would be more matches if it weren't for the defacing of the barrel of the gun."

"Mr. Manning, isn't that like saying, I didn't find the defendant's fingerprints, but if I *had* found them they'd be there?"

"Objection."

"Sustained."

"Mr. Manning, how can you testify that scratches that aren't there probably exist?"

Manning smiled. "Because I have matched the bullet. So I know if the gun barrel hadn't been defaced, those scratches on the test bullet would match those on the fatal bullet."

"Isn't that circular logic, Mr. Manning? You know those scratches exist because the bullets match, but you base your conclusion that the bullets match partly on those scratches that you assume must be there."

"Objection."

"Overruled."

"No, I do not. And I think I've made a fair and accurate appraisal of the evidence, and given you my professional opinion."

"All right," Steve said. "Let's move on to the other pictures. Did you bring in the photographs of the other test bullet, the one fired from the gun, People's Exhibit Three?"

"Yes, I did."

"Could you produce those pictures, please?"

"Your Honor, I object to the introduction of these pictures in evidence," Vaulding said.

"We're not introducing them in evidence now. We're marking them for identification."

"Nonetheless, I object to them."

"Your objection is noted. The court reporter will mark the pictures. How many are there?"

"Four," Manning said.

"Very well. Let's have them marked Defendant's Exhibits B-One-through-Four."

When the pictures had been marked, Steve Winslow selected one and approached the witness. "Mr. Manning, I hand you a photograph marked Defendant's Exhibit B-Two and ask you what it depicts?"

"That shows a test bullet fired from the gun, People's Exhibit Three, on the comparison microscope with the fatal bullet."

"The bullets are aligned?"

Manning frowned. "Once again, the bullets are *not* aligned. An attempt was made to align them, which I could not do. Let me put it this way. The bullets are aligned in as much as it was possible to do so. There was only one real point of similarity."

"And what does that indicate to you?"

"That the bullets don't match."

"I know. I understand that's your contention. I mean, what do you think that point of similarity represents?"

"That would be an example of class characteristic."

"The class characteristic caused the match?"

"That's right."

"Tell me, would that be the same class characteristic that is shown in the test bullet fired from People's Exhibit Four?"

"As to that, I'm not sure."

"Well, take a look."

Steve handed him back the other photo.

Manning studied the two photographs side by side. "It would appear to be the same mark."

"The same class characteristic?"

"That is correct."

"So these photos show the fatal bullet and the test bullets in basically the same position?"

"Yes, they do."

"I see. Tell me, Mr. Manning. Did you by any chance compare a test bullet from the gun, People's Exhibit Four, with a test bullet from the gun, People's Exhibit Three, on the comparison microscope."

Manning stared at him. "Of course not. What would be the point? We know they're from different guns."

"But they each lined up with the fatal bullet. At least in this one regard. It makes me wonder how well they would line up with each other.

"Your Honor, at this point I would like to ask that the witness be instructed to make that comparison."

"Oh, Your Honor," Vaulding said. "That's totally irrelevant and immaterial. We're talking about two separate guns."

"And bullets that match, at least in one respect."

"It's not a case of these bullets possibly matching. We have the guns here in court. Each one fired a bullet. The test bullets we fired ourselves. We *know* they don't match. There's no reason we should have to prove that."

"I'm obviously not trying to prove that, Your Honor," Steve said. "Both bullets do match the fatal bullet, at least in one aspect. I think I have a right to know how well they match each other."

"I think so, too," Judge Hendrick said. "And it is so ordered. Mr. Winslow, will that conclude your cross-examination at this time?"

"Yes, Your Honor."

"Mr. Vaulding, do you have any redirect on the evidence so far, or would you care to wait till the witness is recalled?"

"You're bringing him back again, Your Honor?"

"I've already said so, Mr. Vaulding. You may question the witness then, now, or both. What is your intention?"

"I have no questions at this time."

"Very well. The witness is excused, but you will return tomorrow morning, having made that comparison."

"Yes, Your Honor."

"Very well. Call your next witness."

"Call Donald Walcott."

As Donald Walcott took the stand, it occurred to Steve maybe he should have coached him a little. The young man exuded resentment. Steve realized Vaulding probably would have had no problem getting him declared a hostile witness. Still, there was no need to dump it in his lap.

When the witness had been sworn in, Vaulding stood up and said, "State your name."

"Donald Walcott."

"What is your relationship to the defendant, Russ Timberlaine?"

"I am engaged to his daughter."

"And were you a guest at the Timberlaine mansion on the weekend of the murder?"

"Yes, I was."

"When did you arrive?"

"Friday afternoon."

"And when did you leave?"

"I haven't left."

"You're still there?"

"Yes, I am."

"And how long do you intend to stay?"

The witness glared at Vaulding. "Until this matter is resolved."

"I see," Vaulding said. "Tell me, Mr. Walcott, the weekend you were staying there—the weekend of the murder—did you have any conversations with your fiancée's father, Russ Timberlaine?"

Donald Walcott set his mouth in a firm line.

"Please answer the question, Mr. Walcott," Vaulding said.

When Walcott still hesitated, Vaulding said, "Your Honor?"

Judge Hendrick leaned down from the bench. "Young man?" he said.

Donald Walcott looked up at him defiantly. "Yes."

"Call me Your Honor."

Walcott took a breath. "Yes, Your Honor."

"You have been called as a witness in a court of law. It is your duty to answer questions, unless they are objected to and I rule you need not answer them, or unless you should refuse to answer on the grounds that an answer might tend to incriminate you. Otherwise, you must answer or I will hold you in contempt of court. Is that clear?"

Walcott took a breath. "Yes, Your Honor."

"Fine. Court reporter will read back the question."

There was a pause while the court reporter shuffled through his tapes. Then he read, " 'Tell me, Mr. Walcott, the weekend you were staying there—the weekend of the murder—did you have any conversations with your fiancée's father, Russ Timberlaine?' "

"Yes, I did."

"Fine," Vaulding said. "Tell me, in any of these conversations did Russ Timberlaine mention a gun?"

"Objection, leading and suggestive."

"Overruled. The witness is clearly hostile. Answer the question."

Walcott took a breath. "Yes, he did."

"Would that be the Colt .45, the Pistol Pete gun?"

"Yes."

"Mr. Walcott, we have two guns present in court. People's Exhibit Three, which is the gun found next to the body of Jack Potter. And People's Exhibit Four, the gun found in Russ Timberlaine's holster on his bedside table. We have also heard testimony from Lieutenant Sanders that Russ Timberlaine identified the gun, People's Exhibit Three, as the original Pistol Pete Robbins gun that he owned, and the gun, People's Exhibit Four, as the gun he found substituted for it. Now I ask you, in any of those conversations you had with Russ Timberlaine, did he make any claim about a substituted gun?"

"Yes, he did."

"And what did he say?"

"Just that. That his gun had been substituted."

Vaulding frowned. "I'd like a little more than that. He claimed, did he not, that he owned the original, authentic Pistol Pete Robbins gun. Is that true?"

"Yes."

"He claimed that that gun had been taken and a duplicate left in its place. Is that right?"

"Yes."

"He claimed he no longer had the original gun, he now only had the copy, the fake gun?"

"Yes. That's right."

"The substitution had happened prior to the time you arrived at the mansion that Friday?"

"Yes."

"How long before?"

"I'm not sure. I think the week before."

"The week before you arrived?"

"I think so. As I say, I'm not sure."

"But it *was* before you arrived?"

"Yes, it was."

"Russ Timberlaine mentioned the substitution?"

"Yes, he did."

"Did he show you the gun?"

"Yes, he did."

"The gun he claimed had been substituted?"

"That's right."

"The gun was a Colt .45?"

"Yes, it was."

"With the initial R carved in the handle?"

"Yes."

"Timberlaine showed you the initial R?"

"Yes, he did."

"Pointed it out to you?"

"Yes."

"Did the gun have the serial number ground off?"

"Yes, it did."

"He showed you that too?"

"Yes."

"Pointed out where it had been ground off?"

"Yes."

"He showed you this gun and said it was a fake gun, that his gun had been stolen and this gun had been left substituted for it?"

"Yes."

"He didn't tell you he had purchased this gun?"

Walcott stuck out his chin. "He most certainly did not."

"He didn't mention that he had bought the gun himself at a gun shop on July 16th?"

"No, he did not. And I don't believe he did."

"But he did show you the gun and tell you he had found it substituted for the real Pistol Pete gun?"

"Yes."

"And," Vaulding said casually, "did he tell you any steps he had taken to identify that gun?"

Walcott had relaxed during the latter part of his testimony as he realized the questions he was being asked were simple, the answers to them were already known and didn't hurt Russ Timberlaine.

Which is why he tripped on this one. He opened his mouth to answer, hesitated, blinked twice, frowned and said, "What do you mean?"

Vaulding smiled. "Exactly what I said. When Timberlaine told you about the substitution of guns, did he mention if he had taken any steps to *prove* that there had been a substitution of guns? Did he do anything that would help to identify one gun from the other?

"Oh."

"Well, Mr. Walcott?"

"He had not marked the guns in any way."

Vaulding smiled. "I didn't say he had, Mr. Walcott. I merely asked you if he had taken *any* steps to keep them straight."

"Yes, but—well, the question makes no sense. He only *had* one gun. The gun that had been substituted. The other one was no longer there."

"I understand, Mr. Walcott." Vaulding smiled, but his eyes were hard. "Referring to that gun—the one that was there—did Russ Timberlaine state that tests had been performed on that gun for the purpose of identifying it and keeping it straight and separate from the other gun, should it turn up again?"

Donald Walcott took a breath. He looked at the defense table, as if hoping for an objection.

"Witness will answer the question," Judge Hendrick said.

Walcott looked around helplessly. "Yes, he did," he blurted.

Vaulding smiled. "Thank you, Mr. Walcott. Russ Timberlaine told you that he had performed a test on the gun?"

"Yes."

"What kind of a test?"

Walcott took another breath. "He had had test bullets fired through it for the purpose of identification."

Vaulding smiled again. "He had fired test bullets through this gun?"

"Yes."

"The substituted gun?"

"Yes."

"The gun he claims he was wearing at the time of the auction? The gun that was found in his gun belt on his bedside table? The gun, People's Exhibit Four, that is in evidence here in court and has been identified as the murder weapon?"

"Objection, Your Honor," Steve said. "Leading and suggestive and assuming facts not in evidence."

"Overruled," Judge Hendrick said. "I've allowed leading questions, and those facts *are* in evidence. Witness may answer."

"Is that the gun you are referring to?" Vaulding asked.

"Yes, it is."

"Russ Timberlaine stated that he had fired test bullets through this gun?"

"Yes."

"And had he had those bullets compared to any other bullets?"

"Yes."

"What bullets?"

"Bullets from the original Pistol Pete Robbins gun."

"The original gun?"

"That's right."

"And where did he get those bullets if the gun had been stolen?"

"He said he'd been target shooting with the gun before it was stolen. He'd dug the bullets out of the target."

"And he said he'd had those bullets compared and identified?"

"Yes, he had."

Vaulding smiled. "And who did he have compare and identify them for him?"

Walcott hesitated, then blurted, "Steve Winslow."

There was a shocked gasp, then murmurs in the courtroom. Judge Hendrick banged the gavel.

Vaulding's smile grew broader. "Did you say Steve Winslow?"

Judge Hendrick banged the gavel again. "Already asked and answered, Mr. Vaulding. Ask another question."

"Yes, Your Honor. Mr. Walcott, Mr. Timberlaine told you that he had given the substituted gun and the bullets to Steve Winslow and asked him to fire test bullets through it and to compare and identify the bullets?"

"That's right."

"And did Russ Timberlaine say that Steve Winslow had given him back the gun?"

Walcott frowned. "I don't remember."

"Well, he must have if he showed it to you."

"Objection."

"Sustained."

"All right. Never mind the gun. Did he say anything about the bullets? Did he say whether Steve Winslow had given him back the test bullets."

Walcott hesitated, then said, "Yes, he did."

"He said he *had* been given back the test bullets?"

"Yes."

"Where are those bullets now?"

"I don't know."

"Did Russ Timberlaine tell you what he did with those bullets?"

"No, he did not."

"He didn't tell you where he put them?"

"No."

"But to the best of your knowledge, those bullets are still in Russ Timberlaine's possession?"

"Objection."

"Sustained."

"Did Russ Timberlaine tell you he had given the bullets to anyone?"

"No."

"Or disposed of them in any way?"

"No."

"But he told you he had received them from Steve Winslow?"

"Yes."

Vaulding turned to Judge Hendrick. "Your Honor. At this time I ask the court to take judicial cognizance of the importance of this evidence and order the defense to produce those bullets."

"So ordered," Judge Hendrick said. "Mr. Winslow, you are hereby ordered to bring into court any and all bullets testified to in court, that is, the bullets tested by you and delivered to the defendant Russ Timberlaine. I realize of course you will need to confer with your client. I am therefore adjourning court for the day, and we will take these matters up tomorrow morning at ten o'clock."

36

Russ Timberlaine frowned down at the papers in front of him, then looked at Steve Winslow through the wire-mesh screen. "Explain it to me again," he said.

Steve sighed. "The papers you are signing give me power of attorney to open your safe-deposit box and get the bullets."

"And the gun."

Steve took a breath. "I am also having you authorize me to open the safe-deposit box containing the gun."

"So we can show the bullets came from the gun," Timberlaine said.

"Of course."

Timberlaine looked up sharply. "You *are* going to show the bullets came from the gun?"

"In all due time."

"What does that mean?"

"At the moment we are being asked to produce bullets. Eventually we will need to show where those bullets came from. That needs to be done in an orderly fashion. Here's how it will go. We'll produce the bullets. The bullets will be examined by the ballistics expert, who will compare them to the fatal bullet and to the bullets from the original Pistol Pete gun.

"Now, in one of the test tubes that I gave you is a bullet that you say you dug out of the target. A bullet presumably from the original Pistol Pete gun. If it was indeed from the gun, it should match the test bullets fired from the gun, People's Exhibit Three, the gun found by the body, the gun believed to be the original Pistol Pete gun."

"Exactly," Timberlaine said. "And it will."

"Fine," Steve said. "But the bullet in the other test tube—the bullet from the gun you gave me, the gun you found substituted for the original gun—that bullet will not match *any* of the guns in court."

"Of course not," Timberlaine said. "Because they got the wrong gun. I switched guns, so these bullets have absolutely nothing to do with it. The only gun they will match is the gun in my safe-deposit box. Which is why we have to give them that gun."

"Fine," Steve said, "but not now."

"Why not?"

"Because we're not putting on our case. They are. They've asked for the bullets, so we give them the bullets. They haven't asked for the gun, so we don't give them the gun."

"That's silly."

"No, it isn't. Try and understand the situation. Vaulding's putting on his case. Any evidence he brings out, he's got to explain. We give him these bullets, he gives 'em to the ballistics expert to match 'em up with the fatal bullet. The guy tries and they don't match. That shoots Vaulding's theory full of holes and makes him look like a fool. He's gotta explain the evidence, and he can't. And there's no reason for us to help him. Because if he can't make a case, the judge is gonna dismiss. You hear what I'm sayin'? We don't have to do anything. The burden of proof is on the prosecution. *Let* Vaulding putz around and mess things up. Let him look like a schmuck. Then when it's our turn up to bat, we'll explain everything and look like champs. The jury will say, 'Oh, so that's how it is, thank you so much for clearing it up, not guilty, Mr. Timberlaine.' "

Timberlaine shook his head. "I don't like it."

Steve took a breath. "Why the hell not?"

"The witness says I bought a gun."

"Yeah. So?"

"And Vaulding's claiming it's the gun in court."

"Yeah, but he can't prove it. So what?"

"That's what he's claiming, and people will believe him. So we gotta produce the other gun and prove the gun I bought *isn't* the gun in court."

Steve shook his head. "Here we go again."

"Why is that the wrong thing to do?"

"I just told you why."

"Yeah, but I don't agree."

Steve shrugged. "You are free to fire me and hire another lawyer."

"I don't want to hire another lawyer."

"Then you have to follow my advice."

"That isn't fair."

Steve looked at him. "What, are you ten years old? You want fair? I don't think it's fair that you're up for murder, but you are. Just because it's unfair, nobody's gonna let you off the hook. It's a sad fact, but that's life."

"I know, damn it," Timberlaine said. "It's a hell of a position to be in. That's why I want to do everything I can to get out. And when we have the evidence in our hands—it just seems stupid to sit on it."

"O.K.," Steve said. "I'm glad you told me how you felt."

"You gonna act on it?"

"I'll take it under advisement."

"What does that mean?"

"I means I'll think about it. I know what you want, and I know what you're going through. I'm gonna do my best to get you out of this as quickly as possible. That's all I can do, it's the best I can promise you. O.K.?"

For a few moments Timberlaine didn't say anything, just stared at Steve Winslow. Then he looked down, picked up the pen, signed the papers and pushed them through the slot in the wire-mesh screen.

"O.K.," he said.

But he did not look happy.

37

TRACY GARVIN LOOKED UP FROM HER DESK in the outer office when Steve Winslow came in the door. "Did you get it?" she asked.

"Yeah, I got it. Any calls?"

"Just Mark. He's in his office waiting for reports, but nothing much is coming in."

"At this point, I don't know whether that's good or bad."

"Yeah, I know. Right now you've got your hands full, don't you?"

Steve Winslow looked down at the briefcase he was holding. He grinned. "That I do."

Steve went into his inner office, put the briefcase on the desk, popped it open. He reached in, took out the test tubes containing the bullets.

Tracy, who had followed him in, said, "Now where have I seen those before?"

"Yeah, really," Steve said. "Boy, that seems a long time ago, doesn't it?"

"I'll say." Tracy jerked her thumb at the briefcase. "What else you got in there, mister?"

Steve shrugged. "Papers. Books. A few odds and ends."

"You wouldn't happen to have a Colt .45 with the initial R carved in the handle, would you?"

Steve reached in and pulled it out. "Doesn't everybody?"

"Everybody in *this* case," Tracy said. "So what are you gonna do with this stuff?"

"I thought I'd put it in the safe."

"That safe there?"

"Yeah. Why?"

"Isn't that where the other gun and bullets are?"

"Is it? It's been so long, I don't remember."

"Take my word for it."

Steve shrugged. "You could be right."

"So you're gonna put 'em in the safe?"

"Yeah. Listen, why don't you give Mark Taylor a call, tell him to come down here?"

Tracy took off her glasses, folded them up, put her hands on her hips and grinned. "Nice try," she said.

Steve raised his eyebrows. "I beg your pardon?"

"Sure, play innocent," Tracy said. "You're going to switch guns, aren't you?"

Steve looked at her. "Whatever gives you that idea?"

"Why else would you have it?" Tracy said. "Vaulding didn't ask you for the gun, just the bullets."

"Well, Timberlaine wants me to produce the gun to match the bullets."

"Oh, yeah?"

"Yeah. He was most adamant. I managed to talk him out of it, but he's not happy. I know he's going to ask me again."

Tracy nodded. "Which is why you have to switch the gun."

"I don't quite understand. You have no reason to suspect I would be switching a gun."

"Oh, yeah?" Tracy said. "I happen to know it for a fact."

"How could you know that?"

She looked at him, smiled. "Moron," she said. "You're happy."

"What?"

"The first time since this case started, you're feeling good. You know why? It's 'cause you're gonna be a bad boy and switch the gun, and you love it. You know how I know? I know from what happened in court today."

Steve frowned. "What are you talking about?"

Tracy waved her hand. "No, not the witnesses or the case or the evidence or anything. I'm talking about before that even started.

Judge Hendrick's opening remarks—when he held up the newspapers and bawled Vaulding out about the headlines?"

"What about it?"

"I was watching you when it happened. Considering the prosecutor was getting himself reprimanded by the court, that should have been just fine. But you were not happy at all. And suddenly I knew why. It's not the fact that Vaulding's young or good or that all the evidence is going against you or your client's lying to you or the whole bit—what really got to you was that Vaulding had reversed fields on you. *He* was the bad boy, pulling all the quasi-legal shit and pissing off the judge. Having the judge reprimanding him and protecting you was more than you could bear."

Steve looked at her, grinned. "Tracy, I'm not saying you're wrong, but what the hell has all this got to do with the gun?"

"It's got everything to do with it. You're happy now. Why? Because you're about to switch guns and be the bad boy again."

"That's very interesting, Tracy. But as it happens, no one has asked for this gun. So I'm not switching it with anything. I'm merely locking it up in the safe."

"In which there happens to be an identical gun, which happens to have fired the bullets you have there on your desk."

"Well, isn't that a coincidence?"

"I know it's been some time," Tracy said, "but aren't there also duplicates of those bullets in your safe?"

"You could be right."

"In addition to the *third* test bullet, fired from the gun Mark bought. The gun you carved the R in the handle and filed the serial number off of. The gun you gave to Timberlaine." Tracy pointed to the gun on the desk. "The gun that is presumably *that* gun."

" 'Presumably' is well advised, Tracy," Steve said. "After all, we have only Timberlaine's word for the fact that he did switch guns."

"Imagine if he didn't," Tracy said.

"Yeah? What then?" Steve said.

"Well, in that case," Tracy said, "this gun is the gun Timberlaine bought. And the bullets from it won't match anything. Not the bullets in court. Not the bullets in your test tubes. Nothing.

"In that case, the gun in court, the murder weapon, will be Mark Taylor's gun. In which case, you would have a test bullet in your safe that would match absolutely with the fatal bullet, which was fired before the gun barrel was altered."

"Right," Steve said. "Unless Timberlaine switched guns on me *before* he came to my office."

"There's always that," Tracy said.

"If so, what's the situation then?"

"Well, then we have two more possibilities. One, when Timberlaine left the office he switched guns again. Or at least thought he did, since he didn't know you'd switched guns with the one Mark Taylor bought. Anyway, in that case he'd switch guns again, switching Mark Taylor's gun with the gun he originally found substituted. In that case, *this* gun, the gun he put in the safe-deposit box, would be Mark Taylor's gun, and the gun in court would be the gun he originally found, from which you had never fired any test bullets. The gun you *had* fired test bullets from, the gun in your safe, would then be the gun Timberlaine bought.

"Same thing if he didn't switch guns again. I mean about the gun he bought being in the safe. As to the other guns, if he *didn't* switch back, then this gun here is the gun he found. Which we can't prove, because no test bullets were ever fired from it. And in that case, the gun in court, the murder weapon, is Mark Taylor's gun, and the test bullets in your safe will match it."

"Right," Steve said. "So that covers all the eventualities." He ticked them off. "One, Timberlaine brings me the actual gun he found. I switch it for Taylor's gun. Timberlaine switches it for the gun he bought. The gun he bought is the murder weapon in court, Taylor's gun goes into the safe-deposit box and is therefore the gun on my desk, and the gun he found is the one in my safe.

"Two, Timberlaine brings me the gun he found, I switch it for Taylor's gun, he doesn't switch it, in which case Taylor's gun is the murder weapon, and the gun he bought is this one and the gun he found is in my safe.

"Three, Timberlaine switches guns before and after coming to my office. In that case I have the gun he bought in my safe, he had Mark Taylor's gun in his safe-deposit box, and the gun he found is the murder weapon.

"And four, Timberlaine switches guns only before coming to my office. I have the gun he bought in my safe, Mark Taylor's gun is the murder weapon, and this is the gun he found substituted."

Tracy exhaled, shook her head.

"Yeah," Steve said. "Through all that, there is only one constant."

"What's that?"

He pointed to the bullets on the desk. "This bullet. The one marked RT-SUB. Whatever gun Timberlaine may have brought me, either the gun he bought or the gun he found substituted, whatever gun that was, this bullet came from it. That we know for sure. This bullet came from it, and therefore had absolutely nothing to do with the murder. Absolutely nothing to do with any of the exhibits in court. Because the gun it came from—whichever gun it is—is in my safe, and has been ever since Timberlaine first came to my office."

Steve pointed. "So this bullet—which Vaulding has made such a big deal of and which I've been ordered to produce in court—is the one thing in this case that is utterly meaningless and has nothing to do with anything."

Steve smiled. "So you talk about me being happy. If it weren't for Timberlaine pressing me to turn over the gun, turning over these bullets would be an absolute pleasure. Because Vaulding's going to choke on 'em. He's gonna compare 'em and come up empty. Be left with egg on his face. And it will be all his own doing."

"I can see you're crying all over."

Steve shrugged. "Hey, those are the breaks."

There came a crash of the outer office door flying open and Mark Taylor burst into the room, wide-eyed and breathing hard.

"Shit's hit the fan!" he gasped out.

"What the hell?" Steve said.

Taylor held up his hand, waved it while he caught his breath. "I just got a call. That reporter."

Steve's mouth dropped open. "Vaulding held *another* press conference?"

Taylor waved his hand. "No, no. Not him. Timberlaine."

"Oh, good lord."

"Right. He spilled the beans."

"About what?"

"Everything. You name it, he said it. About testing the bullets. About buying the gun. Once he got started he just couldn't stop."

"Shit. What, specifically, did he say?"

"Well, first he confirms everything Walcott said. About finding the gun and bringing it to you and having the bullets tested. Then he confirms everything that other witness said. About buyin' the other gun."

"And grinding the number off and carving an R in the handle?"

"Yeah."

"Jesus Christ."

"Hey, I don't make the news, I just bring it."

"Yeah, I know," Steve said. "But what else? Did he say he switched guns and put the one I tested in a safe-deposit box?"

"Oh, sure."

"Did he say he wrote me out a power of attorney and told me to get it?"

"Yeah. The way I hear it, he was really worked up over that."

"Shit," Steve said. "Then we haven't much time."

Taylor frowned. "Time? Time for what? I don't want to—Say! Is that my gun?"

"Is what your gun? Oh, good lord!"

There came a sound from the outer office.

Steve whirled around as if at a gunshot, lowered his voice and barked out orders. "Someone's here. Tracy, get out there and stall him. Mark, go with her, but whoever it is, just keep on going. If it's the papers, no comment. If it's the cops, same deal; if they hold you, I'll be there. Now go."

Taylor turned, found Tracy was already out the door before Steve had finished. He hurried after her into the outer office, closing the door behind him.

The moment the door was closed, Steve whirled and grabbed the gun and the bullets. He rushed to the safe. Felt a moment of panic when he realized he didn't have the combination. Then he remembered where Tracy had left it written down for him. He jerked open the drawer of his desk, looked up the combination, spun the dial. He jerked open the safe, thrust the gun and bullets in, slammed the door and spun the dial again.

Steve straightened up and hurried away from the safe, expecting the door to burst open at any moment. It didn't. He crossed to the door, pulled it open.

The outer office was not, as he'd feared, full of cops. A lone man in a suit and tie stood next to Tracy's desk.

The man turned to face him. "Steve Winslow?"

"Yes."

The man thrust a paper into his hands. "Subpoena *duces tecum*. You're a lawyer, you know the drill. It's all in there. Don't blame me, I'm just doing my job."

The man nodded to Steve, nodded to Tracy and walked out.

"What do you make of that?" Tracy said.

Steve held his finger to his lips, pointed to the door.

Tracy got up from her desk, went to the door, opened it and looked out. "No, he's gone," she said. "A process server, just like he said. So what is it?"

"Just what I thought it would be. The natural consequence of Timberlaine's interview. A subpoena *duces tecum*, ordering me to produce the gun in court."

"Then why are you grinning?"

"Because of the wording."

"What about it?"

"Listen to this," Steve said. He read, " '. . . hereby ordered to produce the gun described by your client, Russ Timberlaine, to wit, the Colt .45 revolver with the serial number ground off and the initial R carved in the handle, given to you by him for the express purpose of testing and identifying bullets from said gun.' "

"Son of a bitch," Tracy said.

"Do you get it?"

"Yeah, I get it. But in legal terms, what does it mean?"

"Legal terms, hell," Steve said. "What it means is I'm off the hook. In terms of switching guns, I mean. It's the best of all possible worlds. He doesn't ask for the gun from the safe-deposit box, he asks for the gun Timberlaine gave me to check. And do you know what that means?" Steve grinned and pointed to the subpoena. *"Vaulding just switched guns."*

38

Judge Hendrick looked around the crowded courtroom, pursed his lips, cocked his head and said dryly, "Yesterday I began by remarking on the media coverage."

That produced a roar of laughter from the spectators in the courtroom, who could not have missed the barrage of headlines such as, PISTOL PETE: TIMBERLAINE TALKS and PISTOL PETE: ANOTHER GUN, which assaulted their eyes on their way into the courthouse.

When the laughter had subsided, Judge Hendrick held up his hand. "Yes, I know, Mr. Vaulding. This is not of your doing. Let's press on. This is the time Mr. Manning was to have returned to court having made a comparison of the two test bullets. Is he here?"

"Yes, Your Honor," Vaulding said.

"I assume he has made the comparison?"

"Yes, he has."

"That's good. Though recent matters would seem to have rendered the matter moot. Now, with regard to the other bullets. Mr. Winslow?"

"Yes, Your Honor."

"Yesterday you were ordered to produce the test bullets referred to in the testimony of the witness, Donald Walcott. Do you have those bullets with you?"

214

"Yes, Your Honor."

"Produce them please."

Steve Winslow opened his briefcase and took out the two test tubes. "Here, Your Honor."

Judge Hendrick motioned to a court officer to bring them to him. He picked them up, said, "Let the record show in response to my order the defense has produced two sealed tubes, each containing a single bullet. One is marked RT-ORIG, the other, RT-SUB." He handed them back to the officer to give to the court reporter. "Let's have these marked for identification as People's Exhibits—what are we up to?"

"Five, Your Honor," the court reporter said.

"O.K. Mark them People's Exhibits Five-A and Five-B." Judge Hendrick turned back to Steve Winslow. "Now then, as you, I, and everyone else in this courthouse—with the exception of the jurors, who have been instructed not to read the papers—are aware, last night Mr. Timberlaine made a statement. I understand as a result of that statement a subpoena *duces tecum* was served on the defense, asking them to produce a certain gun. Mr. Winslow, have you complied with that subpoena?"

"Yes, Your Honor."

"Do you have that gun in court?"

"Yes, I do."

"Produce it, please."

Steve Winslow reached into his briefcase and pulled out a gun.

"Fine," Judge Hendrick said. "Let's have the gun marked People's Exhibit Six."

When that had been done, Judge Hendrick said, "Fine. At this point the court is going to make another order. The court intends to keep this evidence straight, and the court intends to see that this evidence is presented in an orderly manner. Or as orderly as possible, considering the dramatic and unexpected developments in this trial. Above all, I intend to see that this evidence is preserved. Is Mr. Manning in the courtroom?"

"Here, Your Honor," Manning said.

"Mr. Manning, we were to have had your testimony today regarding the two bullets the defense asked you to compare. In light of this new evidence, that can wait. I am therefore asking you to return one more time, tomorrow morning at ten o'clock, and to bring with you at that time the evidence you were to have given today."

"Yes, Your Honor."

"I also direct you to take this new evidence, People's Exhibits Five-A and -B and People's Exhibit Six, consisting of two bullets and one gun, and test them and compare them in every way possible to all of the ballistics exhibits present now in court."

"Very well, Your Honor."

"We will hear your testimony on this evidence tomorrow morning at ten o'clock. We will all hear it together. And for the first time. Do I make myself clear?"

Manning frowned. "I beg your pardon, Your Honor?"

"What I mean is, I do not want you communicating your findings to either the defense or the prosecution prior to your appearance tomorrow morning in court."

"Oh, Your Honor," Vaulding said.

"Sit down, Mr. Vaulding," Judge Hendrick said. "Would you want to have Mr. Manning communicate with the defense?"

"Certainly not."

"Well, what's good for the goose is good for the gander. We will have this evidence tomorrow morning in court. If I can't control publicity one way, I'll control it another.

"And you, Mr. Manning. You will absolutely under no circumstances communicate any of your findings to the press. Have I made myself clear?"

"Yes, Your Honor."

"Fine. I want a full report on all aspects of the evidence tomorrow morning at ten o'clock. I assume you have test bullets remaining from your original tests, so if you want to get started now, you are free to go. I will send over the actual exhibits as soon as we adjourn."

Vaulding frowned. "Are your preparing to proceed, Your Honor?"

"I am, Mr. Vaulding. I have no intention of adjourning court prematurely yet another time. I assume you have other witnesses to call?"

"I do, Your Honor. Only I had anticipated Mr. Manning's testimony would take some time."

"Well, it didn't," Judge Hendrick said dryly. "Are you prepared to proceed?"

Vaulding turned and conferred with a trial deputy, then turned back to the judge. "I have witnesses I can call, Your Honor."

"Well, line them up. And bring in the jury."

When the jury had been brought in, Judge Hendrick thanked them for their patience and informed them the testimony they expected to hear from Mr. Manning would be heard at a later time. He then turned back to Vaulding and said, "Call your next witness."

"Call Henry Crumbly."

As the portly gun collector took the stand, Timberlaine leaned over and whispered, "Why are they calling Hank?"

Steve Winslow gave him a look. As one might have expected, their precourt conference had not been harmonious and Steve was not feeling entirely cordial. "Motivation," he said shortly.

When the witness had been sworn in, Vaulding said, "Mr. Crumbly, are you familiar with the defendant, Russ Timberlaine?"

"Of course."

"How long have you known him?"

"Several years."

"How is it that you know him?"

"We are both gun collectors. I believe my wife and I originally met him at an auction."

"A gun auction?"

"Yes, of course."

"Did you know the decedent, Jack Potter?"

"Yes, I did."

"How did you know him?"

"He is a renowned expert in the field of guns. I have met him on several occasions in that capacity."

"Including the weekend of his death?"

"Yes."

"You were a guest at the Timberlaine mansion that weekend?"

"Yes, I was."

"You saw Jack Potter at that time?"

"Yes, of course. He was the expert there for the auction."

"Did you discuss guns with him that weekend?"

"Actually, I did."

"Guns that were to be bid on at the auction?"

"That's right."

"Were you present at the auction?"

"Yes, I was."

"Did you bid at the auction?"

"Yes, I did."

"Tell me, did you make any bid on any gun at the auction that was somewhat out of the ordinary?"

Crumbly hesitated a moment. "Actually, yes, I did."

"And what might that be?"

"I bid on a gun for Russ Timberlaine."

"That's what I was getting at, Mr. Crumbly. Could you tell us about that?"

"Well, that's basically it. There was a gun Russ Timberlaine wanted. He suspected if Melvin Burdett knew he wanted the gun, Burdett would try to outbid him for it. So he asked me to bid for him."

"He asked you to buy the gun for him?"

"At least to try to."

"What instructions did he give you?"

"Simply to bid on the gun as if I were bidding on my own. Make every effort to purchase it, but not go over thirty thousand dollars."

"That's what you did?"

"Yes, I did."

"And did you buy the gun?"

"No, I did not."

"Why is that?"

"Burdett outbid me."

"How much did he bid?"

"Thirty-one thousand dollars."

"Which you had been instructed not to go over?"

"That's correct."

"What did you do then?"

"I stopped bidding. As I'd been instructed."

"Before that happened—did you make any effort to communicate with Russ Timberlaine to see if he wanted you to go higher?"

Crumbly hesitated a moment, then said, "I looked over where he was standing."

"Did he give you any sign?"

"No, he did not."

"Did he see you looking at him?"

"Actually, no."

"Why not?"

"Objection."

"Sustained."

"When you looked over at him, what was Timberlaine doing?"

"He was just standing there."

"Standing there doing what?"

"Nothing in particular. Just standing."

"You say he wasn't looking at you?"

"No."

"Who was he looking at?"

Crumbly hesitated. "The room was crowded."

"I'm sure it was. Tell me, in your mind, who did it appear to you that he was looking at?"

Crumbly took a breath. "Melvin Burdett."

"So," Vaulding said. "Correct me if I am wrong. You bid on the gun. Burdett outbid you. When that happened you looked over to Timberlaine for instructions. He gave none because he did not see you. And to the best you can determine, it was your impression that he was looking at Melvin Burdett?"

There was a pause, then Crumbly said, "That's right."

Vaulding nodded. "I see. And what expression did Mr. Timberlaine have on his face at the time?"

"Objection."

"Sustained."

"How did Russ Timberlaine appear to you?"

"It was hard to tell. He wasn't looking at me."

"What was your impression?"

"Objection. Calling for a conclusion."

"Sustained."

The smile never left Vaulding's face. "Tell me, Mr. Crumbly. When you got no response from Russ Timberlaine you stopped bidding. Is that correct?"

"Yes."

"The bidding was closed and the gun was marked down for Mr. Burdett?"

"That's right."

"When that happened, did you happen to notice Russ Timberlaine then?"

"Yes, I did."

"What did he do?"

"He left."

"He left the auction?"

"Yes, he did."

"How did he leave?"

"Objection."

"Sustained."

Vaulding frowned. "Your Honor, this witness is clearly hostile. Some latitude here would be appreciated."

"Well, he hasn't shown any hostility yet. Rephrase your question."

"In your own words, can you describe how Russ Timberlaine left the auction?"

"I don't know what to say. He just turned around and walked out."

"Was the auction over?"

"No."

"There were other guns left to be auctioned off?"

"Yes."

"How many?"

"I don't know. Five or six."

"Timberlaine didn't stay to see them auctioned?"

"No, he did not."

"I see. And what time was this, when Timberlaine left the auction?"

"I wouldn't know exactly."

"Would you know approximately?"

"It was around four o'clock."

"Now, it was later that evening that the police arrived at the mansion, was it not?"

"Yes, it was."

"And what time would that be?"

"I'm not sure. I think sometime between six and seven."

"And had you seen Mr. Timberlaine between the time he left the auction and the time the police arrived?"

"No, I had not."

"You had not seen him, spoken to him, or had any contact with him in any way?"

"No, I had not."

"Did you look for him? After the auction, I mean. To apologize for not getting the gun, or to commiserate or to discuss what went wrong?"

"Actually, I did look around for him. But he wasn't in any of the usual places."

"Oh? And what were the usual places?"

"The places he would be apt to mingle with the guests. Like the patio or the bar."

"Or the gun room?"

"No. I didn't look there."

"Was it one of the usual places?"

"Not in the same sense. More like one of the special places."

"So you didn't look there?"

"No."

"Did you try his apartment?"

"No."

"Why not? Wasn't that a natural place to look?"

"I wouldn't want to bother him there."

"Why not?"

"I just wouldn't."

Vaulding smiled. "You mean if he was upset enough to hole up in his apartment and ignore his guests, you didn't want to tangle with him?"

"Oh, Your Honor," Steve said.

Vaulding held up his hands. "I'm sorry. I withdraw the question. No further questions, Mr. Crumbly."

"Does the defense wish to cross-examine?"

Steve Winslow stood up. "I have one or two questions. Mr. Crumbly, you've testified Russ Timberlaine asked you to bid on the gun?"

"That's right."

"*When* did he ask you to do so?"

"Earlier that day."

"Can you be more precise?"

"Yes. It happened that I had brunch with him. I say, it happened, because brunch is served all morning long, but we happened to eat at the same time. And he asked me if I would mind bidding for him."

"Did he tell you why?"

"Of course. He was afraid Burdett would outbid him."

"Tell me, had you ever done this before—bid for Mr. Timberlaine?"

"No."

"Why do you suppose he asked you this particular time?"

"There were two items in the auction Russ particularly wanted. One was a derringer. Russ said Burdett had seen him examining the derringer and knew he wanted it, and was sure to outbid him for it. He figured he'd lost the derringer, and he wanted to make sure the other gun that he wanted didn't get away."

"And you agreed to this deception?"

"Well, I wasn't particularly happy about it. But Russ Timberlaine is a dear and valued friend. I wasn't going to turn him down. I wanted to help him."

"Thank you. No further questions."

"Any redirect, Mr. Vaulding?"

"No, Your Honor."

"This witness is excused. Do you have another witness to call?"

"Yes, Your Honor. Call Melvin Burdett."

When Burdett had taken the stand, Judge Hendrick said, "I remind you that you are still under oath. Proceed, Mr. Vaulding."

"Mr. Burdett, directing your attention to the auction that took place at Russ Timberlaine's mansion on the afternoon of the day of the murder—were you present at this auction?"

"Yes, I was."

"Did you bid on any of the guns?"

"Yes, I did."

"Among the guns you bid on, do you recall a derringer that you outbid Russ Timberlaine for?"

"Yes, I do."

"You purchased that gun?"

"Yes, I did."

"By outbidding Mr. Timberlaine?"

"That's right."

"This auction—did it have an intermission?"

"Yes, it did."

"This derringer you bid on—was that before or after the intermission."

"I think it was before the intermission."

"You're not sure?"

"I think it was, but I couldn't swear to it."

"Well, do you recall another gun you bid on—a cavalry piece, which you also purchased that afternoon?"

"Yes, I do."

"Was that before or after the intermission?"

"That was after."

"Are you sure?"

"Yes, I'm sure."

"Do you know if you bid on that gun before or after you bid on the derringer?"

"After."

"Are you sure?"

"Yes, of course."

"How can you be sure?"

"Because . . . I'm just sure."

Vaulding grinned. "Were you going to say because Russ Timberlaine left right after you bought the gun?"

"Objection."

"Sustained."

"Did you notice when Russ Timberlaine left the auction?"

"Yes, I did."

"When was that?"

"After I bought the gun."

"The cavalry piece?"

"That's right."

"Now, regarding the cavalry piece—when you bought it, who were you bidding against?"

"Hank Crumbly."

"He was the other principal bidder?"

"That's right."

"And you outbid him and bought the gun?"

"That's right."

"And it was immediately after that that Russ Timberlaine left the auction?"

"Yes, it was."

"You noticed that in particular?"

"Yes, I did."

"Why did you notice that in particular?"

"Because I wanted to see how he would react to my buying the gun."

"Why, if you were bidding against Mr. Crumbly?"

"I knew Hank was really bidding for Russ."

"You knew Mr. Crumbly was bidding for Mr. Timberlaine?"

"Of course I did."

"How did you know that?"

"It was perfectly obvious."

"Did anyone tell you Crumbly was bidding for Timberlaine?"

"No."

"Or suggest to you Crumbly might be bidding for Timberlaine?"

"No. Of course not."

"What about the decedent, Jack Potter? You already testified to having several conversations with him that weekend. Were any of those conversations about guns?"

"Of course they were. They all were. He was the gun expert. I was naturally asking him the value of guns."

"But not who was bidding on them?"

Burdett stuck his jaw out. It had been several days since his first appearance in court, and he had obviously made every effort to control himself and prepare a cool and rational answer to that particular question. But his indignation was still quite apparent. "Certainly not," he said evenly. "That would be unethical."

"And in order to bid on guns, you wouldn't do anything unethical."

Burdett exhaled. "Come on, give me a break. In the first place, I wouldn't ask. And if I did, Potter wouldn't tell me. He's a professional. In fact, if someone was making improper inquiries, the first thing Jack Potter would do would be report it to Russ."

"Report to Mr. Timberlaine? Why would he do that?"

"Don't be silly. He was Russ's expert. Russ hired him."

"Russ Timberlaine hired Jack Potter?"

"Of course he did."

"You mean Jack Potter was being paid for being there that weekend?"

"Of course he was. He was working. He was there as the resident expert."

"So Russ Timberlaine had every reason to expect and demand loyalty, not only as a friend but also as an employer?"

"Objection."

"Sustained."

Vaulding, having made his point, smiled at the jury and said, "No further questions."

Steve Winslow stood up. "I have a few questions, Your Honor. Mr. Burdett, you say Jack Potter didn't tell you Timberlaine intended to bid on the gun?"

"Of course not."

"And no one else told you?"

"No, they did not."

"And yet you said you *knew*. Not you thought, not you suspected, not you guessed, you *knew*."

"That's right. I knew."

"How? How did you know?"

"It was obvious."

"That's what you said before. It may be obvious to you, but it's not obvious to me, and it's probably not obvious to the jurors. Could you please explain what you mean? *Why* was it obvious? What convinced you that Henry Crumbly was actually bidding on that gun for Russ Timberlaine?"

"O.K.," Burdett said. "To begin with, I expected Russ to bid on the gun. Even without anybody telling me anything. Just from reading the program description. It was a period piece, it was a collector's item, it had a history. It was just the type of gun he would naturally want. When Russ didn't bid on it, I was surprised. Then when Crumbly started bidding, I knew what had happened."

"How did you know? How could you tell Crumbly wasn't bidding for himself?"

"It was obvious. First off, it wasn't Hank's type of gun. It was a period piece with a history, and Hank and Judy—that's Hank's wife, Mrs. Crumbly—they have a more contemporary collection."

"Second, the price was way out of line. Hank went thirty thousand for the gun. No offense, but the Crumblys don't have that kind of money. That's a good twenty-five thousand more than I've ever seen the man bid for a gun. It did not take a genius to know the man was bidding for someone else. Since I expected Russ to bid on the gun, and since Hank is friendly with Russ, when I say I knew, trust me, I knew."

"I see. So when you say you knew, you don't mean that anyone told you anything? What you mean is you deduced this yourself from your knowledge of the parties involved?"

"Exactly."

"So basically, you knew Crumbly was bidding for Timberlaine because Timberlaine really wanted the gun?"

"That's right."

"And yet you bid against him. Made a point of outbidding him and getting the gun away from him."

"Yes, of course."

"Why? Do you hate him that much?"

"Hate him?" Burdett looked shocked. "Don't be silly. Russ Timberlaine is a gentleman and a collector. I admire and respect him."

"Then why would you go out of your way to thwart and frustrate him in this matter?"

"Are you kidding me? Competition is what it's all about. What do you think an auction is? Why do you think people bid? All right, for some people it's a hobby. For some people it's a job. But to me it's sport. It's a game. And Russ Timberlaine is one of the star players." Burdett smiled. "It's a pleasure to play in the same ballpark with him."

39

VAULDING LED OFF THE AFTERNOON SESSION with Martin Kessington, who even without his white suit and clipboard, still managed to give the impression of being in charge.

"Mr. Kessington," Vaulding began, "are you familiar with the defendant, Russ Timberlaine?"

"Yes, I am."

"How do you know him?"

"He is my employer."

"In what capacity are you employed?"

"I am in charge of his household. I suppose in England you would call me his butler. But I'm actually more than that. In the household, I am his second in command."

"Is that a considerable job?"

Kessington smiled. "Somewhat. Mr. Timberlaine's mansion has forty-eight rooms. He has a staff of fourteen. He likes to entertain, has frequent guests, and often holds auctions or other functions that attract other gun collectors. Most weekends the mansion is full."

"I see. And this particular weekend—how many guests were there?"

"Around fifty."

"They were there for what purpose?"

"They were collectors and dealers invited specifically for the gun auction."

"Which was on Saturday afternoon?"

"That's right."

"Directing your attention to Saturday evening following the auction—did anything out of the ordinary happen then?"

"Yes, indeed."

"Could you tell us what that was?"

"Yes, sir. It was around five-thirty. I was out on the patio with the guests seeing that cocktails were served prior to dinner. I was approached by one of the guests at that time."

"And who might that be?"

"Miss Tracy Garvin."

"Miss Tracy Garvin? You say she was a guest there that weekend?"

"That's right."

"Aside from being a guest, did you know who Miss Garvin was?"

"I knew she was the secretary of Mr. Winslow, the attorney."

"You are referring to Steve Winslow, the defense attorney present in court?"

"That's right."

"He was also a guest there that weekend?"

"Yes, he was."

"And you say his secretary, Miss Garvin, approached you?"

"Yes, she did."

"Without getting into what she said, can you tell us what you did?"

"Yes, sir. I followed her from the patio to the gun room."

"What did you find when you got there?"

"I found Mr. Winslow standing watch over Jack Potter, who was lying dead on the floor."

"Dead?"

Martin Kessington held up his hand. "I take that back. I am not a doctor. It is not my determination to make. He looked dead to me, but I couldn't swear to it."

Vaulding smiled. "Well, let's talk about what you *can* swear to. What, specifically, did you see?"

"I saw the body lying on the floor. The body appeared to me motionless. I went over and looked closely, but could not see any sign of breathing. There was a wound in the head, from which blood had come. I assumed at the time it was a bullet wound, though of course I had no way of knowing for sure."

"What led you to believe this was a bullet wound?"

"There was a gun lying next to the body."

"Can you describe the gun?"

"Certainly. It was a Colt .45 revolver with the initial R carved in the handle."

"You're certain of that?"

"Absolutely."

"Did you touch the gun?"

"No, I did not."

"But you could see the R in the handle?"

"Yes, it was facing up."

"Tell me, had you ever seen that gun before?"

"Objected to as leading and suggestive," Steve Winslow said.

"Sustained," Judge Hendrick said. "Mr. Vaulding, this is an area where for obvious reasons care should be taken not to lead the witness."

"Yes, Your Honor."

"Rephrase your question."

"Yes, Your Honor. Mr. Kessington, at the time that you saw the gun, did you *think* that you recognized it?"

"Yes, I did."

"What did you think you recognized it to be?"

"When I saw the gun, I thought it was a gun from Russ Timberlaine's collection. Specifically, a collector's item, a gun once owned by Pistol Pete Robbins."

"You were familiar with this gun?"

"Yes, I was."

"You had seen the gun before?"

"Yes, I had."

"You are familiar with all of the guns in Russ Timberlaine's collection?"

"No, I am not."

"Why were you familiar with that particular gun?"

"It had been brought to my attention."

"By whom?"

"By Russ Timberlaine."

"Russ Timberlaine brought that gun to your attention?"

"Yes, he did."

"When was that?"

"The week before the murder."

"Can you be more specific?"

"No, I can't. It was on one of the days of the week before the murder. I believe it was toward the beginning of the week. Might have been Monday or Tuesday. Possibly Wednesday."

"At any rate, Russ Timberlaine brought it to your attention?"

"Yes, he did."

"How did that happen?"

"He called me into the gun room and showed me the gun."

"Where was it?"

"In a glass-topped case."

"Was the gun in the case at the time?"

"Actually, the case was open and Russ Timberlaine had taken it out of the case."

"And he showed you the gun?"

"Yes, he did."

"Did he make any statement to you at the time?"

"Yes, sir. He said this was not his gun. He said he believed his gun had been stolen and that this was a duplicate that had been left in its place."

"Why was he pointing this out to you?"

"He wanted to know who could have had the opportunity to have taken the gun. See, the case it was in had been kept locked. Unfortunately, one of the keys to it was kept in the office, which was *not* kept locked."

"Did you point this out to Russ Timberlaine?"

"Yes, I did."

"What did he say?"

"He seemed to think if the gun had been taken, it must have been two weekends before when there had been guests at the mansion. He wanted to know if I had seen anyone going in or out of the office on that occasion who might have taken the key."

"And had you?"

"No, I had not."

"Getting back to the gun that you found lying next to the body—

you said when you saw the gun you first thought it was the original Pistol Pete gun?"

"That's right."

"If I understand your testimony, you knew that that gun had been stolen."

"Yes, I did."

"Then why did you assume that the gun next to the body was the stolen gun and not the one that had been found substituted?"

"From what Mr. Timberlaine said. When he called me in and showed me the substituted gun."

"What was that?"

"He suspected something like this would happen."

That answer was greeted by a loud murmur in the courtroom. Judge Hendrick silenced it with his gavel.

"That was the week before the murder?" Vaulding asked.

"That's right."

"And Russ Timberlaine told you he suspected something like this would happen?"

"Not this exactly, of course."

"Yes, but something similar?"

"Objection."

"Sustained."

"Mr. Kessington, to the best of your recollection, what exactly was it Russ Timberlaine said?"

"He said he was afraid someone had stolen his gun to frame him for a crime. He said, 'What if my gun were found at the scene of a crime? Everybody knows it's my gun. I'd have a devil of a time proving I didn't do it.' "

"I see. So when you saw the gun lying next to the body . . . ?"

"I thought of what Russ Timberlaine said, of course. That's why I immediately thought it was the stolen Pistol Pete gun."

"I see," Vaulding said. "Now, tell me. When you first found the body of Jack Potter, who was there?"

"Mr. Winslow and Miss Garvin."

"As I understand your testimony, she came and got you and brought you to the gun room. When you got back there, who else was there?"

"Just Mr. Winslow."

"The three of you were alone with the body?"

"That's right."

"What happened next?"

"I phoned the police."

"You did?"

"That's right."

"Why you? Why not Mr. Winslow or Miss Garvin?"

"Because it would have been awkward. They didn't have access to a phone."

"Could you explain that?"

"Yes. There are very few outside lines in the Timberlaine mansion. There are phones in the rooms, but they are for internal use only. More like an intercom system. There are very few outside lines."

"Why is that?"

"Mr. Timberlaine used to have a multilined system with regular phones in the rooms. But with so many weekend guests it was almost inevitable that people would abuse the privilege. Having people call California was one thing, but we had people calling Europe. Phone bills were astronomical. So the phones were switched over to an in-house system for the rooms, with only a few select outside lines. I, of course, had access to the one in the office, so I placed the call."

"I see. And that is why you went to call, instead of staying with the body?"

"That's correct."

"And while you went to call, did you take any steps to see that the body was left undisturbed?"

"Yes, I did."

"And what did you do?"

"I left Mr. Winslow and Miss Garvin to watch it."

"You left them alone with the body while you went to call the police?"

"Yes, I did."

"When you finished calling the police, what did you do?"

"I went back to the gun room and waited with Mr. Winslow and Miss Garvin for the police to arrive."

"Mr. Winslow and Miss Garvin were there when you returned?"

"Yes, they were."

"How long were you gone calling the police?"

"Not long. Maybe five minutes."

"When you returned from calling the police, did you look at the body and the gun?"

"Yes, I did."

"Was it just as you had left it?"

"Yes, it was."

Vaulding picked up one of the exhibits, extended it to the witness. "Mr. Kessington, I hand you a gun marked People's Exhibit Three and ask you if you have ever seen it before?"

Kessington took the gun and looked it over. "I can't be sure. It looks like the gun I found next to the body."

"But you can't swear to it?"

"No, I cannot."

"I hand you another gun marked People's Exhibit Four and ask you if you have seen *that* gun before."

"Again, I can't say. It also looks like the gun I found next to the body."

"You can't tell which of these guns that was?"

"No, sir."

"It could have been either of them?"

"That is right."

"I am referring to the gun that you found next to the body when you first discovered the body of Jack Potter. You say that could have been either of these two guns?"

"That's right."

"Then when you returned from calling the police—the gun that you examined on the floor next to Jack Potter at that time—that could have been either of these two guns?"

"That's right."

"You could not say which gun it was?"

"No, I could not."

"In other words, you can't tell these guns apart, can you?"

"No, I cannot."

"It could have been either gun you saw the first time?"

"Yes, it could."

"And it could have been either gun you saw the second time?"

"Yes, it could."

"Can you swear it was the *same* gun you saw both times?"

Kessington frowned. "I think it was."

"But can you swear to it? You say you can't tell the guns apart. Then how could you tell that the gun that you saw when you first entered the room was the same gun that you saw lying there when you returned from calling the police?"

Kessington frowned again. "Actually, I guess I couldn't."

"And you were gone calling the police for how long?"

"About five minutes."

"Who was present in the gun room when you left to call the police?"

"Mr. Winslow and Miss Garvin."

"Who was present in the gun room when you returned from calling the police?"

"Mr. Winslow and Miss Garvin."

"No one else?"

"No one else."

"And you cannot positively identify the gun you saw lying next to the body when you first entered the room? And you do not know whether or not it was the same gun you saw lying there when you returned from calling the police?"

Kessington took a breath. "That's right."

Vaulding smiled. "Thank you. That's all."

40

STEVE WINSLOW SHOOK HIS HEAD. "It's insidious."

"I know," Tracy said. "What can you do about it?"

Steve leaned back in his desk chair, shook his head again. "Nothing. That's the problem. Vaulding's within his rights. Everything Martin said was true. We *were* left alone with the body. And he *can't* tell one gun from another. Two indisputable facts. But taken together in just that way, it's devastating. I mean the son of a bitch is virtually accusing me of switching guns."

"You *did* switch guns."

"Not then."

Steve looked up to find Tracy grinning at him. "All right," he said. "I know it's ironic. But it's not at all the same thing. What he's accusing me of. Or at least insinuating that I'm guilty of. Switching guns with the murder weapon. There's a big difference between doing that and switching guns a couple of days before the murder. In one instance I'm obstructing justice, compounding a felony and conspiring to conceal a crime."

"Right," Tracy said. "And in the other case you're just a good ol' boy switchin' guns."

"There's a huge difference."

"Granted," Tracy said. "But clear something up for me. What would have been the *point* of your switching guns?"

"That's the thing," Steve said. "In the clear light of day, when you think the thing out, not much. But the way things stand, it's a little different. Throughout the whole trial I've been harping on the fact that maybe the cops got the wrong gun. Even in my opening argument—keep your eye on the gun. Then leaning on Lieutenant Sanders about his marking the guns and wasn't it possible he made a mistake. And making the ballistics expert jump through hoops. Always with the insinuation maybe someone mixed up the guns. And here's Vaulding throwing it back in my face—'if anyone switched guns, you're the most likely person to have done it.' "

"Or 'Miss Garvin,' " Tracy mimicked. "Think you could point out I ought to be addressed as Ms.?"

"That's the least of your worries. If they get me for gun switching, you're at least an accessory and most likely an accomplice."

"You still didn't answer my question."

"What question?"

"What did you have to gain by switching guns? For the murder weapon, I mean. The way Vaulding's insinuating. You told me why he's making the argument. That's obvious. But what's *your* motivation? What reason can he give for your doing it?"

"To protect my client, of course. I see the gun lying next to the body and recognize it as Timberlaine's gun. The one he consulted me about. Which the jury already knows about from Donald Walcott's testimony. I send Martin off to call the cops. Then I take the gun, dash upstairs and show it to Timberlaine. Ask him if it's the gun he was wearing at the auction. He says, 'Hell, no, I've got that gun right here.' I tell him he's in deep shit, and ask him for something to scratch up the barrel of the gun. He gives me the rattailed file. I take it, rough up the barrel, swap that gun for his, take his gun back downstairs and plant it next to the body just before Martin gets back from calling the cops."

"Yeah, but why?" Tracy said. "For what reason? What good does all that accomplish?"

"It screws the facts of the case up to the extent that the evidence all comes out cockeyed. It lets me make the arguments I've made against Lieutenant Sanders and this ballistics expert. It lets me imply the cops are the ones who screwed the evidence up. If the cops screwed the evidence up, there's no way Vaulding gets a conviction, and my client goes free."

Tracy frowned. "Yeah, but . . ."

"But what?"

"That still doesn't make sense."

"Why not?"

"Because in that case the cops got the wrong gun."

"What do you mean?"

"Well, no, they don't. They've got the murder weapon. It was in Timberlaine's holster. And it's there because you put it there. After scratching it up with the rattailed file. But that would mean that gun was the gun originally found next to the body. Before you switched it. Right?"

"This is getting very messy," Steve said. "We really should have a map with push pins, you know?"

"Stick with me a moment. This one's simple. If you swapped the gun next to the body for Timberlaine's gun, and that's how the gun in Timberlaine's holster turned out to be the murder weapon, that would mean the gun we originally found next to the body was the duplicate, and the gun in Timberlaine's holster that you swapped it for, the gun he was walking around with all day, would be the original Pistol Pete Robbins gun."

"Yeah. So?"

"It doesn't add up at all. How do you explain that Timberlaine's 'got the real thing, baby,' instead of the can of Coke?"

"Commercials? You're throwing commercials at me?"

"You know what I mean. If the real gun was stolen, how did Timberlaine get it back?"

"We've only got his word for that. If he made it up, then he's got both guns, and he can plant them wherever he pleases."

"In which case he'd be guilty of the murder."

"Exactly."

Tracy gave him a look.

Steve cocked his head. "Sweetheart, in those books you read the client is always innocent. Otherwise there'd be no book. It doesn't always work out that way. Believe it or not, occasionally a person is accused of a crime because he actually did it."

"You think Timberlaine's guilty?"

"No, I don't. But when you start trying to explain facts away and negate theories, if you want to dismiss guilty motives as possible explanations, you're really narrowing your sights."

Tracy frowned. "Yeah, I know."

"And," Steve said. "You have to take into account the fact that, since Timberlaine came to call on us and laid this story in front of us with all due candor, we have found out he neglected to tell us that he had purchased an identical gun."

"Right."

"So, naive as Timberlaine may seem to be, we still have to consider what if that's at least partly an act. For instance, what if Timberlaine wanted to kill Potter for some other reason, something that hasn't come out yet? What does Timberlaine do? He sets up a reason for him to kill Potter that won't hold water. That is on its face absurd. See what I'm saying? *He* employs the moron factor. He goes through the elaborate routine of having Crumbly bid against Burdett on a gun, knowing that Burdett will realize Crumbly is bidding for him and outbid him. And then pretend he's angry at Jack Potter for letting the information out. It's a ridiculous motive that won't stand much scrutiny. You heard Burdett say it wasn't the type of gun Crumbly would bid on, and he'd never bid that high anyway. Timberlaine had to know that. So the deception *had* to fail. And even with circumstantial evidence against him, how can you convict him of murder with a motive as shaky as that?"

"Good lord," Tracy said. "Do you really think that's true?"

"Of course not. He's my client, and I think he's innocent."

"Fine," Tracy said without enthusiasm. "That's convincing as all hell. Look, can we go back to the gun switching a moment?"

"Which gun switching?"

"Yeah, right. Vaulding's theory. You and I find the murder weapon, Martin goes for the cops, you grab the gun and run up-stairs."

"What about it?"

"You said Timberlaine gives you the file to rough up the gun."

"Right. So?"

"Where did he get the file?"

"It was there in his room."

"Why?"

"Because there wasn't time for him to get it from anywhere else."

"I know that," Tracy said. "That's just the point. There *wasn't* time, and there's no reason why he'd have that file in his room, so it couldn't have happened."

"But the file *was* in his room. It may not make any sense, but it was. Timberlaine even admits it was. He claims he found it."

"Yeah, but you're not going to let him say so on the witness stand. And this is Vaulding's theory, so how's he gonna prove it?"

"He doesn't have to prove it. He just has to plant the insinuation in the mind of the jury."

"Yeah, but it still has to make sense. The theory is Timberlaine had the file and gave it to you to rough up the gun?"

"Sure."

"And why did you do that?"

"So they couldn't match up the fatal bullet."

"Yeah, well then you made a bad job of it. Because they *still* matched up the fatal bullet."

"I was in a hurry. I had to work fast."

"Yeah, but still—"

Mark Taylor burst into the room.

"Got it, Steve!"

"Got what?"

"My operative's back. I got the name of the collector."

"Thank God for that. Who is he?"

"You're a sexist pig again."

"What?"

Taylor grinned. "The collector's a woman."

"For Christ's sake, Mark."

"Sorry. I couldn't resist."

"Maybe not, but—Oh, shit."

"What?"

"Don't tell me the collector's Felicia Ebersol?"

"Who?"

"Didn't you question her? You know. That friend of Timberlaine's."

"I'm afraid you're a sexist pig again."

"What the hell?"

"Thinking there's only one woman collector. Well, it's not her. This collector's name is Veronica Dreisson."

"Can I talk to her?"

"Would you want to?"

"Actually, yes. My instinct is to bury her, but as an attorney, I want to make sure her rights are protected."

"That's what I wanted to ask you about."

"What?"

"She's in California."

"Oh?"

"Yeah. And she's comin' back tomorrow. I was wondering if some business or other might induce her to stay over?"

Steve gave him a look.

Taylor shrugged. "Just a thought."

"No, Mark, let her come back. I want to talk to her when she gets here."

Taylor looked concerned. "You gonna put her on the stand and drop a bombshell by bringing in the other gun?"

"I wouldn't do that unless I absolutely had to."

"That does not cheer me."

"Right now that looks like a sucker play."

"That does." Taylor took a breath. "I certainly don't want you to tell me anything you don't want to tell me."

"What does that mean, Mark?"

"This morning you produced a gun in court."

"Naturally. I'm not going to defy a subpoena."

"Now I know you don't want to tell me anything or you already would have, but I was just thinking."

"What was that, Mark?"

"I was thinking—hypothetically speaking, of course—but wouldn't it be nice if that gun you produced was the gun that Timberlaine originally gave you? The one I tested the bullets from. The one you substituted for the one I bought. The one that's been sitting in your safe ever since. Because in that event, the bullets you gave them would conveniently match the gun you gave them. And the gun you got from Timberlaine's safe-deposit box—my gun—would now be sitting in your safe where no one would ever think of looking for it. And no one would ever find it, unless you yourself, for some perverse reason, brought it into the case. But barring that, no one would ever ask anything about that gun, because no one would ever know that it even existed. And to all intents and purposes, it never would have existed, because the evidence would all be back in order, and the guns and bullets would all match up. And yours truly would be off the proverbial hook.

"Well," Taylor said. "What do you think of that?"

Steve smiled. "Well," he said. "Hypothetically speaking, I hope you're right."

Mark Taylor looked at him. "Are you telling me you did that?"

"Of course I'm not telling you that."

"Too bad," Taylor said. "It would sure take the pressure off. Particularly with Vaulding pointing out you had the opportunity of switching guns."

"Oh, you caught that?"

"I sure did."

"Then it's a cinch everybody else in court did too."

Taylor winced. "Hey, thanks a lot."

Steve grinned. "Just getting back at you for the sexist stuff."

"I was kidding."

"Yeah, well you hit a nerve. Tracy just got through needling me to get on Vaulding's case to get him to call her Ms."

Taylor grinned. "Are you kidding me?"

"I'm kidding too," Tracy said, "but the fact is, the son of a bitch should."

"Maybe so," Taylor said. "But if I were you I wouldn't push it. Kind of a low priority." He shrugged. "I mean, hell, if I can just get out of this damn case without being charged with anything, the D.A. can call me any damn thing he likes."

41

PHILIP MANNING DID NOT LOOK COMFORTABLE on the witness stand. He shifted position, tugged at his collar, elevated his chin. His actions gave him a somewhat defiant appearance. In view of Judge Hendrick's admonition not to communicate his findings to the prosecution, his attitude created the impression that pressure had probably been put on him to do exactly that.

Vaulding didn't look too pleased either. He frowned, looked around the courtroom, then turned to confront the witness.

"Now, Mr. Manning. Yesterday you were furnished with additional materials, People's Exhibits Five-A and -B and People's Exhibit Six, and instructed to perform certain tests on them. Have you completed those tests?"

"Yes, I have."

"Have you communicated the results of those tests to me?"

"No, I have not."

"Or to anyone else?"

"No, sir."

"Are you prepared to do so now?"

"Yes, I am."

"Fine. Regarding the gun, People's Exhibit Six, were either of these new bullets, People's Exhibit Five-A or People's Exhibit Five-B, fired by that gun?"

"Yes, sir. The bullet, People's Exhibit Five-B—the one from the tube marked RT-SUB—came from the gun, People's Exhibit Six."

"There is no question in your mind?"

"None whatsoever. And what's more—"

Vaulding held up his hand. "One moment, Mr. Manning. There are enough guns and bullets that this is rather confusing. Let's try to take it in an orderly manner. That accounts for the bullet, People's Exhibit Five-B. What about the bullet, People's Exhibit Five-A? The one marked RT-ORIG? Did you determine what gun that bullet came from?"

"Yes, sir."

"What gun was that?"

"It came from the gun, People's Exhibit Three."

"The original Pistol Pete Robbins gun found by the body?"

"I have no knowledge as to that. I only know that bullet came from that gun."

"You compared it to a test bullet under the comparison microscope?"

"Yes, I did."

"The barrel of that gun was not defaced, so the bullets are absolutely identical?"

"Yes, they are." Manning cleared his throat. "With regard to that—"

Vaulding held up his hand again. "Please, Mr. Manning. You'll have your say, but I need all these matters cleared up. Now, two days ago you were asked to compare a bullet from the gun, People's Exhibit Three, to a bullet from the gun, People's Exhibit Four, in order to show how many similarities you could find. Did you perform that test?"

"Yes, I did."

"Did the bullets compare?"

"No, they did not. They came from separate guns."

"But the new bullet, People's Exhibit Five-A, did come from the gun, People's Exhibit Three?"

"Yes, it did."

"And the bullet, People's Exhibit Five-B, came from the gun, People's Exhibit Six?"

"Yes, it did."

"Neither of these new bullets came from the gun, People's Exhibit Four?"

"No, they didn't. However—"

"Yes?" Vaulding said. "What is it, Mr. Manning?"

Manning cleared his throat again. "I had hoped that one of these new bullets would prove to have come from the gun, People's Exhibit Four, since it could only have done so prior to the murder, and therefore prior to the time the barrel of the gun had been defaced, and would therefore be a test bullet with which we could make an absolute match. Unfortunately, that was not the case. Nonetheless, as I was instructed to compare all these exhibits against each other, I did attempt to match up these new bullets with test bullets from the gun, People's Exhibit Four. I was unable to do so."

"Naturally," Vaulding said.

"No, not naturally," Manning said. "You see, both bullets lined up in some regard due to the class characteristics. Which made comparison hard, since I had to allow for the tampering done by the file."

"But the bullets did not match?"

"No, they did not. And with bullet Five-A, this was readily apparent. Only one class characteristic lined up.

"Bullet Five-B proved more difficult. In attempting to align the bullets, I was able to find three points of similarity."

Vaulding frowned. "Three?"

"That is correct. That is the same number that I found in comparing a test bullet from the gun, People's Exhibit Four, with the fatal bullet, People's Exhibit One."

Vaulding held up his hand. "Wait a minute." He blinked his eyes, and in that moment his face betrayed the fact that he could feel his case slipping away from him. But he had no choice other than to go on. "Let me be sure I understand this," he said. "Are you saying that because you found three points of similarity between this new bullet from this new gun, People's Exhibit Six, and a test bullet fired from the gun, People's Exhibit Four—are you saying this weakens your identification of the gun, People's Exhibit Four, being the gun that fired the fatal bullet?"

Manning shook his head. He took a breath. "I'm afraid it goes a little deeper than that. You must understand. I was dealing with a gun that had been defaced. With bullets to which additional scratches had been added. I was trying to work around that. I was giving you a professional opinion based on the best information that could be gathered from the materials I had to work with at the time. I—"

Vaulding held up his hand. His face was hard. "Mr. Manning. Let me be sure I understand this. Are you now testifying that in light of this evidence you have *reversed* your opinion? That it is now your opinion that the gun, People's Exhibit Four, did *not* fire the fatal bullet?"

"That is correct."

Vaulding was incensed. "Well, how can you do that, Mr. Manning? Two days ago you testified positively that this *was* the gun that fired the fatal bullet. It's one thing to say that this new evidence creates some *doubt* as to the finding. But it's something else to retract your testimony and now state positively that this gun did *not* fire that bullet."

"I have no other choice. I now have indisputable evidence to the contrary."

Vaulding stared at him. "And how can that be?"

"From the new evidence." Manning took a breath. "As I would have told you to begin with," he said with some exasperation, "if you'd just asked me to state my findings, instead of insisting on putting everything in order. But as it happens, I know the bullet didn't come from the gun, People's Exhibit Four, because I now have a match for the fatal bullet. You see, when the bullet from the gun, People's Exhibit Six, showed the same points of similarity with a bullet from the gun, People's Exhibit Four, as that bullet had shown with the fatal bullet, I next put the bullet from People's Exhibit Six and the fatal bullet under the comparison microscope. And they match absolutely. That's how I know the fatal bullet didn't come from the gun, People's Exhibit Four. There's no question about it. The fatal bullet came from this new gun, People's Exhibit Six."

42

STEVE WINSLOW COULDN'T SIT STILL. He kept flinging himself around his office, practically bouncing off the walls.

"Take it easy," Tracy said.

Steve wheeled on her. "Easy? You're telling me to take it easy? I just framed my own client!"

"It's not that bad."

"No? How is it not that bad? It's exactly what happened."

"You didn't frame your own client."

"Sure I did. I substituted guns on him and handed the murder weapon over to the D.A."

"I don't know how that happened."

"You and me both. But the fact is, I did. It puts me in a hell of a position. Not to mention the position I put my client in. And what makes it worse is, he doesn't even know it. He must *suspect* it. He knows *something* happened. I mean, the poor son of a bitch is sitting there in court. As far as he knows, People's Exhibit Six is the gun he put in the safe-deposit box—a gun he knows *for sure* couldn't have committed the crime, because it's been locked in a safe-deposit box from the time I gave it back to him to the time I got it out of that box and brought it into court. From his point of view, there's no way that gun could have anything to do with the murder. Then, kick in the chops, it does! And the one explanation as far as Timberlaine is concerned, is his attorney switched guns and framed him."

"He can't think that."

"What else *can* he think? And he's right. The fucker's head must be coming off trying to figure out *why* I framed him, but he's gotta know I *did*."

Tracy shook her head. "Jesus Christ."

"And there's no way to straighten it out," Steve said. "Even if I wanted to take the rap for this—which I sure as hell don't— but even if I wanted to beat my breasts and come clean, march into court and say, 'Pardon me, Your Honor. Excuse me, Mr. Vaulding, but I can straighten this out. The reason the gun and bullets match up is it's not really Mr. Timberlaine's gun, I switched guns on him'—well, nobody in the whole fucking court- room is going to believe me. They'd think it was a stupid story I was making up in a desperate attempt to account for the fact that my client had the gun. They'd also think I was a total moron for trying to claim *I* had the gun. And I'd have to agree with 'em there."

"Granted that is not the smooth move," Tracy said. Steve gave her a sharp look and she held up her hand. "But the fact is, you got a kick in the chops just as much as Timberlaine did. And for the same reason. You're sitting in court, and as far as you know, there's no way in hell People's Exhibit Six fired the fatal shot." She smiled. "I believe it was just last night you told me that was the one thing in this case you knew for sure. Then it blew up in your face. You're blaming yourself for not anticipating that? No lawyer in the world could have anticipated that."

"That doesn't help."

"I know it doesn't help. But if you don't mind the question, what the hell happened?"

"What do you mean?"

"With the gun and the bullet?"

"It's the fatal bullet. It's the fatal gun. A slight physical impossi- bility, but there you are."

"Yeah. So what's the explanation?"

"Are you trying to piss me off?"

"No, I'm trying to get your opinion on the problem. I have a feeling you could think your way out of anything, if you weren't emotionally involved."

"Thanks for your support."

"Don't mention it. Hey, you got a right to be pissed. Let's get beyond it and figure out what the hell happened to you."

"Hey," Steve said. "You think I haven't been trying to do that?"

"I'm sure you have. I just think you're too emotionally involved to think straight."

"And you feel that simply telling me that will enable me to do so?" Steve said sarcastically.

She shrugged. "No, but at this point things are so fucked up, I figure it couldn't hurt."

Steve shook his head. "You got me there. You're absolutely right. There's nothing I can do at this point that can make it any worse. There's a certain consolation in that."

He looked at Tracy and started laughing. So did she, and they were both laughing hysterically when Mark Taylor walked in the door.

"What the hell is this?" he said.

"Tracy found the silver lining," Steve said.

"Oh, yeah? What's that?"

"The case is now so totally fucked up, there's absolutely nothing we could do that could make it any worse."

"You could drag in the other gun," Taylor said.

Steve looked at him, sobered up, snapped his fingers. "Son of a bitch," he said.

Mark Taylor's eyes widened in alarm. "Hey, hey, I was only kidding. You wouldn't do that, would you?"

"Right now, Mark, I don't know *what* I might do."

"Steve. I mean, think what you're doing."

Steve Winslow held up his hand. "Take it easy, Mark. I'm not doing anything right now. I'm just exploring possibilities. All we got left is possibilities."

"It seems to me, all we got left is *im*possibilities," Taylor said.

"Ain't that the truth."

"And that bullet matchin' up," Taylor said. "I don't know what gun you gave them—and I sure as hell don't *want* to know—but think about it and the mind boggles. I mean, unless there's another gun in this case I don't know about—and there're already *way* too many guns in this case—the gun you produced was either the gun Timberlaine kept locked in his safe-deposit box, or the gun you kept locked in the safe. In either case, neither gun could have done it. And yet one did."

"Thank you for your assessment of the situation," Steve said.

"Hey, I have to call 'em as I see 'em," Taylor said. "Now, I know this makes problems for you, but doesn't it make problems for Vaulding too?"

"What do you mean?"

"Well, as far as he's concerned, you gave him the gun from Timberlaine's safe-deposit box. And Timberlaine's been in jail since the murder. There's no way he was out switching guns around. If you gave them the gun from Timberlaine's safe-deposit box, how the hell can Vaulding claim that gun committed the murder? See what I'm saying?"

"Yeah, I do, Mark. Unfortunately, it doesn't wash."

"Why not?"

" 'Cause Vaulding only has my word for it that that's where that gun came from." Steve raised his hand. "And never mind maybe I substituted a gun. Think like Vaulding. Assume I didn't. Assume I'm giving him the gun he asked for, the gun Timberlaine had. Now, Timberlaine and I can *claim* that gun's been in a safe-deposit box since well before the murder and I just got it out, but he's only got our word for that. For all he knows, I could have told Timberlaine we had to produce the gun, and he could have said, 'Oh, all right. After the murder I hid it in the shrubbery out behind my mansion. Go get it.' "

Mark Taylor's eyes widened. "Son of a bitch."

"See, Mark. Even without any substitution, Timberlaine can't *prove* he put a gun in that safe-deposit box and I can't prove I took one out. Which is too bad, 'cause if we could, the gun would theoretically have an alibi for the murder."

"And the gun you gave him *does*," Taylor said. "That's the mind-fuck. We're talking informally here, so I'm going to assume you gave him the gun from the safe. In fact, I *know* you gave him the gun from the safe, because Manning matched a bullet from it with the test bullet, RT-SUB. And that gun's been in your safe since before the murder. You know and I know that gun wasn't used for the murder. Unless someone got into your office and rifled the safe."

"It's been done before," Tracy pointed out.

"Yeah, but not this time," Steve said. "I mean, come on, give me a break. The murderer deduces that I have a gun in the safe. He breaks in and steals it, uses it to commit the murder. Now, never mind all the *other* duplicate guns he plants all over the place. The point is, after the murder, he breaks in again and replaces it in my safe."

"Farfetched, but not impossible," Taylor said.

"Oh, yeah? How does he know the gun's there to begin with?"

"Timberlaine could know, if he figured out you switched guns. Suppose he noticed the difference?"

"So he breaks in and steals it?"

"It's possible."

"Yeah, but how does he get it back in the safe after the murder? He's been in jail ever since."

"True," Taylor said. "Well, he could have an accomplice."

"Who, his daughter? Like father, like daughter, and the Timberlaines actually come from a long line of murdering safecrackers?"

Taylor frowned. "That does seem a bit much."

"No shit."

"So what's the answer?" Taylor said. "What the hell *did* happen?"

Steve exhaled. "We're getting dangerously close to Sherlock Holmes territory here."

"What do you mean?"

"At least, I think it's Holmes. You know the bit about once you've eliminated the impossible, what's left, however improbable, has to be true? Or something to that effect."

Taylor frowned. "What the hell does that mean?"

"It means there has to be an explanation for People's Exhibit Six being the murder gun. Or, more precisely, there has to be an explanation for the fact the fatal bullet came from that gun."

"Would it surprise you to hear I can't come up with one?"

"No, it wouldn't, Mark. What about your expert?"

"Who?"

"The gun collector. The woman. Is she here yet?"

"Yeah. As a matter of fact, she's in my office. I was wondering if you'd want to see her."

"I sure do."

43

VERONICA DREISSON WAS A BIT OF A SURPRISE. A frail, emaciated, white-haired woman, she looked more like someone's kindly but fragile great-grandmother than someone who dealt in guns, and try as he would, Steve Winslow could not imagine her holding one. When Mark Taylor had completed the introductions, Steve smiled and said, "So, you're the gun expert?"

Veronica Dreisson's eyes twinkled and her smile was mischievous. "You sound as if you didn't believe me."

"Oh, I believe you all right. I just want to make sure."

"I'm not surprised. People often have trouble relating to an old lady gun expert."

"Guilty as charged," Steve said, "If I'm going to be hung for a sexist pig, it might as well be for just cause."

"That would be hardly just," Veronica said. "Women have trouble relating to me too."

"I have trouble relating to *anything* right now," Steve said. "I'm sorry. I don't mean to skimp on the amenities, but at the moment I have more problems than you could believe."

"So I understand. I only hope I haven't done anything to add to them."

"So do I. I assume Mark Taylor has given you a rundown of the present situation?"

"Oh, yes. He's really been most helpful." Veronica favored Mark Taylor with a smile, which he returned somewhat sheepishly.

"That's good," Steve said. "I was wondering if we could come to some sort of understanding."

"I don't see what there is to understand," Veronica said. "I gather you are trying a murder case." She shrugged and smiled. "But that's your business. As far as I'm concerned, any guns Mr. Taylor may have purchased are entirely coincidental and not to be inferred."

Steve grinned. "Miss—I'm sorry. Tell me. Is it Mrs., Miss, or Ms.?"

"It's Veronica."

"Veronica, I think you and I are going to get along. At the moment I happen to have a little problem involving guns, and I'm hoping you can help me out."

"In what way?"

"I'm confronted with a physical impossibility. The prosecution just matched up a gun with the fatal bullet. And there's no way that gun fired that bullet."

Veronica opened her mouth to speak.

Steve held up his hand. "I know, I know. Ballistics says it did. So let me rephrase that. There's no way that gun was used to commit the crime. At the time of the murder, that gun *was not available*. It could not have been used."

Veronica frowned. "What are you saying?"

"Exactly that. There's no reason for you to know the circumstances—in fact it's better if you *don't* know—but take it as a given that that gun did not commit the crime. That we know for sure. So we have a series of seemingly contradictory statements here. We need to resolve them. This is where I need your expertise."

"In what way?"

"Listen carefully. Here are certain things we know to be true. One, the gun fired the fatal bullet. We know that from the markings on it. We can identify it absolutely as coming from the gun. Two, the fatal bullet is the cause of death. We know that from the autopsy. It was removed from the head of the decedent and identified by the medical examiner as the sole cause of death. And three, the gun, People's Exhibit Six, could *not* have fired that bullet into the head of the decedent, because it was not available at the time of the murder."

Veronica nodded. "An out-and-out contradiction."

"Exactly."

"So some of your data must be wrong."

"If so I would love to have it pointed out to me."

"The ballistics expert could be in error. The medical examiner could be in error. Or there could have been a substitution of bullet or gun at some point down the line."

Steve Winslow nodded. "True, and I've taken those things into consideration. Frankly, I don't see how any of them could have happened."

"So?"

"So, I'm eliminating the impossible and dealing with the improbable."

Veronica frowned. "You'll pardon me if that's not entirely clear."

"Yeah, I know. I'm saying, assume those things didn't happen. Assume the following are true: the bullet came from the gun, the bullet killed the victim, the gun was not there at the time of the murder." Steve shrugged. "That leaves us with an insoluble problem."

"It certainly does," Veronica said. "So what do you expect me to do about it?"

"Solve it."

44

THE PHONE BEGAN RINGING while Steve Winslow was still unlocking his apartment door. He cursed his deadbolt, a necessity in a New York City apartment, even in that relatively respectable section of Greenwich Village. Steve threw open the door, fumbled for the light switch on the wall, missed it, spotted the phone across the room in the faint street light coming through the window, and, spurred on by another insistent ring, decided to go for it. Predictably, he barked his shin on the coffee table, cursed loudly, lunged across the room, grabbed the phone and picked it up.

"Finally," Taylor said. "I've been callin' you for hours."

"I took Tracy out to dinner. What's up?"

"We blew it."

"What?"

"The whole assignment. We fucked it up somehow."

"How is that possible? Carrie Timberlaine set it up."

"Yeah, that part was fine. I took Veronica out there, Carrie let us in. She didn't have the keys to the gun cases, but that guy Martin did, and he let us in and Veronica did her stuff."

"What's wrong with that?"

"Someone tipped the cops. Lieutenant Sanders showed up, mad as hell, wanting to know what the hell was going on."

"Did you tell him?"

"Am I stupid? Carrie Timberlaine stepped in, told him she was

254

having her father's gun collection appraised, and what the hell business was it of his?"

"That go over big?"

"What do you think? At that time of night? The long and the short of it is he kept us tied up there until Vaulding could rush over a subpoena."

"He subpoenaed you?"

"No, her. Veronica, I mean. She's to appear in court tomorrow morning."

"You don't sound happy, Mark."

"Happy, hell. The one person in the world I didn't want involved in this case. The one person in the world I didn't want the cops to find. And what's the upshot? Tomorrow morning at ten o'clock she's witness for the prosecution."

"There's a saving grace."

"What's that?"

"Vaulding won't know what to ask her."

"He'll ask her *everything*. Jesus Christ, Steve. You think he's not going to ask her about guns?"

"That doesn't mean he'll ask her about *your* gun."

"I was there. He may ask her why."

"You're getting worked up over nothing, Mark."

"I'm glad to hear it. I've been going slightly nuts. I've been trying to reach you for the last two hours."

"I told you. I took Tracy out to dinner. I just dropped her off."

"Good for you. I haven't had dinner yet, and I don't think I could eat a thing."

"Where are you?"

"Back in the office. When I couldn't reach you, I told the switchboard to keep trying and drove back to town. Good thing I did."

"Why?"

" 'Cause there's a lot coming in. As you might expect, considering the bombshell Vaulding dropped today. That was just this morning. Now that he's grabbed your expert off, you wouldn't believe what they're saying."

"Who?"

"The cops. The press. There's a lot of speculation going on, but the bottom line is plea-bargain."

"Is that on the level?"

"Absolutely. Wanna hear how they figure?"

"Not really, but I guess I better."

"O.K. Here's the latest line. After Manning's bombshell today you got an adjournment to see if you wanna cross-examine. Tomorrow morning he's first up on the stand. The best the cops and the press can figure, the bit with Veronica was a last-ditch effort to come up with something you can use to cross-examine—your expert against theirs, see? That's why you sent her out there to look at the guns."

"So, the way everyone sees it, Manning's the barometer. You either take him on or else."

"Or else what?"

"If you can't shake Manning's testimony, particularly if you decline to cross-examine, it's all over. It means the case is hopeless and the next order of business is, you ask for a recess to confer with Vaulding over a possible plea-bargain."

"Sounds like they've written the whole scenario."

"They sure have. The next thing that happens is, Vaulding turns you down flat because he's holding every ace in the deck. He's got your expert, he's got your client and he's got you. Vaulding laughs in your face, goes back into court and puts Veronica Dreisson on the stand. At which point I'm diving for the nearest hurricane cellar."

Steve Winslow took a breath, then exhaled noisily. "Well," he said, "thanks for calling."

45

Judge Hendrick was experiencing a severe case of déjà vu. He had just held up and displayed yet another set of newspaper headlines, and discussed the serving of yet another subpoena on yet another surprise witness. Now, with the jury in place, he turned to the witness stand to see—who else?—ballistics expert, Philip Manning.

Judge Hendrick raised his eyebrows, cocked his head, said dryly, "Well, well, Mr. Manning."

That remark broke the tension in the courtroom, and was greeted with a burst of laughter. It was brief, and for good reason. After the events of the day before, the expectation was high that this was the day the prosecution was going for the kill.

"Mr. Manning," Judge Hendrick said. "Once again I must remind you that you are still under oath. When we left off yesterday, Mr. Vaulding had just completed his direct examination. Mr. Winslow. Your witness."

Steve Winslow stood up. He looked at the witness, paused a moment, then looked up at the judge. "I have no questions, Your Honor."

That announcement produced a rumble in the courtroom, particularly among members of the press. This was confirming their expectations. As a result, anticipation was high.

"Very well," Judge Hendrick said. He turned to the witness. "Mr. Manning, this is a bit of an event. You are excused, sir."

Manning smiled. "Thank you, Your Honor."

Judge Hendrick turned to Vaulding. "Call your next witness."

Steve Winslow was still on his feet. "Before he does, Your Honor," Steve said, "I would like to ask for a brief recess."

This created another rumble in the courtroom, which Judge Hendrick stifled with his gavel.

Judge Hendrick looked down at Steve Winslow and frowned. "Mr. Winslow," he said. "I adjourned court yesterday to allow you to decide if you wished to cross-examine the witness. You elected not to do so. You must have known that when you came into court this morning. Therefore, it seems to me you have had adequate opportunity to confer with your client if you wished to do so."

"Granted, Your Honor," Steve said. "But I do not need to confer with my client."

"Then why do you want a recess?"

"I would like a recess, Your Honor," Steve said, "in order to confer with Mr. Vaulding."

That opened the floodgates. Before the recess was even declared, the courtroom was abuzz with activity as reporters raced for the phones.

46

District Attorney Robert Vaulding's smile was ice-cold. "I appreciate your position," he said. "And I hope you appreciate mine. At the present time, I see no reason not to let this case go to the jury."

"Perhaps I can change your mind," Steve said.

"Very unlikely," Vaulding said. "The way things stand right now, the only plea I'd consider accepting would be guilty to the present charge."

"Who's talking plea?" Steve said.

"I thought you were."

"Well, think again. At the moment, I'm merely exploring possibilities."

"You may be exploring them," Vaulding said, "but I can tell you they are *not* possibilities."

"All right, look, Vaulding," Steve said. "Let's back up and start over. Just for the time being, do me a big favor by pretending you actually believe I came here to talk rather than plead my client out."

"I fail to see the point," Vaulding said.

"You'll never see it if you don't get beyond your current position. Now then, stop denying your inclination to listen to a plea-bargain, and it may dawn on you you're not hearing one."

"What *am* I hearing?"

"You subpoenaed my expert, Veronica Dreisson."

"That I did."

"When we go back into court, do you intend to put her on the stand?"

"I most certainly do."

"What do you expect her to testify to?"

"I see no reason to disclose that in advance."

"You'll have to, if I charge you with abuse of process. You'll have to state what you intend to prove."

"Yes, but I don't think you're going to do that."

"Why not?"

"As much as you might love to do that, as much as you might feel you'd have a chance of embarrassing me, maybe even of making the charge stick, I'm gambling right now you wouldn't be that keen on giving me the opportunity of making a speech."

"So, you thought of that," Steve said.

Vaulding shrugged. "Hey, give me a break. Considering the case, my opening argument was sketchy at best. We've had half a hundred twists in the evidence since then. None of which benefit your client. You think I wouldn't love to stand up and summarize that evidence under the guise of stating what I intend to prove? It's just you and me talking here, Winslow, but you think I wouldn't take that shot if I got it? The jury won't hear me, but the press sure will. And just between you and me, there are a lot more voters read the paper than sit on that jury."

"Gee, that never occurred to me," Steve said.

"I'll bet," Vaulding said. "You wanna know my intention? My intention is to go straight back into court and call Miss Veronica Dreisson to the stand."

"Now, there's another thing," Steve said, "that I promised my secretary I'd take up with you."

Vaulding frowned. "What?"

"The word Miss. These days it's Ms. But that can wait. Right now I'd like to stop you from making a big mistake."

"Thanks for your concern."

"Listen," Steve said. "Remember when you first called me into your office? You told me about your talk with Dirkson. And you said you didn't necessarily buy his line."

"This is true, and I don't. But the situation is a little different here. Your client's guilty and that's the bottom line. Your client's guilty six ways from Sunday. He bought the murder gun, for Christ's sakes."

"That remains to be proven."

Vaulding waved it away. "Oh, sure, sure. By the time you get him on the witness stand, I'm sure you'll have thought up some great explanation. But it's no go. You know and I know he bought it. You know and I know he's guilty. Now I don't care if there's some technicality, some legal loophole, some circuitous route by which you think you could get around all that and get your client off. If you can, bully for you, but I'll take my shot. He's guilty and I'm not giving ground. I got enough to nail him, so that's what I'm gonna do."

"Can we get back to your phone call with Dirkson?"

"What's that got to do with anything?"

"You say you don't buy his line, but it's different this time because my client's guilty. Now, assuming there ever *was* a phone call from Dirkson—assuming that wasn't just a ploy to keep me in your office while you served the search warrant and grabbed the file—"

Vaulding's eyes's flicked momentarily, but he maintained his superior smile.

"Assuming you actually spoke to Dirkson," Steve said. "He may have told you I'm tricky, I'm fast, I pull unorthodox shit in court, you gotta watch out for me, I'm dramatic, I'll grandstand, I'll steal the press—that's just for starters and I'm sure Dirkson could do a better job of it.

"But there's one thing I'll bet he didn't say—that I ever sold him a bill of goods. Now, you can call him and ask him if you want, but here's what he'll have to say."

Steve held up two fingers. "I talked to him two times during a case. Like I'm talking to you. One time he listened. As I advised, he dismissed the case, called in the press and took the credit. The other time he didn't listen. That case blew up on him in court." Steve shrugged. "Tough break. But in both cases, he'd have to admit I gave him the straight goods."

"Yeah, but it's different," Vaulding said. "Those clients were innocent."

Steve sighed. "We're talking in circles here. Forget the innocent or guilty for a moment. I know that's hard for you to do, but, hell, you're an elected official. Think newspaper headlines. You've been getting 'em, all right, but they aren't the kind that win elections. What you need here is a victory."

Vaulding frowned. "What are you talking about?"

"We're separating the men from the boys here, Vaulding. This case is gonna break, and it's gonna break soon. When it does, there's gonna be a huge amount of publicity. My question right now is where you fit into it. Would that be the front-page picture of the grinning D.A. expounding his theory of the case? Or is your name only going to be seen by the people who turn to the inside page and read the one-line blurb, 'District Attorney Robert Vaulding could not be reached for comment'?"

Vaulding stared at him. "What the hell are you talking about?"

"I'm making you an offer. It is a limited offer. Today's special. In fact, it is a one-time-only offer. When we walk out of here that offer will be withdrawn. Frankly, I don't expect you to take it, but I make it anyway. So when this is all over and you're licking your wounds and feeling all pissed off over what a slick son of a bitch I turned out to be, you'll have to admit I gave you your chance.

"The best I can do is offer. What you do after that is entirely up to you. But here's the situation. We're at an impasse. You can either walk into court right now, put my expert on the stand and give her a thorough grilling. Or you can take a deep breath, put your prejudices aside and listen to what I have to say. And I have to tell you, right now I'm so fed up with this case, I don't really care which."

Steve shrugged.

"O.K. Your move. What's it gonna be?"

47

Robert Vaulding's face was grim. He looked around the courtroom at the spectators, the reporters, the jurors, the judge, and finally up at the elderly, white-haired woman he had just installed on the witness stand. She was smiling slightly and looked utterly serene and placid, giving the impression of being one of those elderly women who is totally sweet but also slightly dotty and scatterbrained. For a second it flashed on Vaulding, my god, am I doing the right thing? He took a deep breath, plunged ahead.

"Ms. Dreisson?" he began, remembering Steve Winslow's admonition.

It was not his day.

Veronica held up her hand. "One moment, young man. Dreisson is my married name. Not my maiden name. My late husband, Arnold, was a Dreisson. I do not think that he would like to see his name become a Ms. I am *Mrs.* Dreisson, if you please."

Vaulding took a breath, and seemed to roll his eyes heavenward for a split second before smiling and saying, "I stand corrected, Mrs. Dreisson."

The newspaper reporters, frustrated at having called in instructions to hold the front page for a plea-bargain that had not materialized, scribbled gleefully. It was clear this little old lady would make a feisty witness.

"Tell me, Mrs. Dreisson," Vaulding said, "what do you do?"

Veronica smiled. "I don't do anything. I retired more than twenty years ago."

"Yes, but you seem a quite active woman. Aside from any business or profession, is there any hobby or special interest that occupies your time?"

"Yes, of course."

"And what would that be."

"Guns."

"I beg your pardon? Did you say guns?"

"Yes, I did, young man," Veronica said. She added, "Do you have trouble hearing?"

That produced a laugh in the courtroom.

Vaulding never cracked a smile. "No, I do not," he said. "But I wanted to be sure the jurors heard you. Your hobby is guns?"

"That's right."

"You collect guns?"

"Oh, yes."

"You are still actively involved in doing this?"

"Yes, of course."

"How many guns do you own?"

"Between two and three hundred."

That produced a reaction in the courtroom. Judge Hendrick banged the gavel.

"Between two and three hundred? Of different makes and models?"

"Well, I should think so," Veronica said. "It would certainly be silly to have two hundred of the same gun."

"Then you are familiar with different types of firearms?"

"Yes, of course."

"Do you consider yourself an expert?"

Veronica smiled. "I consider myself knowledgeable on the subject. In the past I've been employed as an expert."

"In the past?"

"Yes." Veronica squinted at him. "Let me see. Would that be before you were born?"

That question produced a roar of laughter. The reporters were eating Veronica Dreisson up. They couldn't have asked for better copy.

Vaulding just stood and took it. "But you *are* knowledgeable on the subject of guns?"

"Yes, of course."

"Tell me, have you ever had occasion to examine the guns of the defendant, Russ Timberlaine?"

"Yes, I have. Just last night."

"Last night?"

"Yes, of course," Veronica said. She cocked her head. "Isn't that why I'm here?"

"Yes, it is, Mrs. Dreisson, but it is necessary that we get these things in the record. Had you ever seen Mr. Timberlaine's guns before last night?"

"As to that, I can't recall."

"Well, had you ever met Mr. Timberlaine?"

Veronica smiled. "That's *why* I can't recall. I must admit I have a better memory for guns than for faces." She looked over at the defense table. "I sit here looking at him and the face is indeed familiar. And now he's wearing a suit and has his hair pulled back off his face. I seem to recall a young man with long hair and a cowboy outfit. That is probably him. But I couldn't swear to it." She gestured to the witness stand. "And here I can only say what I can swear to, is that right?"

"Yes, it is."

She shrugged her shoulders. "Well, there you are."

The remark got another laugh.

Vaulding took a breath, forged ahead. "You don't know if you've seen the guns before, but you did see them last night?"

"That's right."

"How did that happen?"

"I went out to his mansion and looked at them."

"Who took you there?"

"Mr. Taylor."

"Would that be Mark Taylor of the Taylor Detective Agency?"

"That's right."

"He took you out there?"

"Yes, he did."

"And who let you in?"

"A nice young man. I don't recall his name, but he opened the door and went and got Miss Timberlaine."

"That would be Carrie Timberlaine, Russ Timberlaine's daughter?"

"That's right."

"She showed you Russ Timberlaine's guns?"

"She tried to, but they were locked up."

"Did she have a key?"

"No, she did not."

"So you couldn't see the guns?"

"No. She went and found the nice young man, and he came and unlocked the cases."

"He had a key?"

"Yes, he did."

"He showed you the guns?"

"That's right."

"Who was present when you examined the guns?"

"Mr. Taylor, Miss Timberlaine and the young man with the key."

"That would be Martin Kessington?"

"If you say so. *I* don't know his name."

"At any rate, you examined the guns."

"Yes, I did."

"How many did you examine?' "

"I don't know. Forty or fifty."

"Was that all of them?"

"No, it was not."

"Why did you stop?"

"The police arrived and made me stop."

"I see. And did they ask you what you were doing?"

"Yes, they did."

"And what did you tell them?"

"Well," Veronica said. "You have to understand I was rather upset. After all, they did make me stop my inspection."

"I'm sure we can make allowances," Vaulding said. "What did you say?"

"I told them it was none of their business."

"You refused to answer their questions?"

"Of course I did. They had no right to ask."

"You're answering *my* questions."

Veronica looked at him as if he were an idiot. "I'm in court," she said. "I'm *required* to answer."

Vaulding nodded grimly. "That you are, Mrs. Dreisson. Tell me, in those forty or fifty guns you examined, did you find anything that you considered significant?"

"Yes, I did."

"And what was that?"

"At least five of the guns I examined were fakes."

That answer produced a low rumble in the courtroom. People looked at each other.

Vaulding frowned. "Fakes? What do you mean?"

Veronica looked at him. "You don't know what the word fake means?"

"Yes, but in terms of a gun. What do you mean, a fake gun? A gun is either a gun or it isn't."

Veronica looked at him. "Come, come, young man. I mean they were not the guns they were supposed to be. The guns are rare and valuable. They are particular guns. They have a history of ownership that increases their value. When I say these guns are fakes, what I mean is, that in all these cases a rare and valuable gun had been taken and a cheap imitation of the same make and model had been left in its place."

"I see. You say five of these guns were fakes?"

"At least five. That's the best I could tell. You must understand, it was late, I'm old, and my eyesight is not what it used to be. And I did not have any equipment with me. But there were at least five I was sure of."

"Five substituted guns?"

"That's right."

Vaulding's smile was skeptical. "Come, come, Mrs. Dreisson. Do you mean to tell me that, never having seen them before, you were able to examine fifty guns in the space of what?—half an hour?—and pronounce forty-five of them genuine and five spurious?"

Veronica stuck out her chin and narrowed her eyes. "You *do* have trouble hearing, don't you? I just got through telling you the best I could tell was that at least five of the guns were fake. That doesn't mean I pronounced forty-five guns genuine. If you asked me, I *did* see genuine guns, but as to how many, I certainly could not say. But, if you'll pardon me, what does it matter? I would think you would be more concerned with the five guns proven to be false."

Vaulding opened his mouth, started to say something, thought better of it and closed it again. That action produced a laugh in the courtroom. Judge Hendrick banged the gavel.

"All right," Vaulding said. "Let's talk about the guns that were false. When you examined the guns, did any of the people present point those guns out to you?"

"The fake guns, you mean?"

"Yes, of course."

"No, they did not."

"Did you point them out to them?"

"No, of course not. I don't do things piecemeal. I had no intention of saying anything whatsoever until I completed my examination." She raised her chin. "Which I was not permitted to do."

"I see. And who asked you to make this examination? Who sent you out to the Timberlaine mansion?"

"Why, Mr. Winslow."

"Mr. Timberlaine's attorney, Steve Winslow?"

"That's right."

"He hired you?"

"Hired is the wrong word. I am no longer a professional. As I told you, I retired long ago. He did not hire me. He asked me if I would go out there and I agreed to."

"But it was Steve Winslow, the attorney for the defense, who asked you to go out there and look at the guns?"

"Yes, of course."

"And you did so?"

"Yes, I did."

"You went out there, examined the guns, and found five of them to be fake."

"That's right."

"So the reason you went out to the Timberlaine mansion was to see if there were any fake guns in his collection?"

Veronica's eyes widened. She shook her head. "No, I did not."

Vaulding frowned. "You did not?"

"No."

"I don't understand."

"Yes, I knew that when you started asking questions."

That sally produced a roar of laughter. Vaulding stood, took it, and when it subsided, said, "Tell me, Mrs. Dreisson, why *did* you go out to Timberlaine's mansion, if not to examine his gun collection?"

"Oh, it *was* to examine his gun collection. That was a part of it. I just wasn't looking for any fake guns. That was a sort of bonus."

"But you were looking for something?"

"Oh, yes, indeed."

"Could you tell us what that was?"

"Certainly. One moment, young man."

Veronica Dreisson snapped open her purse. She fumbled inside a few moments, took out and held up a small metallic object.

"You see this?" she said, holding it up between her thumb and forefinger and extending it for Vaulding to see.

Vaulding looked, saw what she was holding was a metal tube about two and a half inches long and about half an inch in diameter. "What's that?" he asked.

"I guess you're not familiar with guns," Veronica said. "But then, this is something only an expert would know. For your information, young man, this is an adapter. It is used to take a bullet fired from one gun and allow a person to shoot it from another. In this case, the adapter is just the size to allow a .45-caliber spent bullet to be repacked in a shell casing, fitted into the adapter and refired from the barrel of a shotgun. The bullet, of course, would retain only the markings from the original gun." Veronica shrugged. "Which is of course the whole point."

Vaulding blinked. "A shotgun?"

"Yes, of course. I would imagine the murderer used one from Mr. Timberlaine's collection. There were several in the room. And a shotgun is such an awkward weapon—to conceal, I mean—why run the risk of being seen going in or out with it?"

Vaulding stared at her. "What are you saying?"

Veronica cocked her head. "You have the wrong gun. For the murder weapon, I mean. The real murder weapon is most likely still hanging on Mr. Timberlaine's wall. I'm afraid the police overlooked it. Not their fault, really. They weren't looking for a shotgun, you see."

There came the sound of a commotion in the courtroom.

Vaulding turned his head just in time to see one of his witnesses, Melvin Burdett, practically climbing over people in an attempt to push his way into the aisle.

"Officer, stop that man!" Vaulding yelled.

But the court officer was not quick enough. Before he could reach him, Melvin Burdett broke free. But, instead of making for the door, Burdett suddenly wheeled around, swung his fist in a surprisingly swift uppercut and decked Henry Crumbly, who was headed up the aisle. Crumbly went down in a heap just as the court officer grabbed and held Burdett.

On the other side of the courtroom, another man slid unobtrusively from his seat and headed for the door. But despite the sensational disruption of Crumbly and Burdett, the courtroom was not too crowded for his departure to go unnoticed.

"Oh, look," Veronica Dreisson said. She pointed at the retreating figure, cocked her head, smiled and said sweetly but distinctly, "Why, there's the nice young man who showed me the guns."

48

ROBERT VAULDING WAS TORN in so many directions his plight was almost comical. When court broke up he suddenly found himself with an immediate and pressing need to deal with the defendant, the suspects, the media and Steve Winslow, though not necessarily in that order. Deftly tapdancing, he left Russ Timberlaine in the custody of the court officers pending dismissal, turned the processing of Henry Crumbly and Martin Kessington over to Lieutenant Sanders, sicked the press on Veronica Dreisson and escaped to his inner office where he had asked Steve Winslow to meet him, only to discover Steve had brought along Mark Taylor and Tracy Garvin too. This was almost more than the poor man could deal with—he didn't want them there, but he had neither the time nor the inclination to throw them out.

Aside from that, Vaulding was elated. "It's incredible," he said. "Absolutely incredible. But listen, there isn't much time. I have to make a statement to the press."

"Fine, let's wrap things up," Steve said.

Vaulding shot a glance at Mark and Tracy. "We need to talk freely."

"We can," Steve said. "Anything you say to me they're gonna hear. They've been in this case all the way, and they're gonna be here for the wrap-up. If they go, I go."

"They stay," Vaulding said quickly, holding up his hands. "Look, I took a chance on you and it paid off. So we have a deal, right?"

"Sure we have a deal," Steve said. "But I want you to know where it came from. The case would have broken the same way whether we had a deal or not. I told you to go into court and ask Veronica certain questions and play it aggrieved. You did and it worked. If you hadn't agreed, you'd have gone back into court, put Veronica on the stand and questioned her anyway. And whatever you asked her, she'd have managed to pull the same stunt. The only difference is, if it had happened that way, we wouldn't be talking now."

"Right," Vaulding said. "And I appreciate it. And there's no reason we shouldn't go out together to meet the press."

Steve shook his head. "That's your bag, not mine. Your reward for playin' ball. I'm just happy to get my client off."

"Fine," Vaulding said. "Now please, what do I tell 'em? I mean, all I had was your solemn assurance that gun didn't commit the murder and if I questioned Veronica that way the case would blow up in court. Well, you're right on both counts. But you could have given me a little more."

"I didn't *have* a little more," Steve said. "All I knew was exactly that. The gun ballistics said committed the murder couldn't have done it. Plus Veronica's assurance some of Timberlaine's guns were fakes."

"How did that add up?" Vaulding said.

"All right," Steve said. "Last night, all I knew was I had a problem with the ballistics evidence regarding the gun. The gun could not have committed the crime. Unfortunately, I was the only person in the position to confirm this. You and the cops would never have taken my word for that, and who could blame you? I could have come to you and told you that in utter confidence and you'd have thrown me out on my ear. But *I* knew that gun hadn't been used to commit the crime.

"That's where Veronica Dreisson comes in. Faced with a conflict of evidence, namely the identification of the murder gun, I asked Mark Taylor here to get me a gun expert. He brought me Veronica Dreisson. At first I was skeptical of the choice, but she proved me wrong. The woman is sharp, no doubt about it. I told her the basic problem, challenged her to solve it, and damned if she didn't. The

problem, of course, was how does a fatal bullet match up with a
gun that was nowhere near the scene of the crime at the time of
the murder. Which didn't stop Veronica for one minute. Aside from
collecting guns, the woman is a mystery buff. That sort of question
was right up her alley. She said, 'With an adapter, of course.' It
turns out it's very simple. You fire a bullet from the gun into a
bucket of water or a target or whatever. Then you retrieve the
bullet, and, like she said in court, pack it in a shell casing, stick it
in the adapter and fire it from a shotgun. It will of course retain
all the rifling marks from the barrel of the gun from which it was
originally fired."

"And Veronica went out to Timberlaine's to look for this
adapter?"

"Sure."

"Wasn't that a long shot? No pun intended. But wouldn't you
figure if such a thing existed, the murderer would have disposed
of it?"

"Yes. In all instances except one. Timberlaine was a gun collector. It was entirely possible that the adapter was part of his collection. If it was, I figured the murderer would be more likely *not* to
get rid of it. Because if Timberlaine owned it, he would know of it
anyway, so discovering it would not be that big a deal. But discovering it *missing* would give the whole thing away."

"Right," Vaulding said. "But the plan? The scheme? The whole
deal?"

"There you know as much as I do," Steve said. "If I didn't give
you much to go on, it's because I didn't know much. I didn't know
about the parties involved until they showed themselves in court."

"You knew about the fake guns."

"Not until this morning," Steve said. "You grabbed off Veronica
last night. She clammed up on you and I went to bed. She called
me this morning, told me about the fake guns, which is how I knew
to tell you. But I really don't know any more than you do. If I'm
ahead of you it's because I've had the benefit of knowing my client
wasn't guilty and the benefit of knowing that gun hadn't committed
the crime. But for what it's worth, here's how I dope it out.

"Timberlaine originally came to me with a substituted gun—the
Pistol Pete gun that got us into this whole mess. At the time he
was afraid someone would use it to frame him for a crime. The way

I see it now, at the time he was wrong. The gun wasn't substituted to frame him for anything. The gun was substituted because it was a valuable gun—it was stolen, just like the other guns. Timberlaine just happened to notice this one. He brought it here and expressed his fear it might be used to frame him for a crime. So Timberlaine's got a big mouth—he shot that theory around. That's what gave the murderer the idea to actually do it.

"Now, we're never really gonna know for sure unless one of the conspirators talks, but I dope it out like this. Martin Kessington and Henry Crumbly were involved in ripping off Russ Timberlaine's gun collection—stealing valuable guns and substituting cheap imitations in their place. The joker in the piece is Jack Potter, gun expert. You recall Timberlaine's regular expert had moved on and Jack Potter was relatively new. I'd say there were two possibilities here. One, he was involved in the scheme, or, two, he discovered it.

"I lean toward one—Potter's involved in the ripoff, gets cold feet, wants out. Therefore becomes dangerous and expendable.

"The other, less likely, is that he discovers the substitution and has to be silenced. But then he'd go right to Timberlaine—why would he wait around to be murdered? No, the only way that would fly would be if he noticed the substitution, deduced who'd done it and tried blackmail. That I could buy. But the way I see it, in neither case were Potter's hands clean. In a way, he kind of asked for it.

"Now, a big argument for theory number one is the fact the crime took considerable planning. Timberlaine finds the gun, shoots off his mouth, there's been a substitution, someone's tying to frame him for a crime. Which gives the murderer the idea. Before Timberlaine comes to my office, he gets hold of the gun, fires a bullet through it and saves the bullet."

"Why before he comes to your office?" Vaulding said.

"Because as soon as he left my office he switched guns, remember? He put the gun I gave him in his safe-deposit box."

"Which is how you knew it hadn't committed the murder," Vaulding said.

"So we know," Steve said, "that that far in advance the murderer had an idea he might need that bullet. Which would be much more likely if Potter was a coconspirator beginning to show signs of cold feet."

"Fine. So that's why they killed Potter. But why frame Timberlaine?"

"Well," Steve said, "few people like to go to jail for a crime. It's always better to have a scapegoat in mind. And, you have to remember, Timberlaine suggested it. He kept insisting someone was going to frame him with the gun. Fine. Let's fulfill his prophesy and frame him with the gun. No one's gonna believe him, 'cause he's the little boy who cried wolf.

"Particularly the way they set it up. You have to admit, that was pretty artistic. Kill Potter and leave the original Pistol Pete gun by the body. Timberlaine immediately starts screaming, 'Frame-up, frame-up, they stole my gun to frame me with it. See, and I can prove it 'cause here's the phony gun they left in its place.' And he hands over that gun and swears it's the gun he'd had with him all day long.

"And indeed he had. Only they framed him with a bullet from that gun and, surprise, surprise, it's the murder gun."

"Only it wasn't," Vaulding said.

"Right. Because Timberlaine had switched guns. Only that gun barrel had been roughed up so the ballistics expert, taken in by the class characteristics, blows it and identifies it as the murder weapon anyway."

"But why was the gun barrel roughed up?" Vaulding said. "I mean, the murderer would *want* the gun identified."

"Right," Steve said. "But there's the moron factor."

Vaulding frowned. "What?"

"You may have noticed that my client is not the swiftest thing in the world—witness that whole auction thing of having Crumbly bid on the gun. Only the frame-up still has to wash. The murderer wants Timberlaine to say, 'No, no, no, this is my gun,' and produce it and have it turn out to be the murder weapon. But that makes Timberlaine look like a total jerk. I mean, in terms of motivation, why the hell would he do that? If he were the murderer, the only way he would turn the gun over would be if he expected it *not* to match the fatal bullet. If it was the fatal gun, the only way he could expect it not to match would be if he'd altered the barrel."

"So the murderer alters the barrel to make it look like Timberlaine did?"

"Of course," Steve said. He nodded at Tracy. "Actually, it was

one of the things Tracy said that put me in the right direction."
Steve grinned. "We were discussing the fact you'd just made a
damn good case for the fact *I* was the one who altered the gun
barrel. She said if I had, I sure made a poor job of it, since they
still matched up the bullet.

"That got me thinking. The murderer really *had* made a poor
job of it. I mean, four lousy scratches. If you want to deface the
barrel, you run that file up and down it pretty good. That got me
thinking in the right direction. The murderer didn't want to deface
the barrel, the murderer *wanted* the gun and the bullet to match.
The murderer just wanted to make it *look* like someone had defaced
the barrel. That's why the scratches weren't that bad. But the
barrel had to be scratched up or the frame-up wouldn't work.
Because of the moron factor, you see."

"Yeah, fine," Vaulding said. "If that's true, why was it *that* gun's
barrel that was scratched up? That wasn't the murder weapon.
Why didn't the murderer rough up the barrel at the same time he
fired the bullet?"

"Because he didn't come by the plan all at once. It was an evolv-
ing thing, you know. 'If he claims he's gonna be framed, let's frame
him. I'll frame him with the bullet.' So the murderer gets the
bullet, he's ready to make the frame-up. Then he thinks of the
moron factor. 'Hell, how do I take care of that?' Then he thinks of
the file. 'I'll rough it up with a file and I'll leave the file in Timberlaine's room, and that'll double-dork him. The file will become
a piece of evidence in itself.' Which it did."

"I see," Vaulding said.

"The other thing about the file is, it was planted on Timberlaine
on Friday. At least that's when he found it. The day *before* the
murder. That was a great touch. The guy's in possession of the file
before the murder, so if the gun barrel's roughed up *after* the
murder, then he must have done it. But in actuality, the barrel of
the gun was roughed up at the same time the murderer planted
the file. Which didn't affect the fatal bullet, which had been shot
days before that."

"Before Timberlaine came to your office."

"Exactly. And the murderer knew Timberlaine came to my office, and knew he had the bullets tested. That's why it didn't hurt
to pull the stunt with the file. A few light scratches to make it look

like Timberlaine tried to alter the gun, then if ballistics can still match the bullet, great, but if they can't, no big deal. The murderer just tips the cops to the bullets Timberlaine had me test.

"Which he did. That's why you called Donald Walcott. That was an anonymous tip, right? Telling you to ask him about Timberlaine testing the gun."

"Yeah, right," Vaulding said. He was standing between Steve Winslow and the door and sort of teetering back and forth. He put up his hand. "Hang on a minute," he said, opened the door and dashed out.

"What was that all about?" Tracy said.

"Looked to me like a guy who really had to go to the bathroom," Taylor said.

Steve grinned. "No, I'm afraid the poor guy's just torn between the suspects, the press and us."

"Think they're talkin'?"

"Not yet. More than likely waiting on their lawyers. Vaulding should be right back."

He was. Vaulding came in the door, put his hand up, shook his head and said, "Not yet. Crumbly's lawyer's here and we're waiting on Kessington's. Then they'll need some time to confer. But the press won't wait. Veronica's holding her own, but she's such good copy if I don't get out there I'm gonna find out she's aced me out of the whole front page."

"Go to it," Steve said.

"You're really not coming?"

"It's your show, Vaulding. That was the deal."

"Yeah, I know. But under the circumstances, I'd almost feel better with you there. There's gonna be questions I can't answer."

"Yeah, but there's others you can. You lay on a general line of bullshit—there's certain things you can't discuss until the suspects talk—then you give 'em whatever you want."

"Yeah, but what? I need some hard facts. Right now the main thing I got on 'em is they tried to run and flight is an indication of guilt. Aside from that, I got nothing. That adapter Veronica held up in court wasn't the one they used, that was just a bluff."

"Yeah, but one that worked. Without that you got no flight. But you want hard facts, you got hard facts. There're the substituted guns. That backs that theory. And you remember the bump on the head? The one the medical examiner photographed? There's your other theory. The guy was coshed on the head and then shot. It's a nice theory, 'cause it had to be that way. You can whip out a pistol and shoot a guy in the head, but no one's gonna stand there waiting to be shot while you fit a bullet in an adapter into a shotgun and aim it at him."

"Yeah," Vaulding said. "That helps. Would you happen to know who did it? I can charge 'em as coconspirators, but odds are, when they sing one of them's gonna rat the other out. It would be nice to name the shooter."

"Which you can easily do," Steve said. "You said it yourself. The adapter Veronica held up in court was not the one used in the murder. She couldn't *find* the one used in the murder. Why? Because the murderer had gotten rid of it. But when she held it up in court, someone ran. Who? Crumbly. Why? Because he *wasn't* the shooter, so he didn't know this couldn't be the adapter used in the murder because he wasn't the one who disposed of it."

"Kessington ran too."

"Yeah, but not when he saw the adapter. When he saw they got Crumbly. He knew the adapter had to be a plant, but he figured Crumbly would talk. Which he may.

"Incidentally, there's another player in this you shouldn't leave out."

"Who's that?"

"Crumbly's wife."

"You mean she probably knows about it and if I work on her she might break?"

"It's the other way around, Vaulding. You know, for an elected official, you're not very politically correct. For my money Crumbly's a pretty weak tool and I wouldn't be too surprised to find the missus was the brains behind him."

"Son of a bitch," Vaulding said.

"Yeah, but if so, I'll bet she's a tough nut to crack. The way I see it, it's more likely you'll get *him* to rat on *her*.

"But these are details, Vaulding. They can wait. The press won't."

"Right," Vaulding said. He paused in the door. "Give me one more thing. Odds are these guys won't talk until tomorrow, so any prediction I can make in the papers makes me the golden boy.

Aside from running, give me one more thing indicates these guys were the perps."

"O.K.," Steve said. "You got Crumbly's testimony. About him meeting Timberlaine at brunch and Timberlaine asking him to bid against Burdett."

"What about it?"

"Well, that's gotta be part of the plan, right? They're framing Timberlaine so they gotta give him a motive. You twist Timberlaine hard enough, I'll bet you'd find the idea of having someone else bid did not originate with him."

"Right. They planted the idea. That's obvious. But why does that implicate Crumbly?"

"Burdett's testimony was that the deception did not fool him in the least."

"Right," Vaulding said. "It was only meant to fool Timberlaine."

Steve grinned. "Right. But from Timberlaine's point of view it was supposed to work. According to Burdett's testimony there was no way it *could* have worked. Crumbly didn't bid on that kind of gun and Crumbly never bid that high."

"Yeah, so?"

"So Crumbly had to know that. He's not stupid. But here he is, agreeing with Timberlaine to go along with this great scheme. Bullshit. Crumbly more than anyone else knew that his bidding on that gun was out of character for him and would tip Burdett off. Yet he did it. Why? Because that was the whole point. To furnish a motive for Timberlaine killing Potter. You dig around, I'm sure you'll find the idea that Potter tipped off Burdett was indirectly planted by one of the conspirators too."

"Yeah, right," Vaulding said. He hesitated.

"That's not enough for you?" Steve said. "What about Martin Kessington having the key to the gun room so he had the opportunity of switching guns? Or Crumbly and his wife being gun collectors, and therefore having the avenues to move them? Plus what Burdett said about the Crumblys not having any money, which is why they'd get involved in the ripoff in the first place."

"All right, all right," Vaulding said, putting up his hands. "I'll take it from there." He took a breath. "Look, I took a chance on you, I'm glad I did. Thanks."

Vaulding stuck out his hand. Steve shook it.

Vaulding nodded to Mark, "Mr. Taylor," then to Tracy, "Ms. Garvin," then hurried out the door.

"How about that," Tracy said. "He actually called me Ms."

"Nothing surprising about that," Steve said. "When we made our deal, it was practically a prerequisite."

"Well, I'd still have liked to hear him say it in open court."

"Take what you can get," Taylor said. "Well, whaddya say we get out of here?"

"Hang on," Steve said. "Give Vaulding a chance to get the reporters in tow. I don't feel like walking out of here into the arms of the press."

"You and me both," Taylor said. "You can bet one of them would be bound to ask the wrong question."

"Yeah, like what happened to the other gun," Tracy said.

Mark Taylor almost gagged. He threw up his hands, then put his finger to his lips.

"What's wrong with you?" Steve said.

"Oh, nothing. But this is not our office, and who knows what sort of equipment our host has."

"Relax," Steve said. "Even if Vaulding recorded every word we said, I guarantee you there is nothing that would make him go back on what he's telling the press right now."

"Even so."

"Oh, don't be such a worry wart," Tracy said. "Tell me, what *are* you going to do about that gun?"

"There isn't a river deep enough," Taylor said. "Right, Steve?"

Steve considered a moment. "Actually, Mark, I thought I'd hang it on the wall."

Taylor's mouth dropped open. "What?"

"Yeah. Don't you think it would look good over my desk?"

"Steve, don't joke. You don't know how much sleep I've lost over that gun."

"Who's joking? Safest place for it. Look, if I try to get rid of it and get caught, I'm screwed. No way I can ever explain. If I hang it on the wall, no one will give it a second thought. People who make the connection at all will say, 'Hey, is that a gun from the Pistol Pete case? You handled that, didn't you?' I'll just smile and say, 'Yes, I did.' After all, there's so many guns in the damn case, no one's gonna figure out which one this is."

Taylor exhaled noisily. "Jesus Christ," he said. "I hope you're pulling my leg. But what the hell. Right now I'm so relieved I couldn't care. Listen, we gotta stay here, I need a drink. This hotshot D.A. got a bar?"

"In the corner."

"Do we dare?"

"Under the circumstances, I can't see how he'd begrudge us."

Taylor went to the bar, rummaged around, came back with three brandy snifters. He passed them out, raised his and said, "Here's to crime." He took a sip, exhaled with satisfaction. Took another sip and chuckled.

"Feeling a little better, Mark?" Steve said.

"I was thinking about Burdett coldcocking Crumbly."

"Wasn't that something?" Steve said.

"I'll say. That pudgy guy sure packed a wallop."

"Did you see him when court broke up?" Tracy said. "Before they led Timberlaine off. He goes up to him, throws his arm around his shoulders like they were the best of pals."

"Nothing strange in that," Steve said.

"Why? I thought Timberlaine hated his guts," Taylor said.

"Yeah, but they're adversaries. It's a special relationship. In a way, it's more personal than being friends. A good rival, one who puts up a good fight—well, you don't have to like the guy to respect him as an opponent."

"Funny you should say so," Tracy said.

"Oh?"

"I was thinking about you and Vaulding. He was a pretty good opponent, wasn't he?"

"That he was."

"Except now," Taylor said. "I don't get it. The guy was givin' you fits for most of the trial, now he's in here asking you for explanations like he hasn't got a clue."

"That's not so surprising," Steve said. "The man spent the whole case gearing every theory to the fact Timberlaine was guilty. He's had just this morning to adjust to the idea he might be innocent. It's like every notion he had was pulled out from under him. If you consider that, he's doing fine."

"And when you consider how fast the evidence jumped around," Tracy said. "'Keep your eye on the gun.' Boy, was that ever prophetic."

"Why'd you give it to him?" Taylor said. He jerked his thumb. "The press, I mean. Like you said, you could have pulled this off without telling him at all."

"Which wouldn't have been fair. If the guy's decent enough to play ball, he should have a chance to play ball. There's a bottom line here. Vaulding didn't want to win if it meant convicting an innocent man."

"Of course not," Tracy said.

"There's no 'of course not' about it. Some do. Vaulding deserves credit for not being one of them. And if this case gets him reelected, hey, it's nice to know we got a friend in this county."

Mark Taylor set down his glass. "Can we go now?"

Tracy held up her hand. "In a minute. Let's finish the postmortem."

"What more is there to say?"

"There's a lot more to say. Look, Steve, I heard what you said to Vaulding. And I'm sure a lot of it's true. What I want to know is, how in hell did you figure it out?"

"Oh, that was easy," Steve said.

Tracy exhaled. She snatched off her glasses, folded them up, put her hands on her hips. "I *knew* you were going to say that," she said. "Now, then, you infuriating man, at the risk of being strangled, would you tell me what you mean by that?"

"Well, I should think it's obvious," Steve said. "Considering the fact this all started with Timberlaine inviting us out to his mansion for the weekend, then the whole bit with the switching gun and the people changing rooms and the body on the floor of the gun room—all the elements of your basic mystery novel—well, considering all that, and considering who Martin Kessington was, the solution was obvious."

Tracy frowned. "What do you mean?"

Steve grinned, ducked his head and moved well out of Tracy's reach before answering.

"The butler did it."